SARAH'S LEGACY SHARED

Book Two

DAISY BEILER TOWNSEND

Other Books by Daisy Beiler Townsend

Homespun Faith

Sarah's Legacy Series
Sarah's Legacy
Sarah's Legacy Shared

Dedication

This book is dedicated to my beloved daughter, Angelyn Ruth Townsend, who carries on the legacy of prayer handed down to us by her grandmother, Ruth Beiler, for whom she was named.

To Alma,
Blessings on my
dear cousin who certainly
has shared her godly
legacy.

Daisy Townsend
6/3/19

Acknowledgements

I want to thank my husband, Donn, for his ongoing, selfless help in supporting my writing ministry in so many ways. I'm so thankful for who you are and what you do.

Also, a huge thank you to my readers. You have encouraged me more than I can say and kept me persevering to write this second book of the Sarah's Legacy series. You are such a blessing!

Ongoing thanks to the American Christian Fiction Writers Scribes who walked with me through the critiquing process of Sarah's Legacy Shared. Continuing gratitude to Laurie Germaine who critiqued every chapter of the first book of the Sarah's Legacy series. I learned so much that I applied to this second book. Thanks also to Don McNair, whom I've never met, but whose book *Editor-Proof Your Writing* taught me so much.

Thanks again to my faithful prayer partners who continued to encourage me and pray for me through this second book: Angelyn Trumbull, Bonnie Prugh, Cherri McAnallen, DeVonne White, MaryElla Young, and Stacey Pardoe.

Great appreciation to my beta readers, Angelyn Trumbull, Rebekah Crane, and Stacey Pardoe. Since my ACFW critique partners had not read Sarah's Legacy, I recruited people who had read book one to read Sarah's Legacy Shared and give me input before publication.

I want to continue to express gratitude to Isabel Dye without whom these books would not have been written.

Disclaimer

Sarah's Legacy Shared was inspired by the Thomas and Sarah Davis family and the Robert and Margaret Dye family. They lived at 259 Broad Street (now 81 Broad Street) in Sandy Lake, Pennsylvania, in the late 1800's and early 1900's—our home from 1988 to 2008. You will also encounter other professionals and residents who lived in Sandy Lake during that era.

In spite of the fact that the Davis's and the Dye's, and several other characters were real people, and that some of the events in this book actually happened, the characters I've created and the story I've written are a work of fiction.

Chapter One

Sandy Lake, Pennsylvania
February 1912

"Savannah, where are you? I know you're here somewhere." A loud voice boomed up the wooden staircase.

Was that Mr. Burns? Savannah's heart plummeted. Only boarders and approved guests were allowed upstairs in Mrs. Patton's boarding house. How had he gotten up here?

She didn't want to see the business partner from her old life. Scanning the room, she looked for somewhere to hide. Any movement might produce creaks, giving her away.

Mr. Burns's hobnailed boots clattered up the stairs and down the uncarpeted hall in her direction. Savannah crouched next to the bedside table she'd been dusting, willing herself to become invisible. She hadn't seen him since he'd ended their agreement and thrown her out six months ago. She'd hoped never to see him again, wanting no reminder of that life.

The resounding footsteps stopped outside the half-open door. The hinges creaked as Mr. Burns pushed it further open, riveting Savannah with his piercing dark eyes. He took in her crouching position with a cruel leer. "What's a matter with you? You ain't scared of me are ya?"

Savannah glared at Mr. Burns and rose to her full height. "What do you want?" Her voice quavered despite her efforts to control it. "No one except boarders are allowed up here."

Mr. Burns stepped toward her and smirked. She smelled alcohol. "I thought maybe you'd wanna share your room with me, now that Mrs. Patton's got you all set up here."

"I'm not *all set up here.* I do light cleaning for half my rent, and I have a respectable office job with Mr. Young."

"That's just poppycock. A zebra can't change its stripes." Mr. Burns stumbled in Savannah's direction.

"Maybe not, but Garrett's mother says I'm a new creature in Christ." Savannah held her head high.

Her former landlord snorted. "Once a whore, always a whore, I always say."

Mr. Burns reached for her. Savannah's stomach rolled at the smell of unwashed flesh. She took a step back but the bed stopped her escape. "Why are you doing this? You never bothered me when I had my room at your tavern."

"We was business partners then. I didn't want to do nothing that would mess up our arrangement. You were a moneymaker. That all changed when the sheriff threatened to arrest me for running a bawdy house."

He grabbed Savannah and pulled her into his arms. Powerless in his iron grip, she tried to turn her head away as he pressed his lips on hers.

"What's going on here?" Mr. Burns let go of Savannah as Mrs. Patton's stern voice filled the room. Savannah stumbled and fell backward onto the bed as he turned to face her landlady.

"This here *lady* invited me to come and see her new place of business."

Savannah sprang from the bed. "Mrs. Patton, I didn't—"

He belched. "It was nice of you to—"

"Get out of here *now. Men.* You're all alike." Mrs. Patton's lip curled.

"Who's gonna make me?" Mr. Burns towered over Mrs. Patton's diminutive frame.

"You'll leave or I'll call the sheriff."

Mr. Burns teetered on the balls of his oversized feet as he looked back and forth between Savannah and Mrs. Patton. "I'll be back, Savannah, to get what ya owe me." He jerked his thumb in Mrs. Patton's direction. "This broad's gotta sleep some time." He pushed past her landlady and tripped over the colorful rag rug at the door. Clutching the doorframe, he regained his balance, then staggered toward the stairs.

"Mrs. Patton, you have to believ—"

"What did he mean, he'll be back to get what you owe him?" Mrs. Patton's brown eyes were wide.

Savannah gulped. "I have no idea."

After another long, steady look at her boarder, Mrs. Patton turned toward the door. "We'll talk about this later."

As her landlady's footsteps echoed on the bare wooden stairs, tears rolled down Savannah's cheeks. *God, why would you let this happen just when my six-month trial period is almost up? I kept my part of the bargain, not entertaining men in my room even once. What if Mrs. Patton doesn't believe me? What if Mr. Burns comes back?*

The silence was deafening in the boarder's room Savannah had been dusting. She gasped and struggled to breathe. The nauseating smell of alcohol and unwashed flesh lingered on her skin. She rushed to her room at the head of the stairs and poured water into the basin on the cheap pine chest of drawers. Grabbing a clean washcloth from the top drawer, Savannah plunged it in water and scrubbed her mouth and arm until the skin was raw. George Burns's smell lingered.

Clutching her stomach, she leaned over the small, tin wastebasket in the corner and retched until nothing remained of the beans and ham she'd eaten for supper. A voice from the doorway startled her.

"How long has this been going on?" Mrs. Patton stood in Savannah's doorway. "Are you in the family way?"

"No, no. I'm not. I haven't been... There's no way I could be carrying a child. The smell of Mr. Burns makes me sick."

Mrs. Patton said nothing, her gaze never leaving Savannah's face. Was she trying to peer into her soul? "Why did Mr. Burns think I had *set you up* here?"

"I don't know. He must have found out I was living here and assumed I still... assumed I... I hadn't changed. He... He'd been drinking."

"I can't have men coming upstairs looking for you. People will get the wrong idea. Decent people won't want to live here." Mrs. Patton's forehead creased in a frown.

"It's never happened before." Tears dimmed Savannah's vision. "I'm sure Mr. Burns wouldn't have come up here if he hadn't been drinking. I've never seen him so drunk. Please, you must believe me."

Mrs. Patton backed up. She tapped her foot on the bare wood floor, still gazing at Savannah. At last she turned away. "I don't know." She shook her head. "I just don't know."

CHAPTER TWO

Garrett Young whistled under his breath as he stepped out of his car into the crisp night air. There'd be snow before the night was over. Like they needed more snow. Light streamed from the kitchen window where Ma would be cooking something tasty for supper.

Footsteps crunched in the snow behind him. He smelled something foul. Before he had time to turn, someone grabbed his arm and twisted him around. Garrett peered at the burly man in a black winter overcoat. "Mr. Burns? What are you doing here?"

"I've come to get what that no-good slut owes me."

"What are you talking about?" Garrett tried to yank his arm away from Mr. Burns's meaty grasp, but the man tightened his grip.

"I'm sure Savannah must have told ya."

"Savannah is *not* a slut, and she hasn't told me anything about you."

"When she set up business above my tavern, I gave her free rent for a couple of months and loaned her money so she could buy fancy clothes. Now that Mrs. Patton has set her up at the old Sandy Lake House, I figger Savannah owes me at least for the clothes."

"Mrs. Patton does not have her *set up* at the old Sandy Lake House. Anyway, it's a boarding house now, not a hotel. Did you and Savannah have a signed contract with the terms of your agreement?" Garrett tried again to jerk his arm away. He almost succeeded when the tavern owner slipped on the icy driveway. Before Garrett could lunge for the house where he lived with his parents, Mr. Burns regained his footing and renewed his iron grip.

"Don't need no signed agreement with the likes of her. It'll be my word against hers an you know who they'll believe. I'm a respectable business owner."

Garrett stopped trying to escape. "If you don't get off our property, I'll yell for Ma. She'll call the sheriff and then we'll see how much respect you get."

The angry man spit on the ground. "I always took you fer a mama's boy—can't even fight yer own battles." He dropped Garrett's wrist.

Rubbing his sore arm, Garrett glared at his unwelcome guest. "Have you been harassing Savannah?"

"If you knew what that good-for-nothing floozy has been doing behind your back, you wouldn't worry your head about her. She's got you fooled for sure. Don't you know she's still doing her business at Mrs. Patton's?"

"Says who?"

"All the men at the tavern talk about her. You don't think she'd turn her back on paying customers, do ya? She knows which side her bread is buttered on."

Garrett hesitated. He didn't want to believe this foul-smelling loudmouth, but what if he was telling the truth? Were the men at the tavern talking about Savannah? Maybe laughing at him? He shifted his feet and cleared his throat. "You need to go somewhere and...and sleep it off or get some strong coffee before you do something you'll regret. Stay away from Savannah." Garrett turned and strode toward the house.

Mr. Burns's voice followed him. "Mind your own business and don't be telling *me* what to do. If I can't get what's coming to me one way, I'll get it another."

♠

Angry voices outside startled Mildred Young as she dished up the fragrant beef stew. *What in the world is going on?* Still holding the bowl of stew, she dashed to the window. Someone had her son's arm in a death grip. *He was old enough to fight his own battles but still...*

She ran toward the door and lifted the curtain just as the large intruder spit on the ground and dropped Garrett's wrist. He headed for the house as the stranger shouted parting words.

Wiping her perspiring face with a dishtowel, Mildred yanked open the door as Garrett reached for the doorknob. "Who was that?"

"Mr. Burns trying to make trouble. Too much to drink." Garrett wrinkled his nose.

Retracing her steps, Mildred finished ladling stew into the bowl. "Why would Mr. Burns want to make trouble for you? I didn't even think you knew him."

"He owns the tavern where Savannah lived in Jackson Center. He claims Savannah owes him money. Maybe he thought I'd pay him off so he'd leave her alone." Garrett unbuttoned his wool overcoat and hung it on the wooden hook by the door.

Mildred slid slices of homemade bread out of the strawberry-covered tin breadbox. "Do you think Savannah owes Mr. Burns money?"

Dropping into a chair by the table, Garrett put his head in his hands. "I don't know what to think." His voice was muffled.

Placing the slices of bread on a gray and blue plate, Mildred sighed. "What else did Mr. Burns say?" She touched her son's bowed head.

"Lies. I know he's making up lies about Savannah. They have to be lies."

"What kind of lies?"

"He claims she still has paying customers, that the men at his tavern all talk about her." Garrett lifted his head and opened his intense blue eyes, now dark with pain. "I don't want to believe him but... do you think she's lying to us, Ma? Can someone like her be trusted?"

Mildred pulled out a chair and sat across from her son. "I'm afraid Savannah's reputation followed her from Jackson Center. You know how people talk. We shouldn't jump to conclusions because of something Mr. Burns said, especially after he'd been drinking."

"I can't bear to think she might be making a fool of me, might be making fools of *us,* after all we've done for her." Garrett stood and walked to the hall doorway.

"Where are you going? Supper's almost ready. Your father will be home soon."

"I'm not hungry. I don't think I could eat a bite."

"Why don't you go talk to Savannah? It would be better than sitting in your room worrying. You could find out the truth."

"Could I, Ma?" He looked away and his eyebrows sank. Then he turned to go upstairs. "Makes a fellow wonder."

CHAPTER THREE

George Burns pulled a bottle from his pocket and took a long swig as he shambled down Mill Street, slipping occasionally on the thin layer of snow and ice. He paused and squinted at the Grist Mill. Should he turn onto Dunn Street or continue on Mill? He belched and took another swallow from his bottle.

Which way? Where had he left his buggy? Why was he here? Oh yeah, Savannah. He'd come to get what she owed him. As long as she made money for him at the tavern, he hadn't mentioned her debt. Then when the sheriff threatened to arrest him, he'd wanted rid of her in a hurry.

Bad judgment on his part. He'd already been losing money because of the prohibition pushers. Now losing even more since Savannah left. What would happen to his business if Pennsylvania decided to go dry like some states had? Or a National Prohibition Act was passed?

Looking at the brown bottle in his hand, George shook his head. Alcohol used to be something he sold to other people. When had he started helping himself to the brown liquid in these bottles? Probably when his wife left. *I know all too well what happens to those who try to drown their sorrows.* He glanced at the Christian Church across the street and thrust the bottle back in his pocket. *My mother, God rest her soul, would be so disappointed.*

A movement beside the church on the corner caught his eye. A woman. Maybe it was Savannah. He blinked and tried to focus. Putting on a burst of speed, he stumbled and skidded across the street. "Savannah? Zat you?"

Before the young woman could respond, George slid into her and they both crashed to the ground.

♠

Kitt Potter recoiled from the large, burly man with alcohol on his breath. "Get off me right now. What do you think you're doing?"

"You ain't Savannah Stevens, are you?" George blinked at the woman under him.

"Course not. Why would you think that? Get. Off. Me."

The man belched and tried to stand but swayed and crashed down on Kitt again. Who was this drunken lout? He outweighed her by at least a hundred pounds. She could scream but there was no one around to hear.

"Just roll over so I can get up." She turned her face away, holding her breath to avoid the smell. "Who are you anyway?"

He lifted his head and glared at her. "Don't matter who I am. I got business with Savannah."

Taking advantage of his lifted head, Kitt tried to raise up on her elbows. She managed to lift one leg and kneed her opponent sharply. With a guttural howl, he rolled off and sprawled beside the frozen, snow-covered road.

Kitt leaped to her feet and started toward home. The man bellowed like a wild boar. "You can't go and leave me here."

She looked over her shoulder. "Why not? What's wrong with you, besides being drunk?"

"I think I broke my ankle or sprained it real bad. I can't stand up."

Every instinct told Kitt this man deserved whatever he got. Her opinion of men had plummeted after her experience with the fake doctor last year. Maybe this man was a fake too. Maybe he wasn't hurt at all.

She took another few steps toward home. No, she couldn't walk away. Polly Dye said it wasn't fair to judge all men by Dr. Girard's behavior.

Glancing toward the light pouring from her mother's kitchen window, Kitt took a few steps back toward the inebriated man. "I don't think my mother, my sister and I can help you. I'll have to see if Bob Dye can come."

"Where does he live?"

"Just down the road. But I'm not going for help unless you tell me your name. You owe me that much."

"George Burns from Jackson Center." Pushing himself into a sitting position, Mr. Burns wiped snow from his face. "Hurry up. I think I'm getting frostbite."

Kitt gritted her teeth. "You're in no position to give orders, *Mr.* Burns." She strolled down Broad Street, making it clear she would not be hurried.

♠

Polly looked at the clock ticking on the wall as a loud knock sounded on the door. It was unusual to have visitors after dark on a cold winter evening.

She glanced at all the Dyes sitting around the living room. When had they all started huddling together here after supper? Was it when Mother—six months later, she still couldn't bring herself to say the words. Was it since Mother...had gone? Even Maggie had brought her book downstairs to read.

"I'll get it." Polly glanced at Father who made no move toward the door.

He nodded, barely glancing up from the mining journal. He missed Mother so much. Polly worried about him.

Cold air blasted through the door as Polly opened it to find Kitt Potter standing on the porch. "Kitt, come in. Is something wrong?" She reached out to draw her friend into the warmth from the woodstove.

"Not with my family." Kitt shivered and took off her mittens to rub her hands together. "It's George Burns from Jackson Center."

Father looked up, a puzzled frown on his face. "What's wrong with George?"

"You know him?" Kitt turned in Father's direction.

"We used to live in Jackson Center—he owns the tavern there. You remember him, Florence?"

"I know who he is. I never thought much—" Polly closed her mouth. Mother had always discouraged them from making unkind comments about people. "I never knew him well."

Standing up, Father asked again, "What's wrong with him?"

"He's lying beside the road on Broad Street in front of the Christian Church."

CHAPTER FOUR

Polly gasped and opened her mouth.

"What's he doing there? What happened?" Father strode across the room to grab his coat from the hook by the door.

That reaction was more like the one she'd have expected from her father in the olden days.

"He's so drunk he thought I was Savannah Stevens." Kitt rolled her eyes and looked down at her slight figure. "Why would anyone think—"

"Kittie, why is George Burns lying beside the road?" Father pulled on his woolen gloves and crammed on his coonskin hat.

"Because he sprained or broke his ankle when he collided with me. He says he can't stand up." Kitt looked at Polly. "I don't know whether to believe him or not. You know how men are."

"I doubt he'd be lying beside the road in this weather if he could stand up." Father jiggled the doorknob.

"At first he wouldn't tell me his name. Just said he had business with Savannah."

Father glanced at Polly and shook his head. "That can't be good."

"Do you need me to go with you and Kitt, Father?" Polly took a step toward him.

"No, call young Doc Cooley and see if he can meet me at the church."

"I know he's home. I just came from visiting him and my sister when Mr. Burns knocked me down." Kitt shivered.

Polly started for the telephone on the wall as Father turned back to Kitt. "Where's George's buggy?"

"I have no idea. Maybe at the livery on Laycock."

"I'd better hitch up my buggy in case I have to take George somewhere. Why don't you wait inside where it's warm? Then you can tell me if Florence reached your brother-in-law."

♠

Kitt smiled as Bob Dye went out the door. Some things never changed. Everyone else called Florence by her nickname, but not her father.

Polly's little sisters sat on the couch and looked at a worn copy of *The Dutch Twins,* while her younger brothers played dominoes on the floor. Polly had her hands full helping her father raise her younger brothers and sisters since her mother died.

Ending her conversation, Polly returned to stand beside Kitt. "Doc Cooley will be there in a few minutes. He's just finishing his dinner."

"Your father is hitching up the buggy and wanted me to find out if Doc can come." Kitt put her mittens back on. Lowering her voice, she wrinkled her brow. "What kind of business do you think Mr. Burns could have with Savannah Stevens?"

"I don't know." Polly glanced at her younger brothers and sisters and spoke softly. "People gossip about Savannah, but I don't want to think bad thoughts just because she's so—ummm..." Her voice trailed off. "I really don't know her."

"People *do* talk." Kitt looked out the window, watching for Mr. Dye. "In Jackson Center, they say she was a—"

"Kitt." Polly grabbed her friend's arm. "Watch what you say around the children."

"All right, but you know the old saying, 'Where's there's smoke, there's got to be fire,' or something like that."

"No matter what she did in Jackson Center, that doesn't mean she's still doing it in Sandy Lake. People can change. Look at Garrett Young." Polly wrapped her arms around her waist.

"I'm still not convinced his change is real. Besides, I'd imagine you might think the worst of Savannah the way she stole Garrett away from you." Kitt peered at Polly as though trying to read her mind.

"Savannah didn't steal Garrett from me. I don't even think she knew I existed. Garrett's actions weren't Savannah's fault."

Kitt sighed. "You get more like your mother every day, Polly. She never had a bad word to say about anyone and always tried to believe the best of folks. She'd be so proud of you."

"Mother used to say, 'Love always believes the best.' I think it's in the Bible."

Kitt opened the door as she heard the clop clopping of Mr. Dye's horse's hooves. "*Love always believes the best* sounds good, but what if the person is a fraud like Dr. Girard? What then?"

♠

Polly stared at the door with Kitt's words echoing in her ears. "What then?" *What then, Mother? What if we believe the best and the person is a fraud? So many things I want to ask you. So many things I wish I'd learned.*

If you live your life in tune with God's Spirit, His wisdom will become more and more available to you.

Those were Mother's words. God's wisdom was still available to her even though she could no longer go to her mother for answers. *I want to live my life in tune with your Spirit, Father, so your wisdom is available to me. Please show me how.*

A small hand patted hers, and she looked into her youngest sister's eyes. "Polly okay?"

She bent over and gathered Twila into her arms. She was better, but would she ever be okay again?

CHAPTER FIVE

Savannah lay rigid on the narrow bed in her room. It wasn't bedtime, but she'd gone straight to bed rather than going down to help with the dishes. She couldn't bear the thought of facing her landlady. Her stomach was still queasy. What if she'd vomited again at the smell of food? Mrs. Patton might have thought for sure she was pregnant—although, didn't most women throw up in the morning?

Every time footsteps sounded on the stairs, she held her breath. What if Mr. Burns came back? *That broad's gotta sleep some time.* She shivered and her stomach rolled.

Maybe she should have tried to talk to Garrett or his mother. Surely *they* would have believed her. She turned and faced the wall.

I thought if I left my old life and did all the right things, God, you'd take care of me. I thought my life would be different. But now Mr. Burns is coming around telling lies, and Mrs. Patton isn't sure she believes me...

Maybe I was right when I told Garrett you'd washed your hands of me, just like my parents did.

A tear trickled down Savannah's cheek. She didn't bother to wipe it away. *A zebra can't change its stripes. Once a whore, always a whore.* Mr. Burns's words bombarded her. Her mother had said no matter what kind of clothes she wore, people would always know she was poor white trash.

What would she do if Mrs. Patton threw her out? She still had her fancy dresses and a little money saved. It was more than she had when she arrived in Jackson Center. Maybe she could find a way to get to Mercer or Franklin or some other town. She'd just have to be more careful about keeping her clients a secret so the sheriff—

"*No.*" Savannah sat straight up in bed. "*No.*"

Mildred Young said she was a new creature in Christ. Old things had passed away. All things had become new. She was *not* poor white trash. She was *not* a whore. Mr. Burns was wrong.

She swung her legs to the floor and stood up. Opening the door a crack so she could see to light the lamp on her bedside table, she picked up the Bible Mrs. Young had given her. She opened it to the marker at II Corinthians 5:17. *Therefore if any man be in Christ, he is a new creature: old things are passed away; behold, all things are become new.*

♠

Kitt took hold of Bob Dye's hand as he reached out to help her into the black double buggy.

"I'll drop you off at your house." Mr. Dye glanced at her. "Your mother might be worried."

"Oh, she worries all the time, ever since—well, you know." Kitt swallowed hard. She couldn't bring herself to mention Dr. Girard. She'd never talked to Mr. Dye about her bad experience in Atlanta, but it was in all the papers. Everyone knew how stupid she'd been.

Mr. Dye cleared his throat, his voice gruff but kind. "We all make mistakes, Kittie. The important thing is learning from them."

Tears came to her eyes. Polly's father was one of the few people who called her Kittie as her father had before his death seven years ago.

"Whoa, Jasper." He brought the buggy to a stop in front of her house.

"Thank you. I knew I could count on you to help Mr. Burns, even if he doesn't deserve it."

"We can't let a man lie beside the road all night, now can we? Good night, Kittie."

The front door opened as Kitt jumped down from the buggy. Her mother stepped out of the house, holding a lantern.

"Bob, is that you?" Relief oozed out of Mother's voice. "I was just going out to look for Kitt."

Kitt ran up the wooden steps that separated the road from the sidewalk. "I'm fine, Mother. There's no need to worry."

"You were gone a long time. I was afraid—"

"I'll explain everything when we get—"

"Help." A loud bellow came from down the road. "Isn't anybody going to help me?"

"What in the world was that?" Mother peered into the darkness.

"It's George Burns from Jackson Center lying beside the road in front of the church." Kitt sprinted up the porch steps. "He's drunk and he hurt his ankle."

"How do you know?" Suspicion tinged Catherine's words. "You don't even know George Burns."

"I didn't do anything wrong. When will you start trusting me again? He ran into me when I was on my way home from visiting Doc and Lulu. Knocked us both flat."

"Kittie came to ask if I could help George." Mr. Dye's voice was soothing. "Doc's coming too. Nothing for you to worry about, Catherine. Giddy up, Jasper."

♠

Bob's carriage had gone only a few feet when Doc Cooley's car turned onto Broad Street, backfiring twice. His headlamps revealed George Burns sitting up holding his head.

Encouraging his trusty steed to cover the short distance to the church, Bob turned into the parking lot. "Whoa now." He jumped out of the buggy and strode over to George.

Doc was already out of his car looking at the pitiful figure. "What's going on, George?"

"I've either twisted or busted my ankle, Doc." He groaned again as the doctor examined him. "Ouch, be careful."

"How did this happen?" Doc stood up. "From the smell of you, you've had more than enough to drink."

"I came to Sandy Lake on business and took a little spill."

"Who would want to do business with you in your condition?" Doc shook his head. "You're lucky you didn't wind up in the hoosegow. Come on, let's get you in my vehicle." He opened the passenger's side door. "Can you help me hoist him in, Bob?"

"Wait. I don't trust these horseless chariots." George whimpered and tried to pull away.

"You're getting on my nerves, Burns. You're in no position to complain about transportation." Ignoring George's foul epithets,

Bob leaned down to put one arm around the man's waist while Doc did the same. Then the two men joined hands to form a sort of sling to carry the wounded man and hoist him, still resisting, onto the metal seat.

Doc slammed the door and leaned against it, breathing hard. "Thanks, Bob."

Gasping for breath, Bob bent over for a minute, then stood up and headed for his buggy. "Do you need me to help you get him into your office?"

"Good idea. I think my father has a town council meeting tonight. Between George being inebriated and hurt, I'm not sure I can handle him alone."

Bob patted Jasper as he passed him and climbed into his buggy. Dr. Cooley's car roared to life in seconds as he gave the crank a quarter turn. Not bad on this cold night. Maybe one day he'd get a Ford, although Margaret had never—he stopped. Would he ever remember that Margaret was gone?

CHAPTER 6

George trembled as the engine in Dr. Cooley's car roared to life. He had hated automobiles ever since he'd been in Sandy Lake the day the Eberman steamer rattled down Main Street more'n thirty years ago. He'd never forget being spattered with dust and boiling water.

He watched suspiciously as the Doc backed the vehicle into the church parking area and pulled back onto Broad Street. His ankle ached, and his head spun. He straightened his foot and gasped.

"You okay over there?" Doc tugged on the lever to increase their speed as they turned onto Main Street.

"No, I ain't okay. If I was okay, I wouldn't be sitting in this deathtrap. I don't know why anyone would want an automobile."

"*No smell, no noise, no jolt and the ability to ride like a yacht.*" Doc Cooley chuckled as he spouted the advertisement.

"They ain't safe." George pulled the brown bottle from his pocket for one more swig.

"Put that bottle away." The doctor turned left into the driveway of the office he and his father shared. "You're going to have one humdinger of a hangover tomorrow."

"What do you care?" George took another swallow from the bottle before returning it to his pocket. He leaned his head against the metal seat.

Dr. Cooley shook his head, opened his door and came around to the passenger's side. George glared at him as he opened the door wide.

"You gonna be able to fix up my ankle tonight, Doc?"

"Why? Are you still planning to do business with someone

this evening?"

"Nah." George rubbed his hand over his aching head. "It'll be better if I take care of it when she's not expecting me."

Dr. Cooley raised an eyebrow. "She?"

♠

Bob turned into the driveway beside Doc Cooley's vehicle. "Whoa, Jasper." He sprang out of the buggy and scurried to the open passenger door. A puzzled frown wrinkled the doctor's brow.

"Everything okay?"

Doc shook his head. "Probably just the alcohol talking. Let's get him inside. See if you can step out of the car, George, on your good foot."

George scooted to the edge of the seat and lowered his right foot to the running board, but the alcohol he'd consumed interfered with his balance. When his left foot thumped down beside his right one, he let out another howl.

"All right. All right, George. Grab his other arm, Bob. We'll have to lift him down and get him into the office."

The door of old Doc Cooley's residence next to the office opened, and his wife, Sadie, appeared holding a kerosene lantern. "What's going on?"

Joining hands with Bob to create the makeshift sling, her son explained George's mishap. As Sadie Cooley preceded them up the path, the glow of the lantern cast enough light that they managed to get George safely into the building.

"I'll leave the light for you." Sadie set the lantern on the receptionist's desk and closed the outer door behind her. The three men went into one of the examining rooms.

Doc helped Bob put George on the treatment table, then turned on the gas light and raised the headrest. With a few swift movements, he removed his patient's sturdy shoe and thick woolen sock, both soaked with melted snow. George yelped and swore, his ankle and foot already swollen and red from the cold.

The doctor's expert fingers pressed and moved George's ankle. Despite the man's groans and howls, the expression on Doc's face didn't change.

Bob leaned in for a closer look. "What do you think, Doc? Is it broken?"

Doc Cooley shook his head. "I don't think so. Badly

sprained. As much alcohol as I suspect he's had, I'm surprised he feels any pain."

"You sayin' I'm making this up?" George pointed to his ankle. "You can see how swolled up it is."

"Just saying most drunks don't feel much pain."

"I ain't a drunk." George glared at the Doc. "Just needed a little refreshment tonight. What are ya gonna do for my ankle?"

"We'll wrap it with strips of cloth. I'll send some ice with you to take down the swelling." The doctor pulled a bandage from one of the drawers in the examining table, wrapped it around George's ankle, and fastened it. "The big question is *what are we going to do with you?*"

George looked at Bob. "Just bring me my buggy and I'll go home."

"Go home?" Bob snorted. "You couldn't get out of Doc's car by yourself. Grieger probably has a room at the Cottage Hotel, or maybe Mrs. Patton at the old Sandy Lake House."

"Who's gonna pay for that? I ain't gonna stay somewhere that's gonna charge me."

"Maybe Mrs. Patton would let you do some work for her later in exchange for a night's lodging." Doc cleared his throat. "Being divorced maybe she could use a hand after you're on your feet."

George shook his head. "Mrs. Patton and me ain't exactly on friendly terms. I don't think she'd even take me as a payin' customer. Anyway, she probably don't take boarders just for one night."

"Then you have no choice." Bob's patience was running out. "You'll have to stay at the Cottage Hotel and pay the going price."

"I'll just go down to Bach's Livery and get my own horse and buggy." George scooted to the edge of the table.

"Be my guest. We're finished here." Doc Cooley stepped back.

George looked from one to the other. "I can't believe neither of you will bring me my rig."

The whine in his voice set Bob's teeth on edge. He shook his head. "You're in no condition to drive a buggy."

The patient slid his legs and feet off the examining table. He grimaced as his left foot hit the floor but clamped his mouth shut.

"I don't think I can squeeze my foot back into this shoe. How am I supposed to walk without a shoe?"

"Good question, Burns. We might have an old sock and a burlap bag to put over it, but no shoes to fit you." Doc started opening drawers. "I'll have to see if my mother has something we can use. As he headed for the door, he looked back at George. "If you let us help you across the street to the hotel, missing a shoe probably won't be much of a problem. If you decide to go get your rig, you're on your own." He disappeared through the open door.

Bob started to say something, then clamped his lips together. He was done trying to talk sense to this man.

CHAPTER 7

Savannah rolled over in bed and got up. Sleep wouldn't come after all the turmoil of the evening. Maybe a walk would clear her head. She dressed quickly and tiptoed down the stairs. Noises from the kitchen told her Mrs. Patton was still cleaning up.

Letting herself out the front door, Savannah started up the wooden sidewalk. A light snow swirled around her. When her foot slipped on a thin layer of ice, she slowed her pace.

She'd forgotten to check the time. Was it too late to visit the Young's? She headed that direction. Mrs. Young and Garrett were the only friends she had. Though she'd gotten to know some folks in Mr. Young's office, sometimes they stopped talking when she came into the room. She suspected they were talking about her. Some customers from her old life were from Sandy Lake, so it was likely word had gotten around. One agent had made suggestive comments to her twice, so she tried to avoid being alone with him.

What if Mr. Young was home and asked questions about George Burns? She blushed. Her boss might fire her if he didn't believe her story. Sighing, she turned back toward the boarding house. The walk hadn't cleared her head.

She sucked in her breath and stopped walking. What was that—a commotion in front of the Cottage Hotel? There was no mistaking the booming voice. Why was Mr. Burns still in Sandy Lake? It looked like Dr. Cooley and another man were trying to keep him upright. Was he *that* drunk? She took a few steps back, not wanting to be seen.

♠

Innis Patton wiped the flowered oilcloth on the table in the dining room over and over, staring into space. Had she made a mistake bringing Savannah here? Mildred Young had assured her she would continue to work with the girl who was deeply repentant for her past. Innis continued to hear rumors about the poor girl, but she herself knew well enough how stories got around.

Since being divorced, Innis had found a lot of wives protective of their husbands where she was concerned. It didn't matter that she didn't care if she never saw another man as long as she lived. *She'd* divorced her abusive husband, not the other way around. Women still didn't trust her, and some men assumed she was lonely and would welcome their advances. She grimaced.

Maybe she was misjudging Savannah. Maybe she was telling the truth and George Burns was just looking for trouble. Innis didn't know the man well, not being the kind to set foot in any establishment that served alcohol.

Heading out to the kitchen, she wrung out her dishrag and took her dishpan to the side door. When she opened it to throw out the dirty water, raucous voices came from the direction of the Cottage Hotel. What on earth was going on?

Looked like young Doc Cooley, somebody else, and—was that George Burns? She'd hoped he was long gone. And who was standing in the shadows near by? Savannah? What was she doing out at this time of night?

♠

"For heaven's sake, George, keep your voice down. If you don't stop making so much noise, they'll throw you in jail." Bob looked at Doc, shaking his head.

"He bumped my sore foot. How d'ya 'spect me to be quiet?" George glared at Doc.

"I didn't bump you. You stumbled into me because you're so drunk you can't walk straight. I hope Greiger has some black coffee."

Mr. Grieger opened the door of the Hotel and peered into the darkness. "What's going on out there?"

"I'm sorry, Mr. Grieger. We need to get Mr. Burns inside." Bob took a firmer grip on George's arm and propelled him toward the door.

"Sounds to me like Mr. Burns had too much to drink."

"You're right, Grieger. We were hoping you'd have some

black coffee to sober him up and maybe a room where he could sleep it off." Doc's eyes pleaded with Mr. Grieger.

The hotel proprietor shifted from one foot to the other. "I hate to turn down a paying customer, but I can't have him disturbing the other guests. Maybe he ought to spend the night in jail. Might learn a thing or two."

"Up to you." Bob shrugged.

"No, please don't do that. It might hurt my business if word gets around I was in jail."

"Maybe you should have thought of that sooner." Mr. Grieger hesitated, then stepped back with a sigh. "Oh, all right. You can come in, but if you give me any trouble, out you go."

♠

Taking a deep breath, Savannah hurried toward the boarding house. She didn't think Mrs. Patton usually locked the door at night. After the incident with Mr. Burns, she might make an exception. It wouldn't do for her to be locked out. She turned the doorknob and breathed a sigh of relief as the door swung open.

"Savannah."

She jumped, shielding her eyes from the lamp Mrs. Patton held. Her heart raced, and heat rose in her cheeks even though she hadn't done anything wrong.

"I just took a walk to clear my mind, Mrs. Patton. I hope I didn't startle you."

"Were you taking a walk or meeting someone?" Mrs. Patton's face was stern. "When I threw out my dishwater, I saw Mr. Burns outside the hotel."

"I told you, I don't want anything to do with Mr. Burns. I never want to see him again. He was part of my old life. I'm different now."

"Maybe so. I want to believe you. It just seems strange, you going out and getting to the hotel the same time he did."

Savannah couldn't hold back her sobs. "I wasn't meeting him. You have to believe me."

"Our agreement didn't say anything about you entertaining men at the hotel, but surely you know I can't allow one of my boarders to do that." Mrs. Patton tapped her foot and stared at the floor. "This is twice today I've had reason to doubt my decision to allow you to stay here. The rumors I've been hearing don't help your case."

Tears rolled down Savannah's cheeks as she continued to shake her head.

At last Mrs. Patton met her gaze. "I won't make you leave because I know rumors are often false. But I think we need to change our agreement to say you'll have to leave if you entertain men here or anywhere else. I'm going to extend your trial period for another six months."

Unable to speak through her tears, Savannah nodded, walked to the staircase and trudged up the steps to her room. Pushing her door closed, she dropped to her knees beside her bed. *God, you know I'm innocent. Why won't Mrs. Patton believe me? Don't you care at all what happens to me?*

CHAPTER 8

George turned over on the lumpy mattress and groaned. He couldn't believe he'd allowed Doc Cooley and Bob Dye to talk him into staying at the hotel. How much was this going to cost? He probably wouldn't get any sleep with his ankle and his head throbbing. The black, bitter coffee Grieger had scrounged up had cleared his head enough to add a new level to the pain.

What was he doing in Sandy Lake anyway? Why had he gotten drunk? He blinked at the modest dresser and nightstand barely visible in the darkness as his memory kicked in.

He'd been doing his books and realized he didn't have enough money to pay his bills. Even though it was the middle of the day, he'd taken his first drink. Then another. Finally, he'd remembered the money Savannah owed him. By 5:00 he'd made up his mind to go and collect.

Now instead of collecting, he was gonna owe Mr. Grieger money in the morning. Bitterness pooled like bile in the back of his throat. He couldn't let that floozy get the best of him.

He threw back the blanket and patchwork quilt, sat up, and swung his legs over the edge of the bed. The room tilted and spun. Drawing a few deep breaths, he started to lean over and changed his mind. Stretching his right leg, he groped for his shoe with his foot.

Ah, there it was. After a few fruitless attempts to thrust his foot into his shoe, he lowered himself to the floor with a heavy thud and succeeded in putting it on. He hadn't taken the burlap bag off his other foot, so one shoe would do. The boarding house where Savannah stayed wasn't far.

Gingerly, he put some weight on his left foot and gritted his teeth. He had to do this. The hinges on the heavy door screeched as he inched it open. The hall was dark and he dragged his hand along the wall, so he'd know when he came to the stairway. Mr. Grieger wouldn't be happy if George woke his guests by falling down the steps.

When his hand dropped into empty space, he knew he'd reached the staircase. Groping with his left hand, he found the railing, then inched his left foot down a step. He clenched his jaw. He wouldn't give up. Slowly, he lowered his right foot, then his left, holding back a groan. At last, he reached the entryway on the first floor, hobbled to the door as best he could, and turned the knob. Ah, Grieger hadn't locked. Probably no one bothered to lock in this town.

The cold night air took his breath, and he shoved his hand in his pocket, reaching for his brown bottle to take away the chill. After a few gulps, he inched his way across the porch to the front steps, grabbed the railing and repeated the process he'd used inside.

Where did Savannah keep her money? Did banks let people like her have accounts? If she didn't have money in her room, he'd take some of what she owed him in services rendered. He smirked, then remembered his sore ankle. That might have to wait for another time, but he'd get *something* from her to make it worth his while.

Determination set his jaw and he walked the few steps to the boarding house. He'd have to be quiet in case Mrs. Patton was still awake. He grabbed the door knob and twisted. The door was locked.

♠

Garrett opened one eye, then closed it again. The sunshine didn't dispel the darkness hovering over him. He was hungry, but the thought of food sickened him. What was wrong with him? He hadn't had this bad a morning since, well, since he'd surrendered his life to Jesus.

George Burns...the accusations he'd made against Savannah. The doubts Garrett had entertained. No wonder he felt sick to his stomach. What if everyone was laughing at him behind his back? Maybe he and his parents had been too trusting. His mother always believed the best of people unless proven wrong.

Even then she went on loving. But what if Savannah had just been pretending to be a Christian?

He sat up, rubbed his eyes, and reached for his Bible. If he didn't read scripture first thing, he wasn't good at doing it later. Opening to I Corinthians, chapter thirteen, where he'd left his marker, he began to read. *Though I speak with the tongues of men and of angels, and have not charity, I am become as sounding brass, or a tinkling cymbal.*

Does that mean if I can speak well but don't give to the poor, I'm just making a lot of noise?

Garrett read verse two, shook his head. Too hard to understand. On to verse three. *And though I bestow all my goods to feed the poor, and though I give my body to be burned, and have not charity, it profiteth me nothing.* Wasn't feeding the poor the same as charity? Sometimes reading the Bible was too hard. He closed it, finished dressing and went downstairs.

"Ma, what does *charity* mean?"

His mother turned from the wood stove where she was frying bacon. "Charity? You know charity is giving to the poor."

"I read it in the Bible." Garrett poured a glass of milk. Maybe it would settle his stomach. "Something about just making a lot of noise if I don't have charity."

"Oh, that means love. Some people call that the Love Chapter. Reverend Lawrence says in the Greek the word is agape, which means God's kind of love."

"So God wants us to love others the way He loves us?"

Ma pulled a small blue serving platter from the cupboard and started arranging fragrant strips of bacon. "That's what He wants. His love is unselfish and unconditional. It bears all things, believes all things, hopes all things, and endures all things."

Garrett squirmed. "Is that in the Bible?"

"It's in the Love Chapter. Love always believes the best."

Sinking into a chair, Garrett buried his head in his hands, ignoring the damage to his carefully combed hair. "What if you believe someone and they aren't telling the truth?"

"That's where bearing all things and enduring all things comes in. There's no guarantee we won't get hurt when we love unselfishly and unconditionally. People break God's heart all the time." Ma dished up the steaming scrambled eggs and brought them to the table with the bacon.

"I think God is asking too much. We aren't God, we're just ordinary human beings. We can't love the way He does." Garrett's stomach rolled at the smell of the food in front of him, food he usually loved.

"Is this about Savannah?" Ma's gaze was kind.

"I don't think God should expect us to believe in her without knowing she's telling the truth. How do we know she's really a Christian?"

Ma put down her fork. "How do you feel when people don't believe you've changed, don't believe you're a Christian?"

Garrett looked at his plate, then stood up. "I don't want any breakfast."

"But Garrett, you didn't eat supper last night."

Grabbing his coat from the hook, Garrett opened the door and slammed it behind him.

CHAPTER 9

Savannah sat at her desk in a back room of Mr. Young's insurance office. She rubbed her eyes, then stared at the typewriter keys. It was hard to concentrate with George Burns's voice ringing in her ears. *A zebra can't change its stripes. Once a whore always a whore.* How many people in Sandy Lake knew about her past? Did everyone see her the way her former landlord did?

Forcing her attention back to the letter she was typing, she finished a sentence on her Remington typewriter, startling when the bell rang to warn that she was nearing the right margin. Mr. Young said her typing improved every day, but she was still slow. Garrett's father was such an understanding employer.

She jumped again when the outer door slammed in the front office. "I need to speak to Savannah Stevens." Despite the distance, she heard every word. There was no mistaking the demanding voice. Her stomach churned. She walked to the door of her office.

"I'm sorry but she can't be disturbed. She's very busy." Her boss had never refused to allow anyone to talk to one of his employees. Had he somehow found out Mr. Burns was harassing her?

"Listen here." Mr. Burns's voice boomed. "I need to speak to her right now. I have important business with her."

"I'm sorry. I can't have my employees' work interrupted for private business." Mr. Young's voice increased in volume, too.

"I've come from Jackson Center. I don't wanna have to make another trip."

"That's up to you, but I suggest you be on your way."

With each word, Savannah's appreciation for Mr. Young increased. She was thankful he was protecting her from the blustering, angry man.

She peeked out the doorway. Dorothy, the other secretary, stood frozen at the counter while Mr. Burns teetered in front of Mr. Young. He tried to peer around him down the hallway. She jerked her head back.

"I dunno why you'd hire the likes of her anyway. You're just asking for trouble."

"I've had no trouble with Savannah Stevens. You're the one who's causing trouble. If you don't leave, I'll have to call the sheriff."

Savannah risked another peek in time to see Mr. Burns back up a few steps, huffing and glaring at her boss. At last, he turned around, yanked the door open and went out, slamming it behind him. She dared to step out in the hall as the whole building vibrated.

Dorothy blew out a deep breath and moved to her desk. "What was that all about?"

"Just a windbag trying to make trouble." Mr. Young massaged his forehead.

"You've never complained before when someone needed to talk to us during office hours." Dorothy's brows drew together.

"I don't usually mind, but I didn't trust that man. Besides, he's been drinking." Mr. Young started down the hall. Seeing Savannah standing by her door, he motioned for her to come to his office.

Holding her breath, Savannah followed him. He nodded at the chair in front of his desk and closed the door. They spoke together.

"Savannah—"

"Mr. Young, I—"

Garrett's father laughed. "What were you going to say?"

"I'm sorry about Mr. Burns coming here and causing trouble." Savannah picked at a thread on her plaid skirt.

He crossed the room and dropped into his chair. "Why did Mr. Burns want to talk to you?"

She hesitated and swallowed. Then swallowed again. "He came to my room at Mrs. Patton's last evening."

"He came to your *room*?" Mr. Young scowled. "I didn't think anyone but boarders were allowed upstairs."

"They aren't but that didn't stop him."

"What did he want?"

Savannah felt heat rise up her neck. She and Mr. Young had never talked about her past but surely his wife had told him. "He wanted...that is he pretended to think Mrs. Patton has...he pretended to think I'm still—"

Mr. Young's voice was stern, yet kind. "Are you?"

"No, no, no." Savannah looked him in the eye. "I'm not. I kept my agreement with Mrs. Patton. But now she doesn't believe me. Last night—oh everything is such a mess." She tried to push down the sobs that rose in her throat. "If I had anywhere to go, I'd leave town. I never thought Mr. Burns would come after me. Sandy Lake is too close to Jackson Center. Too many people know about my old life."

Mr. Young steepled his fingers, elbows resting on his desk. "Sometimes running away seems like the right thing to do. I understand why you'd want to—but once a person starts running, it's hard to stop. They're always looking over their shoulder, always afraid someone will come along who knows about their past."

"But what can I do?"

"You can stay here in Sandy Lake and prove you've changed. You can hold your head high and keep holding it up because *you* know you're not that person any more."

"Your wife said I was a new creature in Christ." Savannah felt the corners of her mouth lift.

"If she says so, then I believe it. Mildred is the expert on spiritual things."

"Thank you. You've been so kind. Not many people would hire someone like me and risk their reputation."

"Well, I have to admit, you have Mildred to thank for that too. She believes in you, and it would take a tougher man than me to say no to *her*." Mr. Young smiled.

Savannah tucked a dark curl behind her ear and stood up. "Thank you for protecting me. I heard what you said to Mr. Burns."

"Why do you think he came here today? He said he had important business with you."

"Last night before he left, he said he'd be back to get what I owed him. He's never mentioned I owed him anything."

Her employer's brow furrowed. He tapped his fingers on the mahogany desk. "I didn't know whether or not to tell you... Last night Mr. Burns came to see Garrett."

Dropping back into her chair, Savannah gasped. "He came to see Garrett? Why?"

"I think he hoped Garrett would give him money."

"Oh no." Savannah covered her face with her hands. "Your family has been so kind to me, and I've brought you nothing but trouble. I can't stay here." She stood up.

"Savannah..."

"No, my mind's made up. I have to go."

CHAPTER TEN

"Hurry up and come down for breakfast or you'll be late for school. Maggie, can you help Elsie and Twila, please?" Polly brushed a strand of hair out of her eyes as she scurried back to the kitchen. Mornings were so hectic. How had Mother managed? Even though Polly had helped a lot in other ways, Mother had never asked her to get up early to help with breakfast.

She opened the bread box covered with red, pink, and yellow tulips that Father had given Mother for Christmas. There were reminders of Mother everywhere. Shivering, she pulled out a loaf of bread. Last Christmas had been difficult, trying to make Christmas special, to fill the huge void. Polly could do the work Mother had done but she couldn't be who Mother had been.

"You're getting more like your mother every day. She'd be so proud of you." Were Kitt's words true? Would her mother be proud of her?

Footsteps thundered on the stairs. Polly looked at the uncut loaf of bread in her hand and shook her head. Still holding the bread, she met her brothers as they dashed into the dining room. "Go ahead and eat your oatmeal. I'll bring the bread and jam in a few minutes."

As she cut a few slices, her brother George's voice floated to the kitchen. "You're sitting in my seat, Robert."

"It doesn't matter where we sit at breakfast. Just eat your oatmeal." Ben didn't often get involved with the younger boys, but he disliked bickering at the table.

Lighter footsteps on the stairs and a loud thump. "What was that, Maggie?" Polly had to raise her voice to be heard over the continued discussion about the rules for where to sit at breakfast.

Maggie appeared in the kitchen doorway, carrying Twila and holding Elsie's hand. Beth trailed close behind. "I just dropped the book I'm reading. Nobody hurt."

Polly sighed as Maggie got the girls settled in their seats. Maggie was trying hard to help more with Elsie and Twila and the house, but the ever-present book in her hand often interfered. She slathered fresh butter on the bread and strawberry jam she'd helped Mother make last summer. Their strawberry patch on the hill had produced an exceptional crop. How would she manage the strawberries, as well as planting, weeding, and harvesting the garden without mother's help?

Rushing into the dining room with the bread on a plate in one hand and a pitcher of milk in the other, Polly tripped on a rag rug inside the door. The bread fell, jelly-side down, on the floor. Milk spilled out of the pitcher on top of it. Polly landed face down in the mess.

Silence reigned for a split second before sobs erupted from Polly's throat. She pounded her fists on the floor, causing milk which had puddled beside the bread to splash in all directions.

Twila wailed. "Polly cwy. Polly cwy."

Chairs squeaked on the bare floor moments before gentle hands patted Polly's back. "It's okay, Polly. It's okay." Beth's gentle voice sounded so much like Mother's.

"We'll clean it up." Maggie nudged her to get up.

"No use crying over spilled milk." Robert's changing voice squeaked at the end.

Polly got to her feet, milk and jam dripping off her chin, and stumbled to the kitchen. She grabbed a dishrag and wiped her face, not knowing or caring if it was clean. With a half-hearted swipe at her dress, she threw the dishrag on the counter and sprinted through the living room. She grabbed her coat and went out, slamming the door behind her.

♠

Savannah raced up the stairs at the boarding house, grabbed a small suitcase, and threw in a change of clothes, toothbrush, comb and a few other essentials. Zipping it shut, she hesitated. Should she leave Mrs. Patton a note? No. Mrs. Patton probably wouldn't believe anything she told her. Better just to leave.

Peeking out her door to make sure the coast was clear, Savannah crept through the hall, down the stairs, and out the front door. Tears blinded her. Where had George Burns gone? What if she ran into him? Did it really matter now?

Still, she looked in all directions, blinking away her tears. No one in sight. Turning left, she started down College Street, the opposite direction Mr. Burns would take if he was returning to Jackson Center. Her pace slowed as she left the boarding house behind. Where was she going? She hesitated at Walnut Street and then turned right. She didn't want to pass the Public School where children would soon be arriving.

Savannah rarely came to this part of town. She usually walked up Main Street to the General Store for anything she needed. Looking straight ahead, she saw the enormous house that resembled a castle. What would it be like to be part of a family who had enough money to live like that? Surely they must be the happiest people in the world. Not a single worry or care.

She lowered her head and turned left on Broad Street. Might as well start toward Greenville. It was as good a place as any, and the chances of anyone recognizing her were slight. She plodded along, head down against the wind that whipped the ends of her red scarf. Another sob escaped her lips. What had she been thinking, leaving Georgia to come *north*? If she'd stayed in the south, at least she wouldn't have had to contend with cold weather. Her tears fell faster.

The crash of a door slamming startled her. She glanced toward the house on her right. A young woman of about her age stood outside the door, head down, putting on her coat. What in the world was in her hair?

If only I had a friend like her. Where had that thought come from? It was no use longing for a friend. When they found out who she was, they'd want nothing to do with her. She ran until the pain in her side forced her to slow down.

♠

Polly stumbled across the porch, down the steps, and across the sidewalk. Then down the wooden stairs that led to Broad Street, not caring that she might fall. Her life was retched and no hope of it getting better. She'd made a promise to Mother to help Father raise the children and even if a man came along who wanted to marry her—unlikely as that seemed—she wouldn't break her word. Twila was only two and a half years old. By the time she was grown, Polly would be a confirmed old maid with no prospects for marriage.

She turned right, head down, with no destination in mind. Who really cared about getting married anyway? Marriage just meant more children to raise. Not that she didn't like children but— *Be still and know that I am God.* She recognized the voice and the Scripture. God had spoken it to her when Mother was having seizures. He'd wanted her to trust Him, then and now. Could she do that? No solutions, no reassurances from God that everything would be fine?

What was that? A muffled sob? Raising her head, she discovered a lonely figure walking ahead of her, head down, steps slow. Her first impulse was to pass the person without speaking. She wasn't in the mood to talk. But something about her hopeless air drew Polly.

She stopped beside the raven-haired young woman who stared at the ground, little hiccups escaping her lips. "*Savannah?*" The words were out almost without Polly's volition. Even though she and Savannah had never been introduced, she would have recognized her anywhere. This was the girl who'd been snuggled up to Garrett in his car months ago. That's how Polly had discovered Garrett had been leading her on.

Savannah lifted her head and gazed at Polly, her deep violet blue eyes tear drenched and questioning. "Yes? How do you know my name?"

Polly fought back her own sobs and the bitterness that rose in her throat. She wanted to scream at Savannah.

She swallowed hard, cleared her throat, and softened her voice. "Someone told me who you were. What's wrong? Why are you crying?"

At the kind words, more sobs burst out of Savannah. She clamped her hand over her mouth.

Polly glanced at the suitcase in Savannah's hand. Her forehead puckered. "Where are you going?"

Hesitating, Savannah stared at the ground, then lifted her eyes. "I'm going to Greenville."

"You're walking to *Greenville* in this weather? That's

eighteen miles away."

"I don't know what else to do." A tear slid down Savannah's lovely face.

Biting her lip, Polly hesitated. Surely God wouldn't expect her to befriend the girl with whom her beau had fallen in love?

You're getting more like your mother every day. She'd be so proud of you.

Those words again. If only they were true.

CHAPTER ELEVEN

Polly studied Savannah, lovely in her cardinal red coat, whose gaze had fallen to the road again. She fought to be objective.

"Has Garrett been unkind to you?" The words were out before Polly had time to consider what the distraught woman's reaction might be.

Savannah's head snapped up to meet Polly's gaze. She blinked tears from her eyes. "No, no. Why would you say that? Do you know Garrett?"

Taking a deep breath, Polly bit her lip. "I'm sorry, I shouldn't have... Garrett and I..." She swallowed and began again. "We all know each other in Sandy Lake. I—I've seen you with Garrett, and I don't understand why you need to *walk* to Greenville unless—"

"Unless we'd had a fight? No, it's more complicated than that." Savannah shifted from one foot to the other, shivering as the wind whirled around them.

Polly hesitated. *If you live your life in tune with God's Spirit, His wisdom will become more and more available to you.* She gave a little nod. "I'm Polly Dye and I live in the last house we passed. Why don't you come have a cup of tea so we can talk?"

"But weren't you going somewhere?"

"Not really." Polly frowned. "It's complicated."

Savannah peered at Polly. Then tentatively reached out and touched her jelly- and milk-matted hair "You, too?"

"Me too. Rough morning." Polly turned and walked toward the house she'd rushed to get away from just minutes before with Savannah close behind.

♠

As Savannah followed Polly into the house, warmth and children's voices surrounded her. She began to relax.

"Polly, Polly." Two little girls squealed as they ran to hug her red-haired rescuer. The smaller of the two clung to Polly, repeating, "Polly okay? Polly okay?"

"I'm okay, Twila. I'm sorry if I scared you."

As Polly hung up her coat and beckoned for Savannah to do the same, a shorter young woman with brown hair came into the room. "Polly are you—"

Before she could finish, Polly interrupted. "Did the children—"

"I've already gotten them off to school. I'm staying home today. I think you need a break."

Savannah looked from one girl to the other, then reached for her coat. "This probably isn't a good time for me to visit."

"It's okay. It'll be good to get my mind off my problems. This is my sister, Maggie."

"Nice to meet you." Savannah's hand lingered on her coat as she peered at the jelly in Polly's hair. What kind of crisis was she having? Maybe she should get on her way to Greenville.

Polly gestured toward Savannah. "This is Savannah, Garrett's friend." Maggie's eyebrows went up but Polly continued. "She's having a bad morning. I'm going to make her a cup of tea."

"No, really. I should go." Savannah edged closer to the door, still clutching her coat.

"Why don't you both sit in Mother's— in the sitting room, and I'll make some tea." Maggie held out her hands to Twila and Elsie. "Come help me, please."

Savannah let go of her coat and followed Polly into the sitting room. Polly sat on the loveseat and motioned for her to do the same.

"Is your mother away or sick?" Savannah sat down beside Polly near the well-filled bookcase.

"Our mother passed away six months ago. We're still trying to get used to life without her."

"Oh, Polly. I'm so sorry. Was she ill?"

"No, she died in childbirth last August."

"What about the baby?"

Polly closed her eyes. "He—he didn't live either."

Savannah shook her head. Did she dare say what she was thinking? Would it sound like she was criticizing God? She leaned toward Polly. "I don't understand why God lets things like that happen."

Opening her eyes, Polly gazed toward the window. "It's hard to understand."

"I can see why bad things might happen to wicked people, but I bet your mother was a wonderful person. It doesn't seem fair."

Polly turned toward Savannah. "I used to feel that way, too."

"I—I haven't always lived the best life." Savannah swallowed and avoided looking into Polly's eyes. "But I thought if I stopped...stopped sinning and obeyed God, things would change. For a while, life was better. Now suddenly everything is going wrong."

"God never promised life would be easy for people who loved and obeyed Him."

"Really?" Savannah's eyes widened as she tried to remember what Mrs. Young had told her. "Then what's the use of being a Christian?"

"Because God promises to go through the trials with us and give us the strength we need. He promises to bring good from our problems."

"I don't see what good God could bring from the bad things I'm going through."

Polly sighed. "Believe me, I know how you feel. This morning I felt that way too. But sometimes we develop qualities through suffering that we wouldn't develop any other way."

Savannah's brows drew together. "But Garrett's mother says I'm a new creature in Christ."

"Becoming new creatures in Christ is only the beginning." Polly pulled her feet up under her. "We still have lots of growing to do."

Springing to her feet, Savannah marched to the window. "Why can't we grow without suffering?"

"Sometimes we can, but suffering comes to everyone some time." Polly joined Savannah at the window. "Pastor Caldwell says we have a choice—to be molded, shaped and changed into the image of Christ or—" she paused, then nodded— "to become brittle, hard and easily shattered by our tragedies."

Sighing, Savannah bowed her head. "I guess being a Christian is harder than I thought."

"I still have a lot of growing to do. The way I reacted this morning showed me that. If we don't grow, our lives will fall apart when the storms come."

"What about when your mother died? How did you survive? Even though you were having a bad morning, I felt the peace and love when I stepped into your house." Savannah gazed into Polly's eyes, hoping to find the answers she needed.

Polly pursed her lips, then guided Savannah back to the loveseat "Have a seat. I have something to show you."

CHAPTER 12

Polly pushed the sitting room door open as Maggie, Twila and Elsie came from the kitchen. Maggie carried two cups of tea, Elsie clutched the sugar bowl and Twila gripped two spoons.

"I'll be right back." Swerving around them, Polly dashed up the stairs.

Reaching the sanctuary of her room, she dropped to her knees beside her bed. *Father, I can't believe this is happening. I know Garrett's shameful behavior wasn't Savannah's fault. But still...* She buried her face in the bright quilt her mother had pieced from leftover scraps of material. If only her mother were...No, this was why God had started teaching her to rely on Him even while her mother was still with them.

Taking a deep breath, she raised her head. *Even though I didn't want to invite Savannah to come in, it's been good for me to share what I've learned, to remember where my strength comes from. I know what I need to do.*

She stood and padded to the bureau she shared with her sisters and opened one of the drawers. Gazing down at the faded, burgundy book lying there, she traced the raised lettering—*Diary.* Sarah's diary... How could she part with it? Especially to share with someone who'd helped cause her pain?

Polly stared at the little book. *The truth is, whether I like it or not, I think Savannah needs it more than I do. If I loan it to her, I'm sure she'll give it back.*

Picking up the precious book, Polly left her bedroom and started down the steps. Twila stuck her head around the doorway at the bottom. She pulled her thumb out of her mouth as Polly reached her. "Polly read book?"

Gathering the youngest in the family into her arms, she thought how tall she'd grown. She wasn't a baby anymore. "No, I'm going to loan this book to Savannah."

"Polly read to me?"

"Later, Twila." She set the little girl down at the sitting room door. "Go find Maggie. She likes to read."

Pushing open the door, she smiled at Savannah who sat drinking her tea. She sat down and set the diary on the loveseat between them, then picked up her cup of tea.

"What's that?" Savannah nodded at the book.

"The diary of one of the original owners of this house, Sarah Davis."

"It looks really old. Where did you get it?"

"Upstairs under a loose floor board in the back bedroom. I thought you might want to borrow it."

Savannah gazed at the book, her eyes questioning. It *did* look boring.

"God used it, among other things, to change my life."

"How?"

"Sarah was a woman who experienced many losses. Yet she still maintained strong faith in God. At first it made me angry. How could she not see that God had failed her? But later, I wanted the kind of faith she had."

Savannah put her teacup on the table and picked up the diary. She glanced at the spidery handwriting on a few of the pages.

"Our neighbor, Blanche Davis, is married to Sarah's grandson. Before Sarah died, she asked Blanche to put the diary back in its hiding place."

"Why?"

"Sarah thought God wanted someone to find it, and I think that someone was me. This diary was her legacy to me, and I want to share it with you."

Lifting her gaze from the faded pages, Savannah looked at Polly with glistening eyes. "Why me, Polly? You don't even know me. I don't deserve to have you share Sarah's legacy with me."

Touching Savannah's hand, Polly forced a smile. "Did you forget you're a new creature in Christ? I read in the Bible yesterday that God removes our sins as far as the east is from the west. When

He looks at us, He sees Jesus. He would want me to share it with you."

Tears poured down Savannah's cheeks, dripping onto the faded cover of the diary. "Thank you, Polly. I was trying to run away from my problems and was being tempted to turn back to my old life. I don't know what I'd have done if you hadn't invited me to come in."

"It was good for me to remember that I'm not the only one with problems." Polly handed Savannah a clean handkerchief. "Mother used to say sometimes the best thing we can do when we're discouraged is to do something good for someone else."

Dabbing the tears from her cheeks and from the diary, Savannah smiled. "I'm glad you're feeling better too. I'm still not sure what to do about my problems, but I don't think running away is the answer. Do you think we could be friends?"

Polly's gaze dropped for a moment, and she hesitated. Then, taking a deep breath, she looked at Savannah. "I don't have a lot of time to go places, but if you don't mind the noise and clutter—" She nodded toward the pile of children's books on the floor. "You're welcome here any time."

"Thank you." Savannah stood and smoothed her long, plaid skirt. "I'd better go talk to my boss. He said I should stay in Sandy Lake and prove I'd changed, but I thought I was causing them too much trouble."

"I'd heard you work for Garrett's father. Why did you think you were causing them trouble?"

"It's a long story. They didn't ask me to leave but I hate feeling like I'm a burden. I need to talk to Garrett to find out..." Savannah bit her lip with perfect white teeth. "Well, it's complicated."

Polly stood too. *She's so beautiful.* Was that a pang of jealousy? Even though Polly had been the one to break things off with Garrett, the sting of rejection had reared its ugly head when he told her he was in love with Savannah. What did Savannah want to ask Garrett? Were they having problems? Maybe there was still a chance... *Stop it.* Things were over between her and Garrett.

"Thanks again for inviting me in." Savannah turned toward the door. "Your brothers and sisters are lucky to have someone like you to take care of them. Your mother would be so proud of you."

"You're welcome." Polly wasn't proud of her thoughts. "Come back any time. Maybe I'll put you to work. There's never a shortage of things to do." She followed Savannah to the living room and watched as she pulled her scarlet coat from the hook.

Twila jumped down from the loveseat where Maggie had been reading to her and Elsie. She stuck her thumb in her mouth and watched Savannah put on her coat. Taking a few steps in her direction, she pulled out her thumb and pointed at her. "Pretty. So pretty."

Polly's heart twinged at Twila's words and at the adoring look on her sister's face as she stared at Savannah. "It's not polite to point, Twila."

"It's all right." Savannah stepped closer to Twila and stooped down beside her. "Do you like my coat, Twila? Maybe someday you can have one like it."

Polly met Maggie's widened eyes. Would mother have approved of the bold color of Savannah's coat? With a shrug in Maggie's direction, she turned back to Savannah. "Thanks again for visiting. I'll be praying for you."

It was a promise only God could help her keep.

CHAPTER 13

Loud voices distracted Kitt as she grabbed her green wool coat to go to the market for her mother. Who could be making so much noise? She strode to the window and squinted at the horse and buggy turning from Broad to Walnut Street. She didn't recognize them. Wait, was that Savannah racing down Walnut Street? Hard to miss her scarlet coat. Maybe that was George Burns in the buggy now keeping pace with her.

Kitt threw open the door and raced down the stairs. In no time, she caught up with the buggy and went around it. The chestnut mare snorted and skidded to a stop as she blocked its path.

"What do you think you're doing?" She glared at Mr. Burns.

"Outa my way." Mr. Burns's voice vibrated and his cheeks were cherry red. "I'm just trying to get what's owed me."

"Not this way, you won't." Kitt stood her ground. She'd promised herself she'd never give in to bullies again. When he yanked on the reins to go around her, she grabbed them close to the bit. A quick glance over her shoulder told her Savannah had stopped her pell-mell race down the road.

"Be careful. I don't want you to get hurt." Savannah was panting so hard, Kitt could barely understand her words.

"Go. Go." Kitt flapped a hand over her shoulder. "Get out of here."

Savannah's loud gasps slowly faded. Kitt risked another quick glance over her shoulder. No sign of her. Then she turned on Mr. Burns. "Haven't you caused more than enough trouble for one trip to Sandy Lake? What is the matter with you?"

"If it weren't for this bum ankle, I'd show you a thing or

two."

They glared at each other. Kitt tapped her foot on the hard-packed, dirt road. "I have half a mind to call the sheriff, see what he'd have to say about your escapades."

"By the time you do that, I'll be long gone. Now get outta my way. I got better things to do than sit here jawing with you."

After another quick look behind her, Kitt stepped out of Mr. Burns's path. "Be on your way then. Just stay out of Sandy Lake."

"Oh, I'll be back. Don't think for a minute this is over." Mr. Burns raised his whip and brought it down hard, causing his horse to bolt straight ahead toward Lake Street.

Kitt cringed. What if he'd used his whip on her? Why was she shaking now that it was over? She took deep breaths and followed at a much slower pace, turning onto College Street and keeping an eye out for Savannah. Someone said she lived at the old Sandy Lake House, now a boarding house at the corner of College and Main. What had she been doing on Broad Street?

Turning right at Main Street, Kitt quickened her steps. That was Savannah coming out of Mrs. Patton's place. Kitt called to her. "Are you okay?"

Savannah turned around and recognition dawned in her eyes. "Thank you so much for what you did for me. You could have gotten hurt. I don't believe we've met."

"I'm Kitt Potter, and I can't *stand* bullies."

"I'm Savannah Stevens. I don't know why Mr. Burns didn't get out of his buggy to chase me. I wouldn't have had a chance."

"I can tell you why. Last night he'd had too much to drink and plowed right into me in front of the church on Broad Street. Knocked us both down. I had to get Bob Dye and Jud, I mean, Doc Cooley—he's my brother-in-law, to take him to Doc's office. I imagine his ankle is still giving him trouble."

"Well, that's a relief. Maybe he'll go back to Jackson Center where he belongs."

"I threatened to call the sheriff. Mr. Burns said he was trying to get what you owed him, and he'd be back."

Savannah sighed. "I don't know what he's talking about. He used to be my landlord, but I paid him my last month's rent. He came to the boarding house last night and got me in trouble with Mrs. Patton." She closed her eyes and shook her head. "I'm sorry. I shouldn't be bothering you with my problems."

"You're not bothering me."

"Do you live in that wonderful house that looks like a castle on Broad Street?"

Kitt nodded. "I live there with my mother and my sister."

Savannah's eyes widened. "That's a really big house for three people."

"There were eight people, but one brother and one sister are married. My father and two of my brothers died."

"I'm so sorry. I guess no one is immune to trouble."

"No, I suppose no one is immune."

"Thanks again for helping me. I should get back to work so Mr. Young knows I didn't leave town." Savannah squeezed Kitt's hand and hurried down the street.

Kitt watched her go, a puzzled frown pulling her brows together. What did Savannah mean by that?

♠

Savannah passed the bank and waited for a minute as a horse and buggy turned left onto Main Street from Maple. Would Mr. Young be happy she'd changed her mind about leaving? The tall man in the buggy stared at her. Did he know about—no, she wasn't going to assume the worst. She held her head high.

Crossing the street, Savannah reached the sidewalk and opened the door to the building that housed both the Furniture Undertaker's business and Mr. Young's insurance office. Pausing to take a deep breath, she turned the knob to go into the office where she worked.

Dorothy did a double-take. "Are you all right? You left in an awful hurry."

"I'm okay. I had an—an emergency." Savannah avoided Dorothy's eyes, hoping she wouldn't ask any questions about Mr. Burns's visit.

Mr. Young came out of his office as Dorothy began to question Savannah. "What did that nasty man want with you? And what did he mean by saying—"

"Dorothy, I need you to get that letter in the mail." Mr. Young tapped his fingers on Dorothy's desk.

"I'm sorry, sir." Dorothy lowered her head.

Beckoning to Savannah, Mr. Young headed for his office

and she followed. He sat at his desk, his kind blue eyes encouraging. "Did you change your mind?"

"Yes. That is, I decided you were right about not running away. I met Polly Dye and she invited me to come in for tea."

"She did?

"Do you know Polly? You sound surprised."

"I do. She and..." Mr. Young cleared his throat. "She's a fine young woman taking on a big job since her mother died."

Savannah told Mr. Young about her conversation with Polly and about Mr. Burns chasing her in his buggy.

"I don't know what he'd have done if he'd caught me."

Mr. Young shook his head. "I don't like the sound of that. He seems very determined."

CHAPTER FOURTEEN

Garrett pulled down the accelerator lever of his shiny black Model T Ford. His car responded in a way that usually gave him a thrill even after driving it for a year and a half. Today nothing seemed to budge the darkness weighing him down.

His father had bought him the car so he could get a job in another town after his cousin, Irv, had fired him. The car had led to him meeting Savannah in Jackson Center while he'd looked for work. He'd never forget the day he and Savannah met. She had been and still was the most beautiful woman he'd ever seen.

With an effort, he shut out her image as he drove into Jackson Center. He glanced at the tavern where he'd found her eating lunch the day he confronted her about entertaining men in her room above the tavern. He had to give Savannah credit for not lying that day. She hadn't denied anything Mr. Sullivan had said.

Garrett tapped the steering wheel. If Savannah didn't lie to him then, why was he assuming she was lying to him now? Maybe his mother was right. He shouldn't jump to conclusions based on what Mr. Burns said.

God, please show me what to do. I've messed up so many times, and I don't want to mess up again. Garrett blew out his breath. *Even though I'm trying to believe the best, it seems awful risky.*

A patch of ice caused his car to slide sideways. Better keep his mind on the road. But his thoughts were as slippery as the slick road, returning again and again to what Mr. Burns had said last night. The drive to Mercer had never seemed so long.

At last he reached Mr. Black's men's clothing store. He enjoyed his job and knew he was good at it. Even BJ, Before Jesus, he'd known how to be nice to people when he'd wanted to be. The problem had been that he hadn't cared enough about most people to make the effort.

Garrett stepped out of his car into the crisp, morning air. The parking lot looked clear. No ice. He started toward the store. In a heartbeat, he was lying on his back beside his Model T. His head throbbed. Black ice. The parking lot had looked deceptively dry. Staring at the sky he asked himself if Savannah was deceiving him too.

Closing his eyes against the relentless suspicion, Garrett pushed himself up. His head still ached, but he could walk and swing his arms, nothing broken far as he could tell. Taking slow, short steps, he went in the store's back entrance. No matter how bad he felt, he *would* go to work today. He couldn't imagine lying at home all day trying not to think.

"Garrett, is that you? Would you come to my office, please?"

What could Mr. Black want so early in the morning? He shucked out of his coat, hung it in the cloak room and entered his boss's office.

"Good morning, sir. You wanted to see me?"

Mr. Black leaned back in his chair. "Close the door and have a seat, Garrett."

Garrett obeyed. *What is this about?*

His boss stared past Garrett out the window, but remained silent.

"What is it, sir? Is something wrong?"

"I've been wrestling for months with whether or not to tell you this." Mr. Black stared into Garrett's eyes, then looked away.

"Tell me what?"

"Are you serious about Savannah Stevens?"

Garrett's brows rose. "Why do you ask?"

"How well do you know her?"

"We've been courting for about six months."

"I'm not proud of this Garrett, but I used to be one of Savannah's, ah, clients. That's—that's why I gave you this job, in exchange for...favors granted."

Garrett clenched his jaw and ground his teeth. Mr. Sullivan had implied that was how Savannah had gotten him this job, but he'd blocked it out. Until last evening, he thought he'd made peace with Savannah's past. Heat crept up his neck. He wanted to walk out the door. How bad did he want to keep this job? He tamped down his anger, jobs were hard to come by. "Why are you telling me this now? I know about Savannah's old life. She says all that has changed."

"And you believe her?" Mr. Black's gaze never left Garrett's face.

"Is there a reason for me *not* to believe her?"

"I don't know." His boss shrugged. "I quit, ah, visiting her when I knew you two were seeing each other. But I've felt bad about not telling you about her past. I thought she'd kept it from you."

"Mr. Sullivan told me and she didn't deny it."

"Was that the day you and Mr. Sullivan had words?"

"Yes. I was angry but I'd had a bad past, too. God showed me if I'd been in her shoes, I'd have done the same thing. Both of us asked God's forgiveness and gave our lives to Him." He couldn't let Mr. Black know he was having his own doubts about Savannah's sincerity.

His boss studied Garrett as seconds ticked by. "I think you're making a mistake, young man. I don't think you can trust someone who's lived like she has."

Garrett bit his lip. How much could he say and still keep his job? "Do you think what she did is worse than what you did, sir?"

Mr. Black thumped down on all four legs of his chair. The breeze created by the movement lifted some papers on his desk. Was that a picture of Savannah under the papers?

"I'm trying to do you a favor, and this is the thanks I get? Watch what you say if you value your job."

When Garrett took a step closer, Mr. Black stood, shuffling the papers into a pile. "That's all I have to say. Don't say I didn't warn you."

Garrett opened his mouth, then closed it again. Maybe it wasn't a picture of Savannah. He could be mistaken. On the other hand, maybe Mr. Black was just trying to break up Garrett's relationship with Savannah so he could justify getting involved with her again.

His head still throbbing, Garrett walked into the store and over to his cash register. It was almost time to open. What if his boss was lying about not visiting Savannah any more? Maybe all the time Garrett and Savannah had been courting, she and his boss had been—had been..."

Swallowing bile and gagging, Garrett hurried to the toilet Mr. Black had recently installed in the back room. He was no good at believing the best and maybe never would be. Maybe his relationship with Savannah was all a mistake. He leaned over the toilet, dry heaves shaking his body.

CHAPTER 15

Savannah pulled on her scarlet coat and shoved her hands into the stylish gloves she'd bought during her old life—BJ as Garrett called it. She picked up the diary Polly loaned her and whisked through the outer office flinging a farewell over her shoulder to Dorothy, not giving her time to ask questions.

Pulling the outer door closed behind her, she stepped into frigid air. Wiggling her gloved fingers to get a better grip on the diary, she smoothed the expensive fabric over each finger and started down Main Street. Sometimes she missed her old lifestyle. Not entertaining men in her room, but the things she could do with the money they gave her. At times, her customers had been very generous.

Occasionally Garrett took her to a show at the Opera House or to dinner at the restaurant on Main Street, but working two jobs didn't leave much time for entertainment. Even with both jobs, she barely made ends meet.

She glanced at the Gents' Furnishings store on her left. Dorothy said the man who used to run it had been declared a lunatic. What would it take for someone to be declared a lunatic? Her parents had often told her she was crazy for not settling down in Georgia, not accepting that she'd be dirt poor all her life. Shivering, she hurried on.

Savannah wasn't proud of the choices she'd made back then. If she'd have asked God, maybe He'd have shown her a better way.

She shook her head. "I'm a new creature in Christ. I'm a new creature in Christ." Mrs. Young said it wasn't good to dwell on the past, but to remember what God said about her now that she was His child.

Stopping at Lake Street to allow a horse and buggy to cross the intersection, Savannah looked at the Clock Tower that rose high above the Feather Building. The tower reigned magnificent and could be seen for several miles. Dr. Frank Feather told folks he owned that land from heaven to hell, and he could build it as high as he pleased.

I wish I understood more about heaven and hell. Can a person who's done what I've done really go to heaven? Mrs. Young says I can.

Her mother had always made it sound like only perfect people went to heaven, people who had never done anything wrong. Savannah wasn't sure her mother thought even she herself would go there.

Five-fifteen—the hands of the tower clock told her she'd better hurry. Mrs. Patton liked her to be there in time to help prepare dinner.

But the enormous Feather building distracted her again. What would it be like to have enough money to build such a huge place? Kitt said no one was immune to trials, but it must be nice to have built a structure that was famous for miles around. Fireproof, too, she'd heard. The Feather doctors would never have to worry about being burned out as their first building had been.

Horses' hooves on College Street startled her. *Oh my goodness, I've gone right by the Old Sandy Lake House.* Savannah retraced her steps and opened the door to the boarding house. She looked for the small suitcase she'd dropped behind the wing chair just inside the door earlier today.

"Looking for something?"

Mrs. Patton's voice startled her and she stumbled into the artificial fern beside the chair. "Yes, I—I left something here earlier."

"A suitcase?"

"Yes." Savannah avoided Mrs. Patton's eyes which didn't miss a thing.

"Did you meet someone at the Hotel?"

"No, no, no." Savannah clamped over her hand over her mouth but couldn't hold back the sobs. She wiped her eyes."I didn't meet anyone. I was...was running away." She could barely speak.

Mrs. Patton's eyes were stern but her tone kind. "Why were you running away?"

Savannah looked straight into her landlady's eyes. "Even though I haven't done anything wrong, no one will believe me."

♠

Innis Patton sat down, stunned by Savannah's answer. How many times had she wanted to run away both before and after she'd finally brought charges against her husband? She closed her eyes against the pain. The divorce had been final for more than seven years, but time hadn't healed the wounds.

Savannah must be hurting, and yet Innis dared not let down her guard. She couldn't be soft and assume her boarder was telling the truth. After all Innis had been through, she couldn't trust anyone.

She pointed at the book in Savannah's hand. "What's that?"

"Oh this. I almost forgot. Polly Dye loaned me this diary. It belonged to one of the original owners of their house."

"You and Polly Dye are friends?" Innis couldn't keep the surprise from her voice. Everyone knew Polly and Garrett had been seeing each other for months before Savannah came on the scene. Of course, everyone also knew that Garrett had been cheating on Polly.

"I just met Polly today. She invited me to come in for tea. She's the one who convinced me to stay in Sandy Lake."

Innis shook her head. "Polly's getting more like her mother every day."

"Mrs. Dye must have been a wonderful person."

"She was. Indeed, she was. The Dye's hadn't lived in Sandy Lake long when Margaret passed, but she already had many friends. We all grieved when she died so unexpectedly."

Savannah nodded. "So hard to understand why things like that happen to good people."

"Oh, believe me, I could write a book." Innis tasted the bitterness as she always did when she talked about the past. Before Savannah could question her, she changed the subject. "Why did Polly loan you that diary?"

"She said God used it to help change her life." Savannah told Innis about her conversation with Polly. "She said we have a choice. We can either become bitter and brittle or allow our trials to mold us into the image of Christ."

Innis bit her lip and turned away. "I guess she's never been through the things I have. I think it's impossible *not* to be bitter."

"I'm sorry, Mrs. Patton. I'm sure going through a divorce isn't easy."

"No secrets in this town." Innis heaved a sigh. "Come on, it's almost supper time. You can help me dish up the food. I'll get your suitcase after we eat."

"I'll be back as soon as I take my coat up to my room." Savannah dashed up the stairs.

Innis watched the beautiful young woman. Perhaps she had made a mistake taking this shapely young lady into her boarding house. She hadn't thought about the kind of message she might be sending to the town. Mrs. Young had been very persuasive and certain that Savannah had changed, but had she? Could a leopard change its spots? She used to think so.

How many times had Hugh assured her *he* would change? *I promise things will be different. I promise this'll never happen again.* A bitter laugh escaped her compressed lips as she went into the kitchen. How many times had she forgiven him? Too many to count.

♠

Savannah hung up her coat and looked at the faded burgundy diary in her hand. It was hard to believe something this old and dull-looking could change someone's life. She smoothed her fingers over the raised letters on the cover. She'd been moved that Polly had loaned it to her, but she had no confidence it would have any magical affect. What was the use? Mrs. Patton still didn't believe her, still thought she'd been meeting someone at the hotel. She put the book into the drawer in her bedside table and closed it with a thud.

CHAPTER 16

Mildred bustled around the warm kitchen setting the table and stirring the chicken soup that simmered on the back of the wood stove. She'd polished every available surface until it shone. It was her favorite time of day. Her men folk would soon be home for supper. Harold hadn't called to say he'd be late as he sometimes did if an emergency arose at the office.

She hummed a little chorus she'd been teaching the children in Sunday School. "His eye is on the sparrow, and I know He watches me."

If God's eye was on the sparrow, then He certainly knew what was happening in Savannah's world. Her son had been so troubled last night and this morning. He was losing confidence in Savannah.

Nothing would convince Mildred that the girl's conversion hadn't been real. Still, no matter how real the conversion, backsliding sometimes happened. But she wouldn't believe even that without more evidence than a drunken tavern owner's word.

Most people knew better than to gossip to her but even so, she'd overheard a few tidbits about Savannah. Mostly the story went *Did you know Savannah Stevens entertained men in her room at the tavern in Jackson Center? Do you think Innis Patton knows? I've heard Savannah still takes customers but it's all very hush hush.*

The last time women were gossiping about Savannah at a church sewing circle, Mildred had heard enough. She'd marched up to them. "Who told you Savannah Stevens still takes customers?"

A stunned silence followed. "Well, uh, I, uh, really can't say." Mrs. Tripley wet her lips and swallowed hard. Mrs. Elder backed away, turned and fled.

Mildred spoke in a voice loud enough to be heard by both women. "If I ever hear either of you talking about Savannah again, I'll take it before the church council. How do you ever expect anyone to change if you continue to spread unfounded rumors?"

The backfiring of an automobile and the whinnying of a horse told her both her men were home. Some day maybe she and Harold would buy a car for themselves, but Harold thought one car in the family was quite enough.

After putting a basket of warm homemade bread on the table, Mildred dished up steaming soup in gray and blue bowls. Footsteps pounded up the stairs, across the porch and a burst of cold air preceded Garrett and Harold as they tramped into the house. Stopping her supper preparations to greet them, Mildred knew before either of them spoke that they were troubled.

Her husband often told her she should have been a counselor because of her intuition. God gave her plenty of opportunities to use her skills without hanging out a shingle.

Harold kissed her check and smiled into her eyes. "How was your day, dear?"

"Fine, except I worried because Garrett didn't eat breakfast."

He looked at his son who was hanging up his coat. "Still worried about Savannah?"

"Ma told you?"

"Yes, and Mr. Burns paid her a visit at our office today."

"He came to your office?" Garrett dropped into a chair, shaking his head.

"What did he want?" Mildred set the bowls of soup on the table. "Wait, let's pray first so we can eat while we talk."

As soon as Mildred said amen, Harold told them about Mr. Burns's visit to the office and everything that had happened to Savannah.

"Polly invited Savannah in for a cup of tea?" Garrett's eyes were wide and unbelieving. "Why would she do that?"

"I imagine Polly's grown up a lot since her mother died. She's probably not the same person you knew six months ago." Mildred refilled the bread basket. "Being a mother to seven children changes a person."

Garrett nodded and tapped his foot against the table leg.

"You're probably right. D'you think Polly told Savannah that she and I used to be, that we used to—"

"I don't think Savannah knows. I didn't tell her either. I'm still not sure she's going to stay in Sandy Lake." Harold wiped his mouth on his napkin. "Mr. Burns told Kitt he'll be back to get what Savannah owes him."

"Garrett, you've barely touched your soup. Is it too hot or too spicy? Are you sick?" Mildred touched the back of her hand to Garrett's forehead.

"I'm not very hungry, Ma." His eyes held a far away expression.

"Did something happen at work to upset you, or is this about Savannah?"

♠

Ever since he walked out of the store today, Garrett had been trying to decide whether to tell his parents about the picture that might have been Savannah on Mr. Black's desk. What if he was wrong?

Little by little, he told them about being called to his boss's office and the conversation they'd had. His parents listened, only interrupting to ask a question now and then.

"Why is he telling you this now if he's known about Savannah all along?" His father tilted his chair back on two legs. "If he was so concerned, you'd think he'd have told you right away."

"That's what I told him. I don't know whether I believe him or not."

"Why wouldn't you believe him?" His mother's gaze never wavered from his face.

"Well, Mr. Black was tilted back in his chair like Pa is now. When he brought his chair down, it made a breeze." Choosing his words carefully, Garrett told his parents about the picture he'd seen on Mr. Black's desk, and all the doubts it had created.

"Maybe he and Savannah have been seeing each other all along, and he's just trying to get rid of me."

Pa squinted and wrinkled his forehead. "Did you ask him about the picture?"

"I was afraid to ask. What if I'm wrong? What if he fires me for being disrespectful and not believing him?"

"On the other hand, can you really go on working for

someone you don't trust? Someone who might be lying to you?" Ma rested her chin on her folded hands, elbows on the table.

"I don't know. Maybe I can if I just stop seeing Savannah. Then it wouldn't be any of my business if Mr. Black has a picture of her."

"I thought you said you loved Savannah. How could you just drop her without finding out the truth?"

His mother's loyalty to Savannah, her refusal to face the facts, ate at him. *If I speak with the tongues of men and of angels, and have not charity...* Garrett wanted to put his hands over his ears to shut out the words that had haunted him all the way home.

"Maybe I was wrong. Maybe I don't love her, not God's kind of love anyway." Garrett pushed his chair back from the table. "How can I go on seeing her when I don't trust her? It's making me crazy."

Chapter 17

Bob Dye opened the door into the cozy living room. The fire in the wood stove crackled with comforting warmth after a long day in the mine. Beth played with Elsie and Twila as they built towers with blocks. Twila jumped up and ran to her father. "Papa, up." When had her baby blue eyes turned to sparkling brown?

"I can't pick you up until I wash." He showed her his dirty hands. "Did you have a good day?"

"Polly fall down. Polly cwy." The sparkle was gone and Twila's eyes were serious.

"What happened? Is she okay?" He stooped beside his two youngest daughters. Florence's happiness was such a huge issue in their world.

"She's fine, Papa." Beth, his big girl of the three, filled him in on Florence's accident and tears. "She went out to take a walk and came home with a new friend."

"That's good. Florence could use a new friend about now."

"Her name is Susanna." Elsie joined the conversation, proud that she could say the new name. "She's so pretty."

"Not Susanna. Savannah." Beth corrected Elsie gently.

Bob stood up, his eyes wide. "Savannah is Florence's new friend?"

Nodding her head with bouncing brown pigtails, Beth confirmed Elsie's story. "I was in school but Maggie said Savannah Stevens was here. Do you know her, Papa?"

"Not really, Shortie." He had taken to calling Beth by Florence's old pet name. It didn't seem to fit Florence now that she had so much responsibility. For some reason, he and Margaret had never called her Polly as everyone else did. "She's Garrett's girlfriend."

"Oh...." Understanding sparked in Beth's eyes. "Oh, I see."

She sounded so grown up—so much like her mother. He reached to pat her head but then remembered the coal dust. "I'll go wash up. Does Florence need your help setting the table?"

"It's already set. I'm taking care of the girls while Maggie and Polly make supper. "

Bob watched his two eldest daughters from the kitchen doorway. They'd always helped their mother, but now her work rested solely on their shoulders, especially Florence. She glanced up and smiled at him. "Did you have a good day?"

"The usual. I heard yours wasn't the best."

Florence shrugged. "Maggie was a big help. I don't know what I'd do without her. She stayed home from school."

Bob nodded. It was a blessing Maggie would soon graduate and have more time to help Florence with the children and the housework. What would he do if his girls decided to get married? Most girls did. Florence had promised Margaret to help raise the children but that was a lot to ask. "I heard you made a new friend."

Florence's cheeks flushed. "Savannah was having a bad day too. It was good for us to help each other."

"I'm surprised you'd want to befriend Savannah after, well, you know—Garrett and all." Bob bit his lip. He still felt awkward discussing things like this with his daughters. Margaret was so much better at it—had been.

"What Garrett did wasn't Savannah's fault. Maybe it wasn't his fault either. She's so beautiful, how could anyone expect Garrett *not* to choose her over me?"

Bob pumped some water into a basin in the sink. "We're each responsible for our own behavior when we're courting someone. No matter how beautiful or handsome another person might be, it's unfair to date them secretly." He picked up a towel to dry his hands. "But I'm proud of you for being kind to Savannah in spite of the past. What a good example to your siblings."

"Am I, Papa? I'm trying so hard. This morning when I tripped over the rug and spilled the milk and bread, I acted like a child."

"You've been under lots of pressure the past six months. If

we don't find ways to relieve the pressure, we might explode when unexpected circumstances happen." Margaret used to tell him that when he got upset about things at the mine.

Florence's hand stopped in midair as she sliced the homemade bread. She bit her lip and nodded. "Like those new pressure cookers I heard about. They're made with a little jiggler on top to release steam so they don't blow up."

"Yes, just like that."

Florence started cutting again, but her green eyes were puzzled. "How can I release the pressure? I don't have time to do anything but take care of the house and the children."

"Beth and I can watch Elsie and Twila more often so you have some time alone." Maggie touched Florence's shoulder.

"Good idea, Maggie." Bob paused. What were some of the other ways Margaret had said people released pressure? "Maybe if Maggie watched the children, you could go for a walk or talk to a friend. Or maybe you could buy a journal to write in."

"A journal. Or maybe a diary." Florence nodded again, hope glinting in her green eyes. "Maybe that was one of the ways Sarah released her pressure."

Father's brows drew together. "Sarah who?"

"Sarah Davis. One of the original owners of this house. Did Mother tell you about me finding her diary in the back bedroom?"

"Now I remember. She was Harry's grandmother wasn't she? Harry and Blanche who live next door?"

"That's the one. I learned so much from her diary, but I never thought about keeping one myself. That might be just what I need." Florence straightened her shoulders and lifted her head.

"I believe they have some at the General Store." Maggie picked up the water pitcher. "You can go look for one tomorrow when I get home from school. I'll watch the little ones."

"Thank you." Florence went back to slicing. "Go ahead and fill the water glasses. Supper is almost ready."

Bob turned to leave the kitchen, then turned back. "Did Savannah say what kind of business George Burns had with her last night?"

"Not really. She was walking to Greenville when I met her outside our house."

"*Walking* to Greenville?" Bob took a few steps back into the kitchen. "Whatever for?"

"Running away from her problems. Being tempted to turn back to her old life." Florence began dipping soup into bowls of assorted colors. "We had a good talk and I loaned her Sarah's diary. Maybe it will help her as it helped me."

Bob raised up on his tiptoes and then back down. "I hope so. I'm glad being tempted isn't a sin."

Florence put down the dipper and gazed at the floor, then back into her father's eyes. "How do you know the difference between a temptation and a sin?"

Backing up a few steps, Bob gazed out the kitchen window, lifting a silent prayer. *Father, I'm way out of my league here. Margaret always answered these questions. Help me please.* He looked at his daughter. "Can you tell me what this is about?"

"Savannah is so beautiful. Even Twila noticed how pretty she is and acted like she *adored* her. I don't know if I'm jealous of Savannah or being tempted to be jealous."

"Your mother used to say, 'You can't stop birds from flying over your head but you don't have to let them nest in your hair.'"

"What does that mean?"

"If a jealous thought pops into your mind, you have to choose whether you're going to entertain it or get rid of it."

Florence sighed and picked up the dipper. "Easier said than done."

Chapter 18

Savannah ran down the steps and joined Mrs. Patton in the kitchen. The fried chicken smelled wonderful and her mouth watered. She picked up one of the meat platters and the metal tongs beside it and began transferring pieces of chicken from the heavy iron skillet. Would she ever learn to cook like Mrs. Patton? With firm movements, her landlady smashed the boiled potatoes and milk into creamy mashed potatoes.

Taking a deep breath, Savannah relaxed. Eventually, she would prove to Mrs. Patton she hadn't done anything wrong. She would stay in Sandy Lake and prove to people she'd changed. Uninvited, the words George Burns had spoken returned to her. *I'll be back...that broad's gotta sleep sometime.*

"Savannah, what's the matter? You look like you're in a trance." Mrs. Patton stared at her.

She shook herself mentally. "Nothing, nothing at all. I—I just remembered something." Savannah picked up the last piece of chicken. "This chicken smells so good."

Taking the platter into the dining room, she forced herself to breathe. Her door had a cheap lock on it. Would it hold if Mr. Burns came back? Especially if he'd been drinking. She gazed longingly at the door that led to the entryway of the boarding house. Was it foolhardy to stay in the very place where Mr. Burns would look for her? At least he didn't know which room was hers—she'd been dusting in the room of one of the other guests when he'd attacked her.

Her pulse slowed. She took more deep breaths and returned to the kitchen. Mrs. Patton handed her a big bowl of mashed potatoes and nodded toward Savannah's small suitcase in the corner. "There's your suitcase. I can understand you wanting to run away. Sometimes we have to leave a situation. Other times, it's like jumping out of the frying pan into the fire."

"In some ways, it's tempting to leave." Savannah looked into Mrs. Patton's clear brown eyes. "Especially when it seems like most people don't believe me. Do you think I should stay?"

Mrs. Patton shrugged and looked away. "I have enough trouble making my own decisions. I can't tell you what to do."

♠

Polly had finished cleaning up the kitchen after supper and curled up with Twila on her lap when a car pulled up in front of the house. She looked at her father. "Are you expecting Doc Cooley?"

He shook his head. "Maybe he has some word on George Burns."

Father got up and started for the door. A good sign he was taking more interest in life. Maybe helping George Burns last night had had a good effect on him. Before he reached the door, a shadowy figure ran up the porch steps. Even *young* Doc Cooley didn't run up the steps. It looked like—no, it couldn't be…

A loud knock ended Polly's doubts. Garrett was the only one who knocked that hard on their door. What could he possibly want? Her heartbeat quickened.

Opening the door, her father stepped back in surprise. "Garrett. Wasn't expecting you."

"Can I come in, Mr. Dye?" Garrett shivered in the brisk night air.

It was impossible to miss Father's reluctance. Good manners alone coerced him to step back and let Garrett in. He'd made it clear to Polly he didn't care for Garrett and didn't trust him, even after his conversion.

"What can I do for you?" Father's tone was brusque.

"I need to talk to Polly. Could I take her for a ride?"

Father turned to look at her, eyebrows raised. "That's completely up to her."

Polly set Twila gently on the davenport and joined her father and Garrett by the door. "I don't think that's a good idea." She lowered her voice. "Aren't you still seeing Savannah?"

"I'm not asking you for a date. I just need to talk to you."

Shifting from one foot to the other, Polly wavered. He

wasn't asking her for a date. "All right." She reached for her coat and mittens, and put one arm in her sleeve. Then she stopped. "Let's talk in the sitting room. I don't want to hurt Savannah the way I was hurt." She stuffed her mittens back in her pocket and hung her coat on the hook. Her father beamed his approval.

"Give me your coat, Garrett." Polly hung it on an empty hook next to hers, then led the way into the sitting room. She closed the door, sat on the far end of the loveseat and motioned for Garrett to sit down. Her heartbeat had quickened again, but she was glad she'd insisted on staying in the lighted room. Too many memories of times spent in Garrett's car and his buggy.

Waiting for Garrett to begin, she watched him. He wouldn't meet her eyes, just stared at the floor. "What did you want to talk about?"

At last he raised his head. "My father told me Savannah came to see you today."

"Not exactly. We met on the road in front of our house. She was upset, and I invited her to come in for a cup of tea."

"What did you talk about?"

"I don't think that's any of your business. It was a private conversation." Polly had forgotten how blue Garrett's eyes were.

He licked his lips and swallowed. "Do you know what Savannah did for a living in Jackson Center?"

Polly's cheeks reddened. "I've heard rumors."

"Thing is, the rumors are true. What I really need to know is whether Savannah has changed or whether she's just been trying to make me believe she's changed?"

"Why do you think I would know that? I just met her today."

"I trust your judgment, Polly. I need to know what you think."

Polly closed her eyes and leaned her head back. "Why are you questioning whether Savannah has changed *now*? She's lived at the old hotel since right after Mother—since August."

"Her old landlord, George Burns, says Mrs. Patton has her set up there, says all the men at his tavern talk about her."

"Have you asked Savannah about this?"

"No, but how could I trust her to tell me the truth? Mr. Burns says she's making a fool of me."

"You mean like I couldn't trust you to tell *me* the truth when you were making a fool of me?"

Garrett scowled. "That has nothing to do with me and Savannah. I'm a Christian now and I've changed."

"Have you? How do I know I can trust you? How do I know you've changed?"

Jumping to his feet, Garrett glared at Polly, his face and neck stained a deep red. "I should have known there was no use talking to you. You won't let the past go."

Polly scooted to the edge of the loveseat. "Sit down. This is not about you and me. I'm making a point."

A puzzled frown raised Garrett's eyebrows and he hesitated, then sat down. "What point?"

Taking a deep breath, Polly sent up a silent prayer. How could she explain to Garrett what she suspected? "Garrett, do you think it's possible that because you weren't trustworthy and didn't tell the truth in the past, you are projecting those same qualities onto Savannah?"

Garrett's frown deepened. "That sounds like something your mother might have told you."

The scorn in his tone hurt and Polly's temper rose. She scooted as far from Garrett as she could. "It wasn't my mother. It's a theory I read about in the newspaper. I didn't believe it, but it's beginning to make a lot of sense."

"Just sounds like a bunch of psychological mumbo jumbo."

"Maybe so but I think it could be true. Besides how can it be fair that you want people to believe you've changed, but you won't believe Savannah has changed?"

On his feet again, Garrett turned toward the door. But Polly wasn't finished. "You know what I think is at the root of all this? Your pride. You can't bear to think Savannah might be making a fool of you, making you look bad to other people."

Without a word, Garrett opened the door, stormed through the living room and out the front door. Polly got up and followed just in time to see the door open and Garrett reach for his coat. She could hardly contain her chuckle until the door had closed. Meeting her father's twinkling eyes, she laughed out loud.

"That went well." Father's sarcasm made her laugh harder. "What was that all about?"

"He wanted to know what Savannah and I talked about today."

"Did you tell him?"

"Wasn't any of his business."

Her father nodded. "Is that why he was angry?"

"No." Polly gazed at the closed door. "He was angry because I told him things he didn't want to hear."

CHAPTER 19

Savannah trailed up the stairs, dragging her small suitcase behind her, letting it hit each mahogany baluster. The suitcase wasn't heavy. She could have carried it, but it was a reminder of the decision she needed to make. To stay or to go? To unpack her suitcase or to leave in the morning? Reaching the top of the stairs, she pulled the deep purple suitcase into her arms, went to her room, and tossed it on her bed.

She lit the gas lamp on her bedside table and dropped down beside her bag on the drab coverlet Mrs. Patton provided with every room. When she reached for her Bible, it fell open to the deep blue satin ribbon where she'd marked her place—Proverbs 3. "Please show me what to do, Father. I'm so confused."

A few days ago, she'd read verses one through four of Chapter three, so she began at verse five. *Trust in the Lord with all thine heart; and lean not on thine own understanding.*

"I don't know how to trust you, Lord. Maybe I've been *leaning on my own understanding* all my life. I didn't want a life like Mama and Papa had, so I set out to get the life *I* wanted—no matter what the cost. Is that leaning on my own understanding?"

Savannah glanced at verse six. *In all thy ways acknowledge him, and he shall direct thy paths.* She wanted God to direct her path, but what did it mean to acknowledge Him in all her ways? This was one of those promises with a condition Mrs. Young had told her about. Promise: God would direct her path. Condition: Acknowledge God in all her ways. She didn't know how to do that.

Maybe it was time for a visit to Mrs.Young. They met every Monday for Bible study, but Garrett's mother had told her to come any time she had questions. She wouldn't be able to sleep tonight with the icy block in her chest and all these unanswered questions churning round and round.

She slipped into her bright red coat that reminded her of the scarlet tanagers she used to see in Georgia, pulled on her gloves, and picked up her Bible. Maybe she should tell Mrs. Patton where she was going. It might be a good way to regain her trust.

A few minutes later, mission accomplished, Savannah went into the chilly night. No new snow today. Her heart was lighter just knowing she'd see Mrs. Young soon. Garrett might be home too. She hadn't seen him since George Burns had been to his house. What had Mr. Burns said to him? Would Garrett be upset with her? Or doubt her like Mrs. Patton did?

♠

Garrett's car wasn't in the driveway. Savannah walked up the steps and across the porch. The kitchen light was on, and Mrs. Young was putting a water glass in the cupboard. Savannah tapped lightly on the door.

Mrs. Young bustled across the kitchen and swung the door open. "Savannah. Come in, come in. What are you doing out in the cold?"

Savannah hesitated. "Do you have time to answer some questions?".

Garrett's mother pulled her into the warm kitchen. "Of course, I have time. I'm always glad to see you."

The frozen block in Savannah's chest began to thaw. Mrs. Young didn't seem angry. Maybe Garrett wouldn't be upset either.

Mr. Young poked his head through the kitchen doorway and smiled at her. "Glad to see you."

"Thanks, Mr. Young."

"Come sit down." Mrs. Young took Savannah's coat. "Let me make you a cup of tea to help take off the chill. Would you like one, dear?"

"No, thanks. I'm reading the paper." Mr. Young disappeared into the living room.

Mrs. Young hung Savannah's coat over the back of a chair near the stove. "That'll warm your coat before you go outside."

"Thank you. I know that'll feel good. Can I help make the tea?"

"You can choose one of the tea cups in that cupboard by the

sink. Get one for me too." Mrs. Young filled the teakettle and set it on the shiny black stove.

When they were seated, she smiled at Savannah. "We can talk while we wait for the water to heat. What's on your mind?"

Savannah played with the spoon Mrs. Young had placed on a napkin for her. "How do you know what God wants you to do?"

"That's a very big question. The better we get to know God by reading the Bible and talking to Him about everything, the more easily we discover what He wants us to do. But there is another condition."

"What's that?" Savannah gazed into Mrs. Young's kind blue eyes.

"We need to be willing to do whatever He tells us. I don't think we should even *ask* what He wants us to do if we haven't made up our minds to obey."

"Is that what it means to *acknowledge Him in all our ways*?"

"That's one of the ways we acknowledge Him. It means to admit He's God and He has a right to tell us what to do. If we've asked Him to be our Lord and Savior, He has authority over us." Mrs. Young went to the stove and picked up the whistling teakettle, filled their cups, and dropped a tea bag in each one.

Savannah sighed. "I've been rebelling against my parents' authority all my life. This isn't going to be easy."

"God wants us to honor our parents, but He's very different from them. He loves us unconditionally and always knows what's best. That's why we can trust Him."

Opening her Bible, Savanna cleared her throat. "This is what I read this evening." She read verses five and six aloud, then gazed at Mrs. Young. "Not leaning on my own understanding and acknowledging God in all my ways is going to be a tough assignment. I want God to guide me, but I don't know if I can fulfill the conditions."

"It's not easy. We can't do it in our own strength."

Savannah nodded slowly. "Did you ever wish you could turn back the hands of time and start over?"

"Everyone wishes that now and then." Mrs. Young patted Savannah's hand lying on her Bible. "When I was young, I had a quick temper and often said and did things I regretted later. Even though God forgives our sins, we have to deal with the consequences."

"Did your husband tell you that Mr. Burns came to my room in the boarding house last night?"

"He said Mr. Burns came to the office and that he'd come to your room last night. Did he hurt you?"

"Not really. Not physically. Mrs. Patton came in when he was trying to kiss me. She made him leave, but now she's added another six months to my trial period. I'm scared because Mr. Burns said he'll be back. I don't know what he'll do. Is it wise for me to stay in Sandy Lake since he knows where I am?"

A loud backfire rattled the teacups on the table before Mrs. Young could answer. Savannah gripped her cup with both hands. "Garrett's home."

Mrs. Young's eyes didn't light up like they usually did when her son arrived. She glanced at Savannah, then dropped her gaze.

CHAPTER 20

Garrett jumped out of his Model T Ford and slammed the door so hard the car shook. His mother had talked about how much Polly'd changed. She hadn't changed at all. You couldn't *tell* her anything. What a know-it-all. Coming up with her own theories that sounded just like her mother. He'd done the right thing breaking up with her. He ignored the quiet voice reminding him that she had broken up with him.

He stomped up the steps, flung open the door, and walked into the warm kitchen. Savannah. What was *she* doing here? He was in no mood to talk to her.

Savannah smiled at him. "Hi Garrett."

Turning away from the warmth in her deep violet blue eyes, he mouthed words at his mother who'd come to greet him. *"What's she doing here?"*

Ignoring his question, his mother asked one of her own. "Where've you been? You didn't say where you were going when you left."

Garrett shrugged. "Doesn't matter now."

"We're having a cup of tea. Would you like to join us?"

Shaking his head, Garrett threw his coat on top of Savannah's and headed for the stairs.

Savannah jumped up. "Garrett, can we talk?"

He hesitated, not meeting her eyes. "I'm not really in the mood to talk, but I guess now is as good a time as any."

"Shall we take a walk?"

"I can join your father in the living room if you want to talk here." His mother motioned to the table. "It's pretty cold out there."

"This shouldn't take long. We'll be fine." Garrett covered

the floor between him and his coat in three strides and shoved his arms into the sleeves.

♠

It was obvious Garrett was upset. Savannah struggled to keep up with his long strides in the crisp night air. "Are you mad at me?"

Ignoring her question, Garrett's eyes never left the snow-covered road beneath their feet. "What do you want to talk about?"

"I wanted to say I'm sorry Mr. Burns came to your house last night. I know he'd been drinking."

Garrett sighed. "That's only the tip of the iceberg."

"What do you mean?"

"Things just aren't working out between us, Savannah. I think it would be better if we take a break from seeing each other."

"But you said you loved me."

"I'm so confused. I don't think I have any idea what love is. I just need some time."

Their footsteps crunched in the snow as the silence stretched. Savannah bit her lip. "What did Mr. Burns say to you?"

"I don't want to talk about it. I don't know whether the things he told me are true or not. I can't pursue a relationship with you until I know."

"Can't you tell me what he said?"

"Just forget it. There's nothing you can do to change my mind."

"Do you think it would be better if I moved to another town?"

"What would you do there? Find someone like Mr. Burns to set you up in business?"

Tears slid down Savannah's cheeks. "You don't believe in me at all, do you? You don't believe I've changed or that I'm a new creature in Christ."

Garrett stopped and turned to Savannah. "I told you I don't know what to believe. It's driving me crazy. This conversation isn't helping." He turned around. "Why don't you go on back to the boarding house, and I'll head for home."

Without a word, Savannah walked away. When she reached the end of Mill Street and turned onto Main, she pulled a handkerchief from her pocket, blew her nose and wiped her eyes.

How had this evening gone so wrong? Was this God's way of showing her she needed to leave town? Or was she just leaning to her own understanding again.

Mrs. Young had said Savannah needed to be willing to do whatever God said. Garrett's rejection had just made it easier to meet God's conditions. *Father, I'm willing to do whatever you say. Polly said you promise to go through our trials with us and even bring good from them. Help me trust you.*

Savannah started walking again, taking deep, steadying breaths. *If you want me to leave Sandy Lake, I will. I'll rent a horse or ask someone to take me to Greenville to look for work. I won't go back to my old ways. I think Mr. and Mrs. Young believe in me. Maybe Polly too.*"

Opening the door to the boarding house, Savannah stood up straight. She crossed to the staircase, holding her head high. "I'm a new creature in Christ."

♠

Before she turned out the gas lamp beside her bed, Savannah reached for her Bible again. She never got very far because she always needed time to digest what she'd read. Mrs. Young said that was better than racing through lots of verses and understanding nothing. She began where she'd left off earlier at Proverbs three, verse seven.

Be not wise in thine own eyes: fear the Lord, and depart from evil.

She reread the first part of the verse. Almost every argument she'd had with her parents had started because she thought she was smarter than they were. They weren't always right, of course, but neither were they always wrong. What had she said to them? *I'll never make the mistakes you made. There's no reason for anyone to be poor. Anyone with half a brain can figure out a better way to live than this.* She cringed at her own arrogance.

It was obvious she hadn't feared the Lord, and instead of departing from evil, she had embraced it in all her choices. *Oh, Father, forgive me for all my sins. I sinned against my parents, and I sinned against you. I'm so sorry. I've made such a mess of things.*

Opening her bedside drawer, she pulled out a tablet and a fat yellow pencil. She hadn't communicated with her parents since her mother had said she'd brought shame and disgrace on the family. Would they forgive her or would they act like she was beyond redemption?

If her grandma were living, Savannah was pretty sure *she* would forgive her. The only place Savannah had ever felt close to God back then was when she sat in the little white country church beside her grandma.

She'd never measured up to her parents' God. They took the family to church sometimes. A church where folks acted like she and her brothers and sisters had a contagious disease. One day when they'd seen Savannah headed their way, one of the girls had stuck out her tongue. "You can't play with us." Savannah had laughed and pretended not to care.

Gripping the stubby pencil, Savannah caught her tongue between her teeth and wrote, *Dear Pa and Ma. I imagine you're surprised to be hearing from me.*

CHAPTER 21

Garrett clomped down the stairs without tying his shoes, almost tripping over the laces. The sun was shining, a rare occurrence in western Pennsylvania that usually lifted his spirits. Today he didn't care. The fragrance of pancakes and bacon didn't even draw a comment as he slouched into a chair at the table.

Ma smiled as she set a steaming plate of food in front of him. "Here you are. I bet you're hungry. You haven't eaten much for a couple days. Let me get you a glass of milk."

He stared at the food. His stomach growled even though he wasn't hungry. Could he work on an empty stomach? *Maybe I should go back to bed.*

Where had that thought come from? He hadn't missed a day of work for months. He'd given up "playing hooky" when the Holy Spirit had convicted him that it was the same as lying.

Picking up the maple syrup, he poured a generous amount, then cut into the stack of nicely browned pancakes. Ma watched him. He'd gone straight upstairs when he got home last night. Sooner or later, he'd have to tell her what he'd done. He took a big gulp of milk to force down the pancakes stuck in his throat.

He and Savannah had been so happy, he'd been sure nothing could ever come between them. Now everything seemed to be falling apart.

He set down his glass. "Ma, are you going to eat something?" Stalling and he knew it.

Ma flipped the last pancake out of the skillet. "I'm coming. Do you need anything else?"

"No, I'm fine. I'm sorry I didn't talk to you last night when I got home. I just wasn't ready to talk."

"I understand, son." Ma sank into her chair. "Life can be worse than confusing sometimes."

Garrett nodded. He scooted his chair back and bent over to tie his shoe laces. Anything to avoid meeting his mother's eyes. "I broke up with Savannah last night. At least for a while."

"I'm not surprised. I knew you were struggling with your suspicions about her." Ma sighed. "But I hope you understand I need to go on being her friend. She's like a daughter to me, and she doesn't really have anyone else to help her learn more about Jesus."

"I know. It might be a little awkward. I'll try to make myself scarce when she's here."

"And of course, she'll continue to work for your father."

"I understand. I feel bad that I got you and Pa involved with Savannah, and now I'm backing out. I never thought this would happen."

"It's okay. You and Savannah are both new Christians. It takes time to grow and learn God's ways. He goes on loving us even when we stumble around and get confused. Just keep talking to Him." Ma patted his hand. "Ask Him to make you like Jesus."

"I'll try. Thanks for not giving up on me."

His mother smiled as he kissed her good bye. How did she go on loving him after all he'd put her through? Why couldn't he keep loving Savannah? After he'd come to Christ, he'd thought his problems were over. Instead it seemed like he had a whole new set.

♠

Garrett closed the outer door and glanced into Mr. Black's office. "Good morning."

"Good morning, Garrett." Mr. Black didn't look up from the paperwork spread over his desk.

Going to be a long day if his boss chose to avoid him. He hung up his coat and looked at the clock. About fifteen minutes until the store opened. Plenty of time for his morning routine. He walked around straightening men's shirts and trousers, as well as making sure all the shoes were paired with their proper mates. What a shame one couldn't check a size to discover one's mate for life.

Savannah. The warmth of her eyes when she'd smiled at

him last night. The deep hurt and tears when he'd suggested she might get someone to set her up in business again. That had been a low blow. He closed his eyes in an attempt to shut out the images. Maybe he should go see one of the Tripley sisters to take his mind off Savannah.

No, that was the way the old Garrett had dealt with his problems. BJ. There had to be a better way. How would a true follower of Christ deal with this?

"Garrett."

He jumped and turned around. Mr. Black stood a few feet away.

"I'm leaving to take care of some business. Can you handle things here?" Mr. Black shrugged into his overcoat. "I'll be gone most of the day."

"Of course. Take all the time you need." Garrett tried to smile and act like he would have acted before Mr. Black talked to him about Savannah. He didn't want to get fired again.

"All right. I'll be back by closing time." His boss turned and headed toward the door.

Garrett watched and hunched his shoulders at the burst of cold air that blew in as Mr. Black left. His employer had never been gone for any length of time. What could be so important to take him away for most of the day? He should have asked if someone in his family was sick. He'd never talked to his boss about his personal life. Was he married? Did he have children? Seemed like Garrett should know the answers to those questions after working here for well over a year.

If Mr. Black had a wife, did she know about Savannah? Probably not. What if his boss was going to Sandy Lake to see Savannah now? Garrett hadn't asked her about her relationship with his boss. What good would it have done? No way to know if she was telling the truth.

The door to Mr. Black's office stood open. *What's to stop me from looking for that picture? I need to know if it was Savannah.*

Garrett took a few steps, stopped and rubbed his chin. How should a follower of Jesus approach this? Was it wrong to go through Mr. Black's desk? Maybe God had provided a way for him to find out for sure who was in that picture.

In a few quick strides, Garrett reached the office. He looked through the papers on his boss's desk. No picture. He opened drawers and shuffled papers in each one with no results. He yanked open filing cabinets and sifted through folders. Had he imagined the whole thing?

He even took books from the bookshelves, fanned their pages and shook them. Nothing. Maybe Mr. Black had taken the picture with him.

At last Garrett sank into his boss's chair and tilted back on two legs, scanning the office and the desk. Something peeped from under one corner of the huge, dark green blotter that covered most of the desk's surface. He crashed down on all four chair legs and lifted the left side of the blotter. There it was. A picture of Savannah in a seductive pose, wearing a filmy negligee.

CHAPTER 22

The walls of Mr. Black's office began to close in on Garrett as he stared at the picture, his stomach churning, pulse racing. How could Savannah claim to have changed when—his pulse slowed. He turned the picture over. No date. Nothing written on the back. He had no proof of when this picture had been taken, before or after Savannah claimed to have received Jesus.

His boss had already told him he'd been one of Savannah's customers. Confirming he had a picture of Savannah proved nothing about their present relationship. All it proved was that Garrett was still fighting his battles the same way he'd always fought them—by sneakiness and deception.

The bell above the outer door jangled. He leaped to his feet, glancing toward the door. Only a customer. His secret was safe, but his stomach churned at the underhanded methods he'd used once again.

♠

The Dye's front door opened and Polly dropped her broom and headed into the living room. It was tempting to go on sweeping—the floor needed it, but Mother had always greeted the children when they came home from school. Beth was already stuffing mittens into her pockets, while Robert and George lounged on the couch without removing their coats. Ben's footsteps told her he had headed upstairs to his room. Polly hugged Beth while cautioning the boys to keep their voices down since Twila and Elsie were sleeping.

"Where's Maggie?" Polly peered out the window and saw her sister stumbling up the porch steps, book in hand. Yanking the door open, Polly called to her. "Put your book down before you fall."

Maggie looked up and grinned. "You sound just like Mama."

"She must have said that to you a thousand times or more." Polly smiled at her sister. She'd made a valiant effort to curtail her reading.

"I'm good at reading and walking. I've had lots of practice." Maggie closed her book and followed Polly into the house.

"What are you reading?"

"Little Women." Maggie showed Polly the book.

"Haven't you read that before?"

"Many times. I never get tired of it. Are you ready to go buy your diary?"

"This might be a good time before the girls wake up. I'll ask Ben to listen for them." Polly made a quick trip upstairs, then grabbed her coat. "Listen to Maggie." She gave Robert and George a stern look. "I'll be back soon."

She took deep breaths of fresh air as she headed for Simcox's General Store. Mr. Simcox had other partners now but it would always be Simcox's to her.

Even though it wasn't a long walk, it felt good to be alone. She loved her brothers and sisters but sometimes the responsibility weighed on her. A bell jingled as she opened the door and went into the store. Polly loved the smells here. You could buy anything from groceries and dry goods to books, tobacco, and hardware.

She walked up and down the old hardwood floors, breathing in the smell of the homemade bread and red-cheeked apples she passed. At last she came to the stationery aisle. She looked at every diary and journal, wanting one that said *diary* in raised letters as Sarah's did. Some had only a few lines for each day. She wanted more room than that. She wanted lots of blank pages to fill as Sarah had.

Finally, Polly settled on one that was dark blue and leather-bound. The cover said *Journal* in raised gold print. As she flipped through the empty pages, her muscles tensed. Who knew what events would come in the days and years ahead? If they were as filled with hardships as Sarah's had been, would her faith survive? She put the journal on the shelf and walked away.

Father, I'm still a beginner at following Jesus. I don't have

*much confidence in my ability to be faithful for as long as it would
take to fill that journal. Please help me.*

"Hello, Polly."

She turned to see who had spoken. "Oh hello, Blanche." She
hadn't seen their neighbor, the wife of Sarah's grandson, for quite
awhile. "How are you doing?"

"We're okay. How are you? You've taken on a big job
helping your father raise those children."

"It's hard. I don't feel like I have nearly enough wisdom for
the job. Mother was so wise."

"Your mother must have believed in you. You were the one
she asked to help raise the children."

"Maybe she just asked me because I was the oldest girl."

Blanche studied Polly's face. "Just remember the line at the
end of Sarah's diary. *If only I had...*

"*...taught my children to put their trust in you, Lord.*" Polly
raised her eyebrows. "That's what you thought Sarah was going to
say... Right?"

"Right."

Polly stared into space. "The most important thing I
learned from Sarah's diary was that it wasn't enough to have faith
in my mother and in her faith. I needed to have faith in God
myself."

"I think that's why your mother chose you—she knew you'd
learned that lesson. She wanted you to teach your brothers and
sisters to put their trust in God, not in you. You don't need to have
all the answers. Just point them to the One who does."

"Thank you so much, Blanche. I needed to hear that. I came
to buy a diary. Then I looked at all the blank pages and got scared. I
should stop worrying about the future and go back to trusting God
one day at a time."

Her neighbor squeezed Polly's shoulder and smiled into
her eyes. "I'm glad I didn't know ahead of time the way my faith
would be tested." The bright feather on Blanche's hat bobbed as
she emphasized each word. "The grace to face our trials only
comes in time for the test, not before."

Polly stilled, then nodded. "Not before. I need to remember
that. Thanks again."

"You're welcome. Even though I don't have your mother's

wisdom, I'm praying for you. I'm praying for your whole family." With another bob of her feather, Blanche took her purchases to the counter.

Returning to the shelf of diaries and journals, Polly stared at the thick journal. Her knees still trembled when she thought about the future. Mother had said God didn't promise an easy life just because we put our trust in Him. Sarah and Blanche had both suffered many losses. She sighed and clasped her hands. *Not before.*

Father, make my faith in you real, the kind that holds even when storms come. I'm buying this journal as an act of faith that You will see me through come what may.

CHAPTER 23

Savannah dashed to the post office during her lunch break, letter to her parents clutched in her gloved hand. How long did it take for a letter to get to Savannah, Georgia, from Sandy Lake? She had no idea. After she requested a stamp and handed him her letter, the post master took note of the address. "Sending this to Savannah, just like your name. You have family there?"

"Yes." Savannah shut her lips in spite of Mr. Boyd's inquiring look. The post office often buzzed with people exchanging tidbits of gossip. She didn't want her personal information to be part of it.

"Haven't exchanged news with them for a long time, have you?"

Apparently Mr. Boyd didn't miss a thing, even if one kept one's mouth closed. Savannah shrugged. "How much do I owe you for the stamp?"

"That'll be five cents for the mail train."

She paid him and left. One more stop on her way back to work to open an account at the Mercer County State Bank. Having heard that the predecessor of this bank had been forced to go out of business two years earlier, she hadn't wanted to deposit any money there. But after Mr. Burns's threats about coming back, she didn't want to keep what little cash she had in her room.

What did Mr. Burns think she owed him? He'd helped set her up in business with the understanding that he received half of everything she earned, plus paying him monthly rent after the first two months. He's also helped her buy a few fancy dresses but had never mentioned paying him back. What if he tried to get what he thought she owed him through services rendered? He was stronger than she was.

♠

The sound of horses' hooves brought Savannah back to the present as she reviewed her day on the way home from work. She stopped at the intersection of Lake and Main Streets. *Does opening a bank account, mean I'm staying in Sandy Lake?* She had told God she'd do whatever He wanted, but how would she know?

Savannah ran the last few blocks to the boarding house. She'd been doing all she could to be useful and win her landlady's approval. She hung her coat on one of the hooks by the door to save time and went straight to the kitchen.

Mrs. Patton glanced up from the onion she was peeling. "Savannah. You're home early."

"I wanted to help with supper. What can I do?"

"Break this up for the meatloaf." She gestured to yesterday's bread.

After washing her hands, Savannah tied a white apron around her waist, wrapping the strings around her twice. She and Mrs. Patton worked side by side in silence, chopping the onion and breaking the bread. Was that a tear her landlady wiped from her cheek with the dish towel? "Are you okay?"

"Oh, it's just this onion making me cry, not that I wouldn't have plenty of reasons to cry if I had a mind to."

Touching her shoulder, Savannah gazed at her. "I'm sorry. Life can be so hard. How long have you been divorced if I may ask?"

"I might as well tell you. Everyone else knows. Been divorced since August of 1904."

"I'm sure you had a good reason." Savannah kept her eyes on the bread crumbs.

"Can't believe you haven't heard why I divorced Hugh. We'd been married since 1889, and he hadn't been good to me for a long time." She shrugged as another tear rolled down her cheek. "I left him and brought charges against him for assault and battery a year earlier. He always said he'd change, but it never lasted."

Savannah's parents had often argued but there'd never been physical abuse. Poor Mrs. Patton. "I'm glad you left, even though I'm sure it wasn't easy."

"Oh leaving was easy enough. It's the living and forgiving

that's hard." Mrs. Patton paused. "Have you read any of that diary you borrowed yet?"

"Not yet. I've been pretty busy. It was really good of Polly to loan it to me; but to be honest, it's sort of hard to believe someone's old diary could make that much difference to you or me."

"Yeah, I guess you're right." Mrs. Patton turned away and swiped the dish towel across her eyes.

♠

Garrett's footsteps thudded on the stairs as he went to his room. He'd managed to force down some supper so Ma wouldn't give him the third degree. Whether it would stay down or not remained to be seen.

He'd almost told his parents about what he'd done, going through Mr. Black's office, but in the end he kept it to himself. They wouldn't approve.

Slumping on the edge of his bed, Garrett buried his head in his hands.

Let him who is without sin cast the first stone.

He lifted his head. That was the verse that had convicted him after Savannah admitted how she earned a living. He'd felt differently about Savannah's behavior when God had shown him his own sins. Seems he'd lost sight of that perspective. More and more he'd seen himself as someone well above Savannah spiritually.

Garrett dropped his head in his hands again and groaned. Good thing he had the day off tomorrow so he wouldn't have to face Mr. Black. He'd had a hard time looking him in the eye when he'd come back to the store. The mixture of anger about the picture and guilt over his invasion of his boss's privacy made him ill.

♠

By the light of her gas lamp, Savannah slipped on her warm flannel nightgown. The coal furnace wasn't able to keep all the rooms in the boarding house warm even when they fed it around the clock. Usually that didn't happen, and the rooms became colder and colder as the night progressed. She wrapped herself in the extra blanket Mrs. Young had given her, tucked the warmed brick under the covers for her feet, and crawled into bed.

After bowing her head for a few moments of silent prayer,

she opened the drawer of her bedside table. Grabbing the worn burgundy book, she lifted it out of the drawer. She rubbed her finger tentatively over the raised letters on the front.

On the first page she read, *May 14, 1840.* She did the math—more than 70 years ago. What could she possibly learn from this old diary?

Instead of heeding the old attitude that reminded her of how she'd treated her parents, she turned to prayer. *Jesus, I admit I don't know what I can learn from an old diary, but Polly says it helped change her life. If there's something you want to teach me, open my eyes and ears to see and hear what you want me to learn. Forgive me for my prideful attitude.*

She glanced at the date again. How old had Sarah been when she started this diary? Polly hadn't said. Savannah read the first entry, surprised to find that Sarah's husband, Thomas, was from Ireland. People of Irish descent had been some of the earliest settlers in Savannah, Georgia. Her parents had looked down on the Irish although Savannah had never understood why.

Thomas is as kind a husband as any woman could want. He is a good provider, too, working hard at his trade. He goes from farm to farm making shoes as needed—an ideal occupation for someone who loves to talk and share stories as he does, regaling his listeners with his famous "Paddy" humor which he inherited from his father. He is a welcome visitor at the farms not only for the fine shoes he produces but also for the laughter he brings.

Thomas sounded like a delightful fellow and a wonderful husband. Savannah stilled. Who was the real Garrett? The one who had treated her well in the past, or the one who'd treated her with such disdain? A tear slipped down her cheek. After Garrett said he loved her, she had always assumed they would marry one day. Now she wasn't so sure.

Chapter 24

Polly emptied the dish water and hung up the dish cloth while Maggie dried and put away the last of the plates. "Thanks again, Maggie, for watching the girls and starting supper while I went to the store. It was good for me to get out of the house."

"I should have thought of it sooner. Except for the little ones, the rest of us go to school or to work almost every day. It must be difficult to stay home all the time."

"Do you think Mother ever got tired of being cooped up so much?" Polly raised a questioning eyebrow at Maggie.

"She never complained, although *we* sometimes complained when she went to her WCTU meetings. Remember?"

"I'm ashamed of myself now, thinking I had it so hard." Polly grabbed the broom and swept up a few crumbs.

"*I'm* ashamed when I think how much time I spent reading instead of helping you and Mother." Maggie pushed a strand of brown hair behind her ear.

"It's all part of growing up, I guess."

"We've had an intense course in maturing since—well, since last August. It's not the way I'd have chosen to learn, but I hope I'm not as selfish as I used to be."

Polly hugged her sister and patted her cheek. "Mother would be proud of you. Want to help me get the girls ready for bed?"

♠

Polly helped settle Twila and Elsie, and then headed for the bedroom she shared with her other sisters. She passed Maggie in the hallway and squeezed her shoulder. "Thanks for helping. I'm going to spend some time writing in my new journal."

"Have fun. You don't need to guess what I'm going to do." Maggie grinned. She was always in the middle of at least one book.

Picking up her journal from the bedside table, Polly flopped down on the double bed. She pulled Chartreuse, the name she'd given to her green fountain pen, out of her pocket. It hadn't leaked. She loved this pen and especially loved the color of its ink cartridge. A green stain on the middle finger of her right hand wasn't uncommon.

She uncapped Chartreuse, opened her journal and wrote on the first page: February 16, 1912. Nibbling the top of her pen, she squinted at the blank page. Beginnings were important. How should she start? Stalling, she wrote her name on the inside of the cover in big swirling cursive, Florence (Polly) Lydia Dye. She rarely wrote her legal name which she'd always disliked. No one seemed to know where she had gotten her nickname, but it had stuck.

Wrinkling her forehead in concentration, she began to write.

Father thinks I need to find ways to release the pressure I've been under since Mother— she paused. She hadn't been able to say the words, so maybe writing them would be a good beginning—*died. He said some people release their pressure by writing in a journal or diary. Maybe writing in Sarah's diary helped relieve some of her pressure and maybe it would help me.*

Polly paused and reread what she'd written, reminding herself that it didn't have to be perfect. It was a start.

One of the ways I released pressure in the past was by talking to Mother, although I didn't know it at the time. I'm thankful I learned to talk to God before she died because otherwise, I'd have been even more lost without her. Even so, I miss her terribly and appreciate her even more now that she's gone. I'm determined to be a good role model for the little ones who may not remember her when they're grown.

Wiping a tear before it could fall and smear her ink, Polly sat up, pulled a clean handkerchief from her pocket and blew her nose. She'd heard it was healthy to mourn one's losses. Not that she'd had much time for that in the past six months. Filling Mother's shoes took most of her time. But it felt good to let the tears come.

"You okay, Pol?"

Hiding her handkerchief, she looked up. Ben stood in the doorway. She hadn't closed her door. Next time she wouldn't forget. She nodded and tried to smile. Ben had been fifteen his last birthday. Such an awkward age. "I'm okay."

Ben motioned to her journal. "What's that?"

"A journal I bought at Simcox's today. Papa thought it might help me deal with the pressure I'm under."

"I'm sorry about the other day. I should have done something to help you when you fell and spilled the milk. I'm no good at knowing what to do when people are upset. Seems like I just freeze. Maybe I could get up a little earlier to help get breakfast on the table."

"Thanks, Ben. That's sweet of you to offer, but you often help Papa at the mine when he needs you."

"I know, but it just doesn't seem right for you to have so much responsibility. If the rest of us help, maybe you can do something fun once in awhile. I guess there's no chance of you working things out with Garrett after the other night."

Polly smiled. "I think Garrett is history. Even if he wanted to be my beau, I don't think I could say yes. What about you? Is there anyone special you like?"

"Not really. Seeing how lost Father is without Mother makes me think getting married isn't such a good idea."

"We all miss her, Father most of all I guess."

"Do you think he'll ever remarry? Some people tell him he needs a wife to help him raise the children." Ben scowled.

"I don't know. How can people even suggest that he remarry so soon? It's only been six months."

"Polly, I wanna drink. Bring me a drink. Bring me a drink, pwease." Elsie's voice raised with each repetition.

"I'll get her a drink. You rest, sis." Ben disappeared. "Hold your horses, Elsie. I'll bring you a drink." His footsteps thundered down the stairs.

Staring at the empty doorway, Polly chewed her lower lip. Sometimes she complained about all the work, but Father remarrying had never been a solution she'd entertained. Someone else sitting in Mother's chair, cooking in Mother's kitchen. Someone else taking care of the little ones and telling Polly what to do. Tears pricked her eyelids. Papa would never want another wife, would he?

Footsteps ascended the stairs, followed by Ben's voice soothing Elsie. "Okay, I'll sing you one song."

A smile dried Polly's tears as Ben sang in his adolescent voice. "Row, row, row your boat, gently down the stream. Merrily, merrily, merrily, life is but a dream."

Mother would be so proud of him. *Life may not be too merry right now, Heavenly Father, but help us keep rowing our boat and putting our trust in you. Oh, and is it wrong to pray father won't ever remarry?*

CHAPTER 25

Garrett had been happy he didn't have to work today so he wouldn't have to face Mr. Black. The question was how to get through the day? He raised up on one elbow and stared out the window beside his bed. Usually he spent some part of the weekend with Savannah but that wasn't an option now. He'd slept in as long as he could. It wasn't as easy to sleep in as it used to be. His body clock had adapted to getting up early nearly every morning to go to work. He turned his back to the window and squeezed his eyelids shut.

Every time he closed his eyes, Savannah's face appeared. He probably needed to apologize. But what was the use apologizing when he still didn't know the truth? She might be guilty, his apology misplaced. The picture under Mr. Black's blotter haunted him more than the image of her sorrowful face.

He sat up, dangled his legs over the side of his bed and dropped his head in his hands. *God, I don't know what to do. I'm so miserable and lost. I've disappointed my parents and maybe I've disappointed you by the way I've treated Savannah. But thinking she might be making a fool of me is eating me alive. Maybe Polly is right—maybe it's because of my pride.*

Polly might be right? What a bitter pill to swallow. He scrubbed his hands over his face and through his hair. *You have to help me, God. I can't go on this way. Please.*

Garrett reached for his Bible lying on his bedside table. He'd been reading about Jacob in the book of Genesis for several days. Jacob's twin brother, Esau, was born first. By rights, he should have received the birthright. But when Esau came in from the fields famished, Jacob persuaded him to sell it for some stew.

Later, Jacob joined his mother in yet another scheme to rob his brother of their father's blessing.

He read again the words Esau spoke when he realized Jacob had tricked him again:

Is not he rightly named Jacob? For he hath supplanted me these two times: he took away my birthright; and, behold, now he hath taken away my blessing.

Supplant wasn't a word he'd heard often but it had been in a list of spelling words he'd looked up a few years ago. He wrinkled his brow. Supplanting was to get things by deceitful means. Jacob must mean supplanter.

Ever since he'd been a child, Garrett had been good at getting what he wanted. His mother admitted to spoiling him because she'd wanted a child so desperately, and they'd waited so long for him to be born. His father nearly always let his mother have her way with Garrett.

If he'd had a twin brother who was the older son, he'd probably have done what Jacob did. He sighed, remembering some of the lies he'd told and some of the tricks he'd pulled. He'd apologized to Ma and to Polly when he first came to Christ but not to anyone else. Was that really necessary? Garrett squirmed. Surely, it was best just to let bygones be bygones rather than stir things up.

Closing his Bible, he bowed his head again. *Father, I'm afraid I have a lot of Jacob in me. I don't much like what I see. You're the only one who can change me.*

He smelled sausage and fried potatoes. His stomach growled. He'd better dress and get downstairs for breakfast.

♠

The sun streamed through George Burns's window even though it was none too clean. He'd arranged for some of his workers to come in early today so he could sleep later and rest his ankle. He hadn't removed the bandage Doc Cooley had put on for him. The Doc hadn't charged him that night, though George suspected he might get a bill in the mail. He'd also persuaded Mr. Grieger at the Cottage Hotel to send him a bill, so he'd probably get one from him soon too.

He rolled over on his side, moving the pillow he'd wedged under his foot. It was Saturday. He smiled. After his misadventure in Sandy Lake the other night, he promised himself he'd only drink on weekends. Couldn't afford to drink up all the profits anyway. Losing Savannah had put a crimp in his style. He'd gotten used to the money she brought in. Maybe making her leave was unnecessary. After all, the sheriff had never come back to make sure she was gone.

Savannah claimed she wasn't doing her business at Mrs. Patton's. He snorted. You couldn't trust a pretty face. He'd learned that the hard way when his wife ran off with his best friend. Funny, she'd always preached to him about right and wrong. She never would have allowed him to set Savannah up in business while she was here.

Maybe if they'd been able to have a child, his wife would have stayed. She'd acted like it was his fault she hadn't conceived. One night he'd yelled at her, "Do you think I'm God, that I have the power to give you a child?" He didn't have much use for God but surely if someone was to blame, it must be him.

George sat up and rubbed his eyes. No use thinking about his wife. What's done was done. He needed to come up with a plan to bring in more money. If he couldn't get money from Savannah, maybe he could convince her to come back to her room above the tavern but keep it real quiet this time. Tell her customers not to discuss it with anyone.

A light tap on his door. "Who is it?" He wasn't happy to be disturbed, and he didn't care if the person outside knew it.

"Mrs. Tyler is here to collect on your account. She said you promised to pay her last week."

He despised Carolyn's timid voice. He despised the message the barmaid brought. "All right, all right. Tell her to hold her horses. She's gonna have to wait till I get dressed."

Throwing back the tangled, none-too-clean blankets, he stood up. His ankle was much better—almost normal again. He picked up a pair of socks from the floor where he'd thrown them the night before, then grabbed a flannel shirt and pants he'd dropped beside his bed. He couldn't keep up with his laundry since Priscilla left.

He looked around for a comb. What did it matter? No one cared how he looked or if his clothes were clean. His reflection in the mirror was even worse than he expected. Shrugging, he left the room.

Going through his desk in the office, he found a couple envelopes with money. Enough to pay Mrs. Tyler what he owed. She watched him from the door to his office. He wasn't gracious about it as he stalked over and handed her the money. "You know times are hard."

"Times are hard for everyone. I can't extend credit indefinitely. My bills have to be paid, too." Mrs. Tyler's cheeks were pink. If the situation had been different, George would have found her attractive. She *was* attractive.

He grunted and muttered an apology under his breath. She nodded and walked away. George watched her go. Money was an issue. He needed it bad. But he also needed, well call it companionship now that his wife was gone.

Mrs. Tyler was easy on the eyes but she couldn't begin to compare with Savannah. To be honest, Savannah was the most beautiful woman he'd ever seen. Whether she believed it or not, she owed him, and even if *companionship* was all he could get, he'd get what he could take.

CHAPTER 26

Yesterday had finally ended. It had been interminable. One of the longest days Garrett ever lived through. He pulled a long-sleeved blue shirt from its wire hanger and his best pair of trousers from a drawer. At least today he and his mother would go to church. The outing should help pass the time. But of course, Monday came next and facing Mr. Black.

A few minutes later, he stood in front of the mirror combing his bronze blond hair. He still liked to look nice but it didn't seem as important anymore. Maybe because there was no one he wanted to impress.

When he entered the kitchen, his mother and father were both seated at the table with bowls of fragrant steaming oatmeal. He glanced at his father, and then looked again. "Where are you going, Pa? You have an appointment at the office on Sunday?"

"No, son. I thought I'd go to church with you and your mother. I wanted to hear this Reverend Caldwell she said was preaching."

His mother stood to get Garrett's oatmeal but he waved her back down. "Who's Reverend Caldwell?" He picked up his bowl and began to spoon oatmeal from the pot on the stove.

"I'm not sure where he's from, but he fills in when pastors are away. I believe he's been at the Presbyterian Church a couple times. A few of my friends said he's very good." Ma's blue eyes sparkled.

Garrett's eyebrows raised. "Isn't that unusual for a pastor to preach at both the Presbyterian and the Methodist churches?"

"I guess it's a little unusual, but I think he's sort of an itinerant preacher. I don't think he preaches at any one church."

"That sounds interesting." Garrett blew on his oatmeal. "How does he get paid?"

His mother shook her head. "I'm not sure. Our church will give him an offering. Maybe he lives by faith."

"Sounds risky." Garrett's father chimed in.

"Not if that's what he's called to do." Ma put down her spoon. "Scripture says, *Seek first the kingdom of God and his righteousness, and all these things shall be added unto you.* If we put God and His kingdom first, He promises to provide for our needs."

Pa looked amused. "Should I quit selling insurance and go around preaching at different churches?"

"Not unless God tells you to." Ma didn't smile.

After a few minutes of silence, Garrett glanced at Ma. "I'm looking forward to hearing Reverend Caldwell. I've never known an itinerant preacher. Glad you're coming with us, Pa."

"Your mother talked me into it." Pa patted Ma's plump hand.

She smiled at him. Ma was never one to hold grudges even when Pa teased her about her strong beliefs. She took her relationship with God very seriously.

Scooping up his last spoonful of oatmeal, Garrett picked up all the empty bowls and put them in the sink. "Let's go before all the good seats are taken." Ma knew he liked to sit in the back, but today he would surprise her by sitting near the front.

♠

Savannah dried while Mrs. Patton washed the mounds of dirty dishes after Sunday breakfast of pancakes and sausage. "I started reading that old diary last night. Nothing too helpful yet, but I promise to tell you if I learn anything life-changing."

"Who did you say the diary belonged to?"

"Sarah Davis. Her husband, Thomas, was from Ireland. He sounds like a wonderful person."

"That makes one wonderful husband. I haven't heard of many. How bad could life be with a grand husband?"

"I don't know. Polly said Sarah suffered many losses but still kept her faith in God." Savannah dried the last plain white dish. "Do you need me to do anything for lunch before I leave for church?"

"No, no. You go ahead. I'm glad you're going to church. You

may not get anything out of it, but it might help your reputation." Mrs. Patton emptied the greasy water from her dark blue and white speckled-enamel dishpan.

Heat rose in Savannah's cheeks. Would her landlady ever let her forget her past? She took off her apron and hurried up the stairs. Maybe she should stay home today. She'd always gone to the Methodist Church where the Young's attended. Not such a good idea if Garrett wanted nothing to do with her.

She picked up her Bible and stood straight and tall. There was more than one church in town. How about the Presbyterian Church? She'd find out if they allowed sinners like her to attend.

Putting on her coat, Savannah ran down the stairs and through the entryway. She opened the door and started down the front steps. Reaching the bottom, she almost collided with a warmly-dressed little girl with brownish blonde hair.

"Savannah!" The child beamed a bright smile.

Staring at the child, Savannah crinkled her forehead. "Who—" She looked up and found herself gazing into Polly Dye's emerald green eyes. "Polly... It's you."

Polly hesitated, then let go of her younger sisters' hands and gave Savannah a quick hug. "Where are you off to this morning?"

"I'm going to the Presbyterian Church." Savannah smiled at the little girls stroking her red coat. What were their names? She hadn't been in a good frame of mind to remember when she'd first met them.

"I've never seen you at the Presbyterian Church. Is this your first time?"

"I usually go to the Methodist Church but..." Savannah hesitated. "I decided to go to the Presbyterian Church today. Is that where your family attends?"

The rest of Polly's family surrounded her. Her father stretched out his hand as Polly introduced him. "Savannah, this is my father, Bob. My brothers, George, Robert, and Ben. My sister, Beth, and you've met Maggie, Elsie, and Twila."

Savannah's head was spinning, trying to remember all their names. "Nice to meet you." She managed a smile.

Polly bit her lip. "Come on, let's go or we'll be late for church. I think we can squeeze one more into our pew."

"Are you sure?" Savannah didn't want Polly to think she had to include her.

"Of course. We can introduce you."

"But..." Savannah hesitated. Would it ruin the Dye's reputation to be seen with her?

Polly grabbed Twila's hand and reached out to Savannah with the other. "Let's go. Don't forget you're a new creature in Christ."

God knew that but people were harder to convince.

CHAPTER 27

Reverend Desmond smiled at the congregation as he greeted them from the wooden pulpit. Was that a hint of surprise in his eyes as he noticed Garrett sitting near the front? Garrett was serious when he'd told God only He could change him. Sitting near the front seemed like a good way of showing he meant business.

The congregation sang a few hymns, one of which he'd never heard before.

Have thine own way, Lord! Have thine own way! Thou art the Potter, I am the clay. Mold me and make me after Thy will, while I am waiting, yielded and still.

He met his mother's gaze as he sang the words. Were they just words or did he mean them? Maybe the reason he'd been feeling a little disoriented lately was because the Lord had him whirling on the Potter's wheel.

When Reverend Caldwell was introduced and came to the pulpit, Garrett sat up straight. There'd been times even since he'd received Jesus when his mind had wandered and he hadn't paid attention to Reverend Desmond. Today would be different. *God, help me not to miss a thing you want me to hear. Speak, Lord, for your servant is listening.*

Where had that phrase come from? Ah, a flannel graph story about Samuel from Garrett's Sunday School days. He studied the young man on the platform. He wasn't sure what he'd expected of an itinerant preacher, but Reverend Caldwell didn't look weird or strange. He was tall, broad shouldered and had a full head of dark hair.

"Thank you for your kind welcome." The young pastor's eyes were clear and probing as he looked at the congregation. "I have a message today that may not be easy to deliver or easy to hear. Let's bow our heads for prayer."

Bowing his head, Garrett took a deep breath. He'd never heard a pastor give a warning before a message.

"Let the words of my mouth and the meditations of my heart be acceptable in Thy sight, O Lord, my Rock and my Redeemer. Amen." The quiet words permeated the atmosphere as complete silence fell.

"God has been speaking to me about Jacob for almost a month, giving me the message for today. The Scriptures I share probably won't be new, but the conclusions I draw may be different."

Garrett couldn't believe his ears. A message on Jacob, the person he'd been reading about in his daily Bible reading. A message God had told the pastor to preach today. A message for him?

Reverend Caldwell led them through the account of the birth of Jacob and Esau. Jacob manipulating Esau to get his birthright, deceiving his father to steal Esau's blessing too. "The Bible never covers over people's flaws. Jacob was a manipulator and a deceiver, willing to use any means to acquire what he wanted."

Was Reverend Caldwell looking straight at him? Heat rose to his neck and ears, and Garrett looked at his hands. How many people in the congregation knew those words described him?

"If you follow the story, you'll discover Jacob's Uncle Laban was also skilled at deception. During his relationship with his uncle, Jacob did a lot of reaping what he'd sown, although God was still faithful to him in the midst of that season." Reverend Caldwell paused.

"Let's go to Chapter thirty two where God is sending Jacob and his family back home. Home, where he'll see his brother, Esau, for the first time in many years. Jacob is glad to be leaving Uncle Laban's sphere of influence, but he's scared to death of Esau. He fears what Esau will do now that their parents are dead.

"How many of you know that when you've lived by manipulation and deception, there are people you'd rather avoid?" Garrett squirmed. His cousin, Irv, his old boss from the mill, sat across the aisle from Garrett and his parents. Garrett hadn't spoken to him since Irv had fired him months ago for being unreliable and deceitful.

"Jacob does some serious praying and considerable gift preparation as he assembles herds of livestock to give Esau. Once again, Jacob has a plan. He was going to buy Esau's forgiveness with impressive gifts sent ahead of him with his servants. But God had another plan. That night Jacob sent his wives and children over the brook ahead of him, and he was left alone. How many of you know that sometimes God has to get us alone to deal with our character flaws?"

For years, Garrett had filled his life with women to keep from being alone. That's why the break with Savannah and his refusal to deal with his loneliness by finding someone else had been so difficult. This time he would do it God's way.

"While Jacob was alone, a man came and wrestled with him all night. At daybreak, the man had a question for Jacob. He said, 'What is your name?'" Reverend Caldwell leaned toward the congregation.

"Why would the man ask Jacob his name? Why was that important?" The pastor paused, allowing the silence to lengthen.

"After having wrestled all night and having his hip put out of joint by what we can assume was a heavenly being, could it be that Jacob had a moment of shocking realization of being all that his name meant? Supplanter, schemer, trickster, swindler... Could it be that God couldn't change Jacob until he admitted all that he was?

"After Jacob told God his name, God changed Jacob's name from supplanter to Israel, which means contender with God. His new name was symbolic of the change God was making in Jacob."

The young pastor gazed at the congregation like he'd been there too. Like he understood the grip of sin. "Maybe you too have been wrestling with God. Maybe your pride has kept you from being honest about who *you* are. If God is the Potter and we are the clay, we need to let Him make changes in us too. Israel walked away from his encounter with God with a limp that some say he had for the rest of his life. We need to be willing to do the same."

Garrett sat in the pew unable to take his gaze from Reverend Caldwell's face. How had this man known exactly what he needed to hear? Garrett had never seen him before. As far as he knew, Reverend Caldwell knew nothing about him.

The young pastor broke the silence at last. "I've asked Reverend Desmond if we could sing *Have Thine Own Way* as our closing hymn. If anyone wants to come to the altar for prayer, I'll be happy to pray with you."

Come to the altar? Was that really necessary? What would people think? Irv and everyone in church would see him. Garrett gripped the pew, the urge to go forward so strong he could barely resist.

Whiter than snow, Lord, wash me just now as in Thy presence humbly I bow. The congregation finished the second verse.

Polly had said pride was at the root of his problems with Savannah. Pride was the opposite of humility. Was pride the reason he didn't want to go to the altar?

He stood, glad he was sitting in the aisle seat, and walked to the front of the church before he could change his mind. Reverend Caldwell joined him as he knelt. The pastor stooped and put his hand on Garrett's shoulder.

Before Reverend Caldwell could speak, Garrett lifted his head. "Did someone talk to you about me? Is that why you preached this message?"

A spark of humor lit the pastor's eyes. "Well, yes and no. As I told the congregation, the Holy Spirit has been speaking to me about Jacob for almost a month, telling me to preach this message today. If the message was for you, then yes, someone spoke to me about you. It was the Holy Spirit."

Garrett nodded. "My name is Garrett but it should have been Jacob. I've been a Jacob all my life, manipulating and deceiving people to get what I want. Six months ago I received Jesus, but my repentance was shallow. God couldn't make lasting changes because I wasn't willing to admit what I was."

Reverend Caldwell smiled. "It took a lot of courage to say what you just said. I know God will honor your honesty. Most of the time when we've lived life as a Jacob, we need to confess not only to God but to the people we've wronged. Are you willing to do that?"

"I am now. It won't be easy, but I'm willing."

"One more thing. As I said earlier, there are times in our

lives when God has to get us alone to deal with our character flaws. I'm not sure what that means in your life, but if you pray about it, God will make it clear."

The congregation had finished the third stanza of *Have Thine Own Way, Lord,* and the organist continued to play. Pastor Caldwell bowed his head and prayed softly. "Father, you know what's burdening Garrett's heart. You know why my message spoke to him. Give him the courage to follow through and do everything you tell him to do. Don't allow pride to stand in his way. If he's tempted to fall back into his Jacob ways, speak to him clearly so he can understand. Mold him into your image, Lord. Amen."

Garrett returned to his pew, head still bowed. *Have thine own way, Lord. Have Thine own way.*

Chapter 28

Surrounded by a friendly buzz of voices in the unpretentious sanctuary, Savannah smiled and spoke to everyone Polly introduced to her. A few people quickly excused themselves when Polly told them Savannah's name, but most welcomed her. When they sat down, Twila and Elsie positioned themselves on either side of her. Polly sat on the other side of Twila, cautioning the girls to be quiet.

The service began with the singing of a few hymns, and even though it wasn't as rousing as at the Methodist Church, peace washed over her. One hymn in particular spoke to her, and she wrote some of the words on a piece of paper in her Bible.

> *Open my eyes, that I might see glimpses of truth Thou hast for me; Place in my hand the wonderful key that shall unclasp and set me free. Silently now I wait for Thee, ready my God Thy will to see. Open my eyes, illumine me, Spirit Divine.*

"Yes, Lord. I'm ready to see your will. Thank you for this family who've made me so welcome."

♠

After church, Polly introduced Savannah to a few more people, as well as Pastor Lawrence, before they left the sanctuary. Twila and Elsie each grabbed one of Savannah's hands as they walked down the steps. Polly battled twinges of jealousy at her little sisters' fascination with Savannah. After all, Polly was the one who cared for their every need, wiped their noses, made sure their bellies were full.

The girls each gave Savannah huge hugs before her father shepherded them away so Polly and Savannah could talk during the short walk to the boarding house. She breathed a sigh of relief.

As soon as they were alone, the girls looked at each and said in unison, "So how are you doing?" Then burst out laughing.

"You go first, Polly. Last time we mostly talked about my problems." Savannah touched Polly's arm as they started down the snow-dusted sidewalk.

"I'm doing okay. My father suggested some ways to release some of the pressure I'm under. Writing in a journal was one of them. I'm doing that, and I think it will help."

"That's a grand idea. Especially since Sarah's diary helped you so much. Maybe someday your diary will help someone else." Savannah squeezed Polly's hand.

"I don't know if I want anyone to read my journal. Although after I'm dead, maybe I won't care." Polly giggled. "How about you? How are you doing?"

"Life's been hard. My old business partner is making trouble... that's why I was so upset when we met in front of your house a few days ago." Savannah avoided Polly's eyes.

"Is George Burns your old business partner?"

"How did you know?"

Polly told Savannah about Kitt coming to get her father's help and saying that Mr. Burns told them he had business with Savannah. "Did he bother you that night?"

"He came upstairs in the boarding house. My landlady came on the scene just as he tried to kiss me. Now she doesn't trust me."

"I'm so sorry." Polly glanced up at the boarding house on their left. "Would you like to come home with us for Sunday dinner?" Immediately, she wished she'd bitten her tongue.

"I'd love to but I have to help Mrs. Patton. It's part of our arrangement."

"All right. Maybe you can come visit another time. Ben and Maggie are helping more with the little ones." Polly started to leave, then turned back. "Have you had a chance to read any of Sarah's diary yet?"

"Not much. I only know that Mr. Davis was from Ireland and that he seemed like a wonderful husband. Mrs. Patton is interested in the diary too, but she doesn't see how Sarah's life could have been so bad if she had a husband like him."

Polly nodded. "Mrs. Patton went through a lot in her marriage."

"She thinks she has a right to be bitter."

"Whether or not we have a right, bitterness will ruin our lives. Mother used to say it's like drinking poison and hoping the person we're mad at will die." Polly swallowed hard.

♠

"...and give you peace." Garrett raised his head as the last words of the benediction faded. *May as well get started eating humble pie.*

He stepped across the aisle and nodded at Irv. "Do you think we could talk sometime soon? Maybe I could come to the mill tomorrow before you close."

Irv glanced at Garrett's parents across the aisle, then at Garrett. "We can talk, but I'm not giving your old job back. I hired someone I can trust."

Garrett felt heat rise up his neck and ears, but he kept his voice low. "This isn't about getting my job back."

"All right. I'll expect you by six o'clock tomorrow. I hope you do a better job of showing up than you did when you worked for me."

Biting his tongue hard, Garrett nodded. "I'll be there." Irv wasn't making this easy.

Garrett's father caught up with him as Garrett strode up the aisle. "What's that all about?"

"I have some things I need to make right. Irv is as good a place to start as any."

Garrett grabbed his coat from the cloak room, opened the church door and went into the crisp morning air. His parents followed. As they climbed into the family buggy, his father's sleek black stallion snorted and stamped his feet, eager to be on his way.

"But you said Irv was unreasonable and unfair in the way he treated you. I'd think he should be the one to make things right." His father picked up the reins and clucked to Midnight.

"I said a lot of things that weren't true, Pa. It's about time I owned up to the wrong things I said and did."

Pa frowned. "Is that what Reverend Caldwell told you?

Don't you think you're getting a little carried away with this religion stuff?"

"Reverend Caldwell's message was for me this morning. All week, I've been reading about Jacob in the Bible. God is showing me I've been a Jacob all my life, but I want to change."

Ma reached back to squeeze his hand. "I'm so proud of you, Garrett. I know God will honor every effort you make to correct things you've done, even if some people don't receive it well."

"Thanks, Ma. My repentance didn't go deep enough when I received Jesus. I guess God is working on my pride."

♠

Polly closed her door and curled up on her bed with her journal and Chartreuse. Elsie and Twila were sleeping and everyone else had found quiet things to do after lunch—even Robert and George, although that might not last long.

She traced her finger over the gold lettering on her journal, then opened it to page one. She hadn't gotten very far in her first entry, but having the journal to write about anything that concerned her gave her peace.

February 25, 1912 This month will soon be over, although we have 29 days in February this year. Sometimes I wish I'd have been born on February 29 instead of on September 9, just to be different. I always thought I'd be married, or at least engaged, by the time I was twenty years old—not taking care of my brothers and sisters and keeping house for my father. Of course, I was living in a dream world anyway, thinking I'd marry Garrett. It hurts to remember him making a fool of me. Probably half the town knew he was running around with other girls when I thought he was in love with me.

Polly sat up and scrubbed at an ink stain on her middle finger. Chartreuse was better than a dip pen but not foolproof. She crossed her legs and leaned back against the oak headboard.

Today Savannah went to church with us. She really is very nice. I'm trying not to be jealous of how Elsie and Twila adore her. They both wanted to sit beside her in church and then gave her big hugs when Father made them walk with him. I know it's silly but in some ways, it's a little like being rejected by Garrett all over again. He liked her better too.

A tear dripped off Polly's chin, smearing the green ink in her last sentence. She blew on it, trying to dry the words before turning the page.

I'm praying God will remove these jealous feelings because I know He wants me to be Savannah's friend. Mother used to say, "Charity envieth not." I guess that means I need to love Savannah more. Please help me, Jesus.

"Give me that, George. It's mine." Robert's irate voice shattered the silence.

Before Polly could untangle her legs to go quiet the boys, footsteps passed her room.

"Quiet, you two. The girls are sleeping." Ben's loud whisper penetrated the wall between the boys' room and hers.

Bless his heart for taking charge so she didn't have to get up. Too late. Twila's wail followed by Elsie's told her their naps were over. She uncrossed her legs, sprinted to the door and opened it. Ben was already soothing the girls, lifting Twila out of her crib and stretching a hand toward Elsie crawling out of the double bed. "It's okay, Polly. You rest or take a walk. Maggie and I will keep an eye on the girls."

A tear rolled down her cheek at Ben's unexpected kindness. "Are you sure?"

"I'm sure. I don't have anything better to do." He stopped at the doorway to the boys' room. "You two get along now. No more arguing."

Muttering and grunts told Polly the boys didn't appreciate their brother telling them what to do. They'd have to get used to it.

Polly stared out the window. She so seldom had spare time that she didn't know what to do. Maybe she'd visit Kitt. Would she be home on a Sunday afternoon? Taking a deep breath, Polly ran down the stairs, grabbed her coat from the hook, and pulled her mittens out of her pockets. Father was dozing in mother's gray chair, so Polly stuck her head into the sitting room where Ben, Maggie and Beth were playing with Elsie and Twila.

"I'm going to visit Kitt. I'll be at the Potter's if you need me." Maggie smiled and waved while Beth came to give her a hug. Twila and Elsie barely looked up, so engrossed in the tower Ben was building. Probably best that way since she didn't want to take them with her.

Tiptoeing past Father, she left the house and ran down the porch steps. It had been a long time since she and Kitt had gotten together. Polly missed her. Did Kitt still fret about the poor judgment she'd used in allowing herself to be duped by the fake doctor last year? Would she ever trust any man after that experience?

CHAPTER 29

Kitt ran down the steps to Broad Street and hesitated. Which way should she go? She was going to lose her mind if she stayed in that house another minute. How long would it be until she could leave the house without Mother giving her the third degree? How long would it be until she could go to town without being embarrassed, without thinking people were talking about her and without people avoiding her because they didn't know what to say?

Would the mistake she'd made in going to Atlanta haunt her the rest of her life?

She took a deep breath and turned right. Maybe a good talk with Polly Dye would encourage her. Not that Polly didn't have problems of her own. Still, she didn't seem to struggle like Kitt did. Maybe it was because Polly'd had such a faith-filled mother. She'd told Kitt once that praying was just like breathing for her mother.

Staring at the snow-packed road, she headed down Broad Street.

"Hello, Kitt."

The greeting was so unexpected that Kitt jerked her head up. Polly was standing in front of her smiling. "Polly, how did you know I needed to talk to you?"

"I didn't. Maggie and Ben are watching the little ones so I thought I'd see if you were home." Polly pushed a strand of her vibrant red hair behind her ear. "It's been too long since we've talked."

Kitt nodded. "I agree. Want to come to my house or shall we walk? Are you warm enough?"

"Let's go for a walk. I'm tired of being indoors."

"Me too."

The girls headed toward Main Street. "What's happening in your world, Kitt?"

"Not much. Oh, the day after I came to ask for your father's help with Mr. Burns, he chased Savannah down Walnut Street in his buggy."

"What?" Polly's eyes were wide.

"I stood in front of him so she could get away. I hate bullies."

"That was probably the day she told me she was running away to Greenville. We met on the road in front of our house, and I invited her in for a cup of tea."

Kitt stared at Polly and shook her head. "I don't know how you do it."

"Do what?"

"You're always helping people, even people you have reason to dislike. Today you were the person I wanted to see when I needed encouragement. Your life can't be easy, but it doesn't seem like you ever get discouraged or upset."

Polly laughed out loud. "You are so wrong." She told her friend about the bad morning she'd had a few days earlier. "The reason Savannah and I met was because I was running away, too. At least for a little while."

"I'm sorry, Polly. I can't even imagine how difficult it must be to cook and clean and take care of the house and so many children. But still, even on that very bad day, you were willing to help Savannah with her problem. I'll say it again: Your mother would be so proud of you."

Polly chewed her lower lip. "I hope you're right. Sometimes I'm not so sure. Why did you need encouragement today?"

"I don't think my life will ever be normal again. I'm always thinking people are talking about me and remembering the dumb thing I did. Sometimes I just want to run away."

Stretching out her hand to her friend, Polly squeezed her arm and looked thoughtful. "I understand that feeling. Do you suppose that's how Savannah feels?"

Kitt ducked her head. "I said some pretty unkind things about her last time we talked. I didn't stop to think about how she'd feel about people talking about her."

Nodding, Polly's green eyes were kind. "My mother used to say one of the best ways to quit worrying about what other people think of us was to look for something we could do for someone else. Sounds like you helped Savannah the other day, and I'm sure she's grateful. Maybe she could use another friend."

Kitt started to nod, then hesitated. "I'm not sure how my mother would feel about Savannah and me being friends. That might damage my reputation even more."

"Pray about it. Maybe God will show you what to do."

♠

Garrett sat on his bed with his head in his hands. He had spent a long afternoon devising and discarding concrete plans about how to act on what he'd learned at church today. Part of the time, he'd walked in the woods behind their house, thinking and talking to God. Making an appointment with Irv had been a good start even though he dreaded talking to him tomorrow evening.

Restless, he got up and paced back and forth from his door to his window. How far back did he need to go to make things right with people? Would they even remember the things he'd done? Savannah's face kept blocking his attempts to decide. He ached to hold her in his arms and kiss her sweet lips. What had he been thinking, breaking up with her? She was the most beautiful woman he'd ever known. Should he apologize for not believing in her? He still didn't know if she was telling the truth, but how could he live without her?

A longing for Savannah consumed him. The peace he'd experienced in church dissipated. What if she found someone else? In deep agony of soul, he picked up his Bible. How had he so quickly lost his way after his experience in church this morning? The Bible fell open to the book of Jeremiah, a book he'd never read. His gaze dropped to the second chapter, the thirteenth verse. "*My people have committed two evils: They have forsaken me, the fountain of living waters, and hewed them out cisterns, broken cisterns that can hold no water.*"

Sinking down on the bed covered with a multicolored quilt, he lowered his head into his hands again. "I'm sorry, Father. I'm so sorry. Once again I'm trying to substitute a woman for what I need most—You. Reverend Caldwell said I should pray about what it meant for you to get me alone to deal with my flaws. But I already know what it means."

Garrett knelt beside his bed. "I promised, Father, that *this* time I'd do it your way. I'm not going to substitute Savannah or any other woman for the springs of living water. I need to focus on developing my relationship with you, on letting you change me from a Jacob to a man who has power with you, a godly man who puts you first."

As he rested his head on the coverlet, peace flooded his soul. He picked up his Bible and turned to the marker where he'd been reading in Psalms. *Surely I have behaved and quieted myself, as a child that is weaned of his mother: my soul is even as a weaned child*. He wasn't sure he completely understood the words, yet it described his experience. His soul was at peace. He flipped back to another verse he'd marked last week. *Be still and know that I am God.*

Maybe the hardest thing in the world for a Jacob was to be still. Jacobs wanted to be in control, to decide what they wanted and then somehow, make it happen. "Not this time, Lord. Not this time."

CHAPTER 30

George hated Sundays. He hated the blue laws that forbid him to be open on Sunday. They diminished his income. But just because he couldn't sell alcohol on Sunday didn't mean he couldn't drink it. Of course, drinking alone on Sundays also cut into his profit, but he needed something to get him through the long hours.

Before his wife left... No use thinking about that.

He glanced out the window at the setting sun. He couldn't face another lonely night. Picking up his glass, he tossed back a few more swallows of whiskey and selected a smaller, flat bottle from under the counter to put in his pocket.

None too steady on his feet, he went to his bedroom and searched again for a comb. Finding one at last in the pocket of dirty pants lying on the floor, he dipped it in the glass of water on the dresser and used it to slick his hair close to his head. He peered into the looking glass and nodded. Not bad. Not bad at all.

He grabbed a bottle of cologne he'd picked up at the five-and-ten and dabbed it on his cheeks and neck. Could have used a shave but he didn't want to waste time. He had a little drive ahead of him.

♠

Savannah pulled Sarah's diary out of the drawer and curled up on her bed. The glow of the gas lamp matched the glow that had stayed with her all day since going to church with the Dye's. They had welcomed her as though she were one of the family. Mr. and Mrs. Young had also made her welcome, but that was because of Garrett.

What would it be like to be part of a family where you were loved and made welcome just for yourself?

She opened Sarah's diary, turned to the second entry, *July 27, 1840,* and began to read. What an exciting day for Sarah—feeling movement and life in her womb for the first time, anticipating her husband's excitement, planning a name, hoping for more children to come. And yet, even in the midst of her pleasure, fear clouded Sarah's joy...fear of disease, fear that her child's health would be fragile. So many died. Still, she recognized that only God could help her cope with losing a child.

Polly said Sarah had experienced many losses. Having a good husband hadn't protected her from them. Even Kitt, who lived in a house that looked like a castle, had experienced loss. Her father and two brothers had died. Savannah read the last sentence of Sarah's entry again. *Only God could see me through the loss of a child.*

When the possibility of losing a child occurred to Sarah, her first thought was that only God could see her through. Would she respond as Sarah did if she were pregnant and feared losing a child? To be honest, her first thought would probably be to blame God.

She chewed her lip. Polly had explained that becoming a new creature in Christ was only the beginning. She'd said they both still had a lot of growing to do. How long did it take for a Christian to turn to God during hard times instead of blaming Him?

♠

George peered through the darkness as he entered Main Street in Sandy Lake. Not much happening on a Sunday night. His chestnut mare stepped along at a brisk pace. He didn't have to use his whip as often now that she'd tasted it enough to discourage her from loitering. He pulled the reins left to turn Freda. He'd named the horse for a neighbor who had a long, horsy face. The mare marched down Laycock to the livery.

If things went well, he shouldn't be gone long. He took another swallow from the bottle in his pocket.

A few minutes later, he was back on Main Street, taking long strides up the wooden sidewalk. His ankle hadn't pained him today—the bandage was still in place. Next time he bathed, he probably should take it off. Good thing he'd had that bottle of cologne on hand since he hadn't had time to bathe this week.

He passed the Cottage Hotel across the street from Doc

Cooley's office. George cringed as he remembered how much pain he'd been in earlier this week.

On his left loomed the old hotel, now Mrs. Patton's boarding house. Hopefully, she hadn't locked the door for the night yet. She shouldn't be in the dining room at this hour. If he was quiet, she wouldn't hear him. He hesitated. Would have been better to come when she was sleeping, but then the door might have been locked.

Tiptoeing up the porch steps, weaving a little, he reached the porch without incident and tested the door knob. Unlocked. He could hardly keep from whooping. Nothing was going to stop him tonight. Opening the door, he stumbled over a chair to his right. He froze. No footsteps to indicate anyone overheard.

Pulling himself upright, George tiptoed across the entryway and started up the stairs, trying to remember which room was Savannah's. The steps and upstairs hallway were dimly lit from lights downstairs.

He stopped part way up the steps to get his bearings. Savannah had been in the room to the left at the top of the stairs and on the right side of the hall three or four doors down. Maybe the fourth door. The last step creaked under his feet.

Without warning, the door in front of him opened and Savannah stuck her head out. In one huge stride, George shoved the solid oak door open all the way, knocking Savannah backward. She stumbled and fell on the bed as he entered the room, shutting the door behind him. He leapt forward and clamped his meaty hand over her mouth.

"Don't you dare scream. I ain't gonna hurt ya."

Savannah's pupils dilated and she didn't move except for her chest rising and falling.

"I come here to make a deal with ya. Promise ya won't scream?"

As soon as she nodded, George took his hand off her mouth and plopped down on the bed, getting a firm grip on her right arm. She sat up and moved away as far as she could. George pulled her back. "Don't be doing that. I want us to be friends."

"Friends? This is how you treat your friends?" Savannah's tone was heavy with scorn.

"I'm sorry I had to do it this way. I knew you wouldn't talk to me otherwise."

"Why are you here?"

"I told ya, I wanna make a deal." George tightened his hold on her arm.

"What kind of deal?"

"I want you to come back to the tavern. The sheriff never come back to make sure you was gone. We'll keep it real quiet that you're back. Only tell your best customers."

"Mr. Burns—"

"No, no. Wait. I ain't finished. If you'll come to my room and keep me company whenever I'm lonely, I'll only charge you half the rent you was paying. Besides that, in exchange for favors rendered, I won't make ya pay me what you owe me from before."

"Mr. Burns—"

"Ya never know. I might even fall in love with ya, and we could get married. If I ever get around to divorcing my no-good wife."

"Stop! You don't understand. I'm a Christian now. I can't do the things I used to do. I can't go back. You could have a new beginning, too."

George snorted. "I don't want no new beginning. I just want somebody to meet my needs." He turned toward Savannah, yanking her arm behind her and ripping her sleeve. "I was hopin' we could do this the easy way, but looks like it's gonna be the hard way. I'm gonna get what's owed me."

He pushed her down on the bed and flung himself on top of her, pressing his lips on hers. Savannah kneed him in the groin with a lot more spunk than he'd expected and gave a piercing shriek, just as he let out a roar.

"Help! Help! Somebody help me." Savannah kneed him again.

The door burst open and a tall, burly young man flung it wide. "What's going on in here? Get off her. Now." In two steps, the man reached George and yanked him off the bed. George landed with a thud on the floor.

Running footsteps on the stairs and Mrs. Patton appeared in the doorway. "What in the world..." She saw George. "You again? This time I'm calling the sheriff."

George stood and tried to get past her but the other man

blocked his way and spoke to Mrs. Patton. "He was attacking Savannah." He gave George a menacing look.

Mrs. Patton glanced at Savannah tugging at her torn sleeve. "I can see that. Don't let him get away." She hurried down the stairs.

"Thank you so much, William, for coming to my rescue."

"This ain't over yet, Savannah. Just you wait and see." George glared at her. "I don't give up easy."

"I'll tell the sheriff that not only did you attack her, you also threatened her. I think you'll wish you hadn't." William's gaze never left George's face. "What were you thinking, coming in here attacking Savannah in a boarding house?"

"He's been drinking. He gets like this when he's drunk." Savannah wrinkled her nose.

"You know this man?"

"Sorry to say, I used to work for him. That was in my old life." Savannah took a deep breath. "Not any more. Never again."

"Don't listen to her." George scowled. "She's a whore and she'll always be a whore. She can't fool me with all her Bible talk."

CHAPTER 31

As Savannah continued to hold together the torn edges of her sleeve, William turned to her. "What did you say your last name is?"

"Stevens, Savannah Stevens. Why?"

"No reason. I think I've heard that name before. What kind of work did you do for..."

The outside door opened in the entryway downstairs. Sheriff Donley boomed a greeting to Mrs. Patton.

Savannah tried to shrink into invisibility as the sheriff and her landlady came up the stairs. More bad publicity for her and for Mrs. Patton's boarding house. Would she have a place to live when this episode was over? Grandma always used to say there were consequences for bad behavior, but this time she hadn't done anything wrong.

She glanced up and met Sheriff Donley's eyes as William stepped into the hall and let him enter. George held out his hand to the sheriff. "I think there's been a misunderstanding. I just come to do business with Miss Stevens, to try to get what's owed me. I don't know how she ripped her sleeve."

"That's not what happened, Sheriff." William squeezed back into the room. "He attacked her. When she screamed, I opened the door. This man..." William pointed at George, "was lying on top of her."

"Is that right, young lady?" The sheriff's gaze swept over George before moving to Savannah.

"That's what happened. When I wouldn't do what he wanted, he tried to force me." Savannah shuddered. "He's been drinking."

"I can tell." The sheriff stared at George, "I also heard from Doc Cooley this isn't the first time you came to my town after you'd had too much to drink. Let's see if we can find a comfortable place for you to sleep it off and think long and hard about what you've done. There's no excuse for your behavior."

"But Sheriff, the woman owes me money—"

"If that's true, this is certainly not the way to get it. Let's go. Will you come willingly or do I have to give you some encouragement?" Sheriff patted the bulge in his pocket.

George started for the door, then turned back and snarled at Savannah. "You ain't heard the last of this, pretty lady." He spit out the last two words.

After George and the Sheriff left, Mrs. Patton looked at Savannah and then at William. "How did you happen to be so handy when George Burns attacked Savannah? You were mighty quick to the rescue."

"I was leaving my room to go to the hymn sing when I heard Savannah scream, followed by that man roaring like a bull. It wasn't too hard to figure out something bad was going on. You got here pretty quick, too."

Nodding, her landlady sighed. "No shortage of noise to sound the alarm. I'm glad most of my boarders were at the hymn sing over at the Christian Church." She bowed her head and rubbed the back of her neck. "They'll find out though. No secrets here. It'll be in the paper."

Savannah closed her eyes. *God, why did you let this—* No, she wanted to stop blaming God and start running to Him when bad things happened. *Help me, Lord.* She opened her eyes.

"Mrs. Patton, do you want me to leave? I know what Mr. Burns is doing is bad for your business. And even if I didn't do anything wrong, I'm the reason he's causing trouble."

Lifting her head and gazing at Savannah, Mrs. Patton was silent for a moment. "If I make you leave, that bully will have won. If I let you stay, my boarders might leave."

"Give us more credit than that, Mrs. Patton." William stood up straight. "Your boarders will be on Savannah's side when they hear what Mr. Burns did to her."

Savannah shook her head. "I doubt it." A tear trickled down her cheek. "They'll probably say I had it coming. Maybe they'd be right."

"But..." William frowned.

"Let it go, William." Mrs. Patton headed for the door. "We should give Savannah some privacy to fix her sleeve. I don't have to make any decisions tonight."

♠

As Innis Patton closed the door behind them, William put his hand on her arm. "What was that all about?" His forehead wrinkled in a frown.

"I don't want to spread stories about my boarders. Let's just say Savannah made bad choices in her past. Some of the people in this town aren't very forgiving. I should know." Innis's mouth formed a grim line.

William shrugged. "Mr. Burns said she was a whore."

"People can change. Don't be spreading rumors by quoting that drunk." In spite of herself, was she defending Savannah? Before Savannah offered to leave, Innis had been thinking about asking her to go. And yet she identified with Savannah's dilemma, being up against someone bigger and stronger. How could she turn her out?

"Mrs. Patton, are you all right? I've said your name three times."

"I'm sorry. So much on my mind. Thank you for coming to Savannah's defense. I hate to think what could have happened if she'd been alone." Innis shuddered, then frowned. "You and Savannah didn't have plans to meet while most everyone was at the hymn sing, did you?"

"I barely know Savannah." William's puzzled frown was back. "One minute you're defending her and the next, you're acting like you don't trust her."

"You're right. I'd better make up my mind. It's hard being in charge of a business with no partner, no one to agree or disagree with what you're doing. I've worked hard to build this business, and I'm afraid of making a costly mistake."

"My mother always says *Love always believes the best.* Sometimes people just need someone to believe in them."

Innis snorted. "That sure didn't work for me. Every time I tried to believe the best, the worst hit me between the eyes. Maybe I was right to be suspicious about Savannah, suspicious about the two of you."

"You can believe what you want, it won't change the truth. But it will change *you*. Believing the worst changes us into mean, bitter people. You being divorced and people being what they are, I'd think you know how it feels to have people believe the worst."

Innis stared at the broad-shouldered young man, clenching and unclenching her fists. His words had the ring of truth, even though she didn't really want to hear them. "I do know how it feels. But I also know how it feels to trust someone and be betrayed again and again."

William nodded. "But it isn't fair to judge everyone to be untrustworthy because one person failed you." They stared at each other for a long, tense moment. Then William shrugged. "I'm sorry. Maybe I've spoken out of turn. You're the only one who can decide...will you believe the worst or will you believe the best?"

CHAPTER 32

Savannah sank down on her bed. It reeked of George Burns's cheap cologne, making her gag. She ripped off the flimsy quilt and threw it on the floor. She'd have to wash it. Kicking it into the far corner, she dropped down beside her bed. Tears flowed down her cheeks.

"Father..."

She refused to say the words that were ready on her tongue: Why are you allowing these things to happen? Why did you let Mr. Burns come and attack me? Why? Why? Why?

What had Sarah said in her diary? "Only God could get me through the death of a child."

"Father..." Her tongue resisted saying the words but she pressed on "...only you can get me through Mr. Burns coming to my room and attacking me again."

She pulled open the drawer in the stand beside her bed and drew out the little burgundy diary. She opened it to the pink satin marker. *June 25, 1847.*

I'm so filled with sorrow it's hard even to think about putting into words the entry I must make.

Had Sarah's dreaded moment come? Had she faced the loss of a child? The third paragraph confirmed her fears.

Yesterday the battle was finally over. Our little Nancy is now safe in the arms of Jesus.

A battle raged in Sarah's heart after her loss, then these words:

If I turn against God, to whom will I go for comfort and strength to get through the days ahead?

"Yes, Father, if I turn against you now, to whom will I go for comfort and strength to get through the days ahead? Help me win this battle as you helped Sarah."

Savannah opened the drawer again and lifted out her Bible with the marker still at Proverbs 3. She couldn't seem to get past these words: *Trust in the Lord with all your heart and lean not on your own understanding. In all your ways acknowledge Him and He will direct your path.*

"I want to trust you, Father, even when things don't make sense. I want to believe you're going to use this for good in my life, to help me prove I've changed. When Mr. Burns offered me a way to go back to my old life, I refused. Help me keep acknowledging you in all my ways, no matter what happens."

Savannah stood, and then sat on the edge of her bed. "I told Mrs. Patton I'd leave if she wants me to, and I will, even though I don't know where I'd go. I'd even go back to live with my parents in Georgia if I thought they'd take me."

She picked up her Bible again and flipped to the book of Psalms. Mrs. Young had recommended reading Psalms when life was difficult. Allowing the Bible to fall open to Psalm 27, she began to read. *The Lord is my light and my salvation; whom shall I fear? The Lord is the strength of my life; of whom shall I be afraid?*"

Peace and courage settled over Savannah. God was more powerful than Mr. Burns. She would not run from him or allow him to frighten her into doing something foolish. Even though He had used William, God was the one who had rescued her.

She pulled out the piece of paper on which she'd written the words to part of the hymn this morning and read the first two lines:

Open my eyes, that I might see glimpses of truth Thou hast for me; Place in my hand the wonderful key that shall unclasp and set me free.

"Thank you, Father, for the glimpses of truth you're giving me, for the faith you're instilling in me that is setting me free."

♠

Kitt grabbed her dark blue, down-lined winter coat and headed for the door. Mama wanted her to go to the General Store across town this morning to pick up her favorite brand of honey, not that Kitt could taste the difference. She sighed. Bess actually went to town for Mama more often than Kitt so she shouldn't complain. Mama swung back and forth between wanting Kitt to stay home so she knew she was safe or worrying because she stayed home too much.

Not hard to understand. Kitt swung back and forth between being bored to death and wanting to avoid people as much as possible. She hated interacting with the town, but Polly had been a good friend to her.

Last night after her talk with Polly, Kitt had prayed about befriending Savannah. In spite of her reluctance to make new friends who would eventually find out how stupid she'd been, Kitt needed to be willing. Maybe it was something God wanted her to do. She chuckled at how Savannah had described her house as looking like a castle. She didn't feel much like a princess.

Kitt ran down the flights of stairs that allowed her to cross Broad Street to Walnut. Then one block down, she cut across College Street to Main. She rounded the corner just as Savannah sprinted down the front steps of the old hotel. Could this be an answer to her prayer?

"Hello, Savannah." The words were out of her mouth before she had time to change her mind.

The raven-haired young woman turned toward her. "Oh, hello...um, is it Kitt?"

"That's right. How are you?"

Savannah shrugged. "Life is...interesting. But I wanted to thank you again for helping me when Mr. Burns chased me in his buggy. I appreciated that so much."

Concern for Savannah overcame Kitt's usual self-consciousness. "Has he left you alone since then?"

Savannah hesitated and glanced around. She stepped closer to Kitt. "He came back last night, drunk again."

Kitt frowned. "What happened?"

"Can we walk and talk? I don't want to be late for work." Savannah turned toward town. "Where are you going?"

"The General Store on the other end of town. I'm in no hurry."

"Okay." Walking briskly, Savannah told Kitt what had happened the night before. "God sent William to help me at just the right time."

Kitt squirmed as she always did when someone talked about God rescuing them from a bad situation. She still struggled with why God hadn't rescued her sooner in Atlantic City. Did Savannah know about her experience with the fake doctor?

"I'm glad you're okay, Savannah. Did Mrs. Patton call the sheriff?"

"Yes, I guess Mr. Burns is in jail. At least that's where he's supposed to be." Savannah shivered. "I'm not sure how long he'll be there, or what he'll do when he gets out. He told me I'd be sorry."

Reaching out to pat Savannah's arm, Kitt looked for comforting words. "I wish there was something I could do to help."

Savannah stopped outside the building where she worked. "Thanks for walking with me. I'd better get on in to work. It was nice talking to you."

"You're welcome." Kitt looked down at her feet, and then raised her gaze to meet Savannah's. It was still hard for her to say these five little words. "I'll be praying for you."

Chapter 33

Garrett walked out of the house, used his crank, and hopped into his automobile. They'd had a fresh coating of snow last night so he'd have to take it easy. He hoped he'd allowed enough time. Even though Mr. Black wasn't a stickler about being on time, Garrett tried not to be late. Irv would have a hard time believing that. He groaned.

When he worked for Irv, he'd been late more than he'd been on time. Not just a few minutes late. On his mornings to open, he assumed Irv would have someone to cover for him. Other days he pretended to be sick so he could go fishing. No wonder his cousin had gotten fed up and sacked him. Garrett owed him a huge apology.

His car swerved on an icy patch. Better pay attention instead of wool gathering. Six o'clock tonight would come soon enough. Garrett gripped the steering wheel and squinted through the light snow.

And then there was Mr. Black. Garrett groaned again. He'd told his parents if he stopped seeing Savannah, maybe he could go on working for Mr. Black and not worry about whether his boss was lying. But could he?

"What do you want me to do, Lord? I guess I was wrong in going through Mr. Black's office. I probably need to ask his forgiveness for not respecting his privacy, but then what?"

Trust me. You do what's right and I'll take care of the rest.

"Are you saying you want me to apologize to Mr. Black?" Peace settled over Garrett, and his anxiety lifted as he processed the gentle impression. "All right, Father. I can do that. "

The rest of the journey to Mercer was uneventful, but when

the Mercer County Courthouse came into view, his pulse sped up again. "I choose to trust you, Lord. *I will trust and not be afraid.*"

He pulled into the parking lot beside the store, turned off the engine, but remained in his car, head down. A light tap on the window roused him.

Garrett opened his eyes as Mr. Black peered in his window. "You all right?"

He opened the door. "I'm fine. Just preparing myself for the day."

"How do you do that?"

"Well, I was thinking of a Bible verse, actually." Garrett got out of the car and felt heat rise in his neck at the admission.

Mr. Black gazed at him. After a moment, he said, "I wouldn't have taken you for a religious man."

"I don't like to think of it as being religious, more like having a relationship with Christ. I've only been a Christian for about six months."

"I see." As they walked Mr. Black snuck looks at Garrett as if he were some sort of circus oddity.

"Are you a Christian?" The question slipped out of Garrett's mouth although he'd never asked anyone that before.

"Well, er, ah." Mr. Black's stammering faded. "I guess it depends what you mean by Christian. My parents had me baptized when I was a baby. I have no *other* religion."

"I don't think being baptized makes you a Christian. I meant have you asked Jesus to forgive your sins and live in your heart?"

Mr. Black unlocked the door without answering and hurried into his office. Garrett hung his coat in the cloakroom, then started a fire in the Belleville cast iron stove. He guessed the conversation was over.

Garrett glanced toward the office in time to see Mr. Black close his door. This wasn't unusual behavior for his boss, although he'd always thought it a bit strange. Why would his boss need privacy? Did he close the door so Garrett wouldn't observe him opening the wall safe or counting the money?

Regardless, today Garrett would knock on that door, something he'd never done before. Might as well beard the lion in his den. He wanted to get this talk over with. He rapped sharply on

Mr. Black's door. Silence, then a few shuffling sounds. "Come in."

Garrett opened the door. If he wasn't mistaken, Mr. Black's face looked flushed. "Could I talk to you?"

His boss glanced at his desk and nodded. "What can I do for you?"

Help me, Lord. Garrett walked into the office. "I have an apology to make."

Raising his eyebrows, Mr. Black frowned. "Why would you need to apologize? Does this have something to do with you getting religion?" He tilted his chair back on two legs.

Garrett took a deep breathe. "Remember when you talked to me about Savannah?"

His boss nodded.

"You were tilted back on your chair just like you are now. When you brought your chair down, the breeze lifted some of the papers on your desk. I thought I saw a picture of Savannah."

The silence in the room was deafening. Neither man moved. Then Mr. Black brought his chair slowly down on all four legs. "Why should you apologize for thinking you saw a picture of Savannah on my desk?"

"Because the other day when you were gone, I came into your office and searched for it."

Mr. Black jumped to his feet. "You had no right—"

Garrett put up his hand. "I know I had no right. That's why I want to apologize. I know it was wrong. I'm sorry."

Dropping into his chair, Mr. Black stared at Garrett. "I could fire you for this, you know."

"I know but I still have to do what's right. I'll take whatever consequences follow."

Another silence. Mr. Black gazed out the window, then met Garrett's eyes. "Why did you want to know if I had a picture of Savannah?"

"I wanted to find out if she had continued to...to see you after she claimed to have become a Christian."

"Savannah is a Christian, too?"

"So she says."

Mr. Black lowered his head, chin on his chest. At last he looked up. "I guess I have a confession to make too. My motive for telling you about Savannah's past was selfish." He cleared his throat. "When she disappeared from the tavern, George told me you'd taken her to Sandy Lake and that you two were courting."

"We were. She's living at Mrs. Patton's boarding house."

"I know. I asked one of my customers who lives in Sandy Lake if she lived at the same boarding house he did. William said someone named Savannah lived there. How many Savannahs could there be?" Mr. Black stood and walked to the window.

"I said I was telling you about her past for your sake, but really it was for mine. I thought if you knew about her past, you'd stop courting her. I thought maybe then she'd find another place to do her business. I might even have helped her find one."

"So you haven't seen Savannah since she moved to Sandy Lake?"

"No, but every time I look at her picture, I get more determined to see her again."

"Are you married, Mr. Black?"

Garrett's boss shrugged. "So what?"

"You stopped seeing Savannah because she and I were courting, but it doesn't matter that you're married?"

"It's the code of honor between gentlemen. As your employer, it wouldn't be right for me to be involved with your girlfriend."

Shaking his head, Garrett backed away from Mr. Black's desk. "Unbelievable. There's a gentlemen's code of honor between you and me, but no code of honor between you and your wife?"

"You're young, Garrett. I wouldn't expect you to understand. Some day you'll know how things work in the real world."

"I hope not, sir. I'm pretty sure there's nothing in the Bible about a gentlemen's code of honor but plenty about being faithful to your wife."

Mr. Black stood up. "I'm not too interested in what the Bible says. And since you don't believe in a gentlemen's code of honor, I take it you'd be okay with me making arrangements to visit Savannah while you two are courting?"

Garrett stared at the floor. He opened his mouth once, then closed it. At last he lifted his gaze to his employer. "To be honest, Savannah and I aren't seeing each other. I don't think God wants me to have a girlfriend right now."

Shaking his head in disbelief, Mr. Black stared at Garrett. "I think you must be from Mars or Venus or some other planet. I've never heard that kind of talk before. You're taking yourself and your religion way too seriously."

"I guess we'll have to agree to disagree on that, unless you've decided to fire me." Garrett returned Mr. Black's gaze. "Are you firing me?"

"I haven't decided yet." Mr. Black sat down and steepled his fingers on top of his desk. "Other than you searching my office, I can't find fault with your work. Just don't try to turn Savannah against me."

CHAPTER 34

Savannah stepped into the insurance office, greeted Dorothy and took off her coat.

Dorothy jumped up. "Savannah, are you all right? I heard George Burns came after you again last night. You know, the man who came here looking for you."

It was all Savannah could do to keep her mouth from falling open. How in the world did Dorothy find out the latest gossip almost before it happened? "I'm okay. One of the other boarders rescued me."

"What did Mr. Burns want?" Dorothy's eyes glowed.

"Nothing I want to discuss with you. He's in jail."

"I heard he wants you to come back to work for him. Are you going to do it?"

Without a word, Savannah plodded into her office and closed the door. She hung up her coat and plopped down in her chair. How could Dorothy have known Mr. Burns wanted her to go back to work for him? Did she know what kind of work Savannah had done?

Feeling completely naked and exposed, Savannah bowed her head, chin resting on her chest. A sick feeling in her stomach and the desire to run away permeated her entire being. She gripped the arms of her chair to keep from bolting from her office. Where would she go?

The Lord is my light and my salvation; whom shall I fear? The Lord is the strength of my life; of whom shall I be afraid?

Was it fear in the pit of her stomach feeding the desire to run away? Fear and shame? Fear of being found out, fear of being shamed. If she ran again, she would be running all her life. God was saying He was her light and her salvation, the strength of her life, and she didn't need to be afraid of anyone.

God knew the worst about her and still loved her. He didn't shame her or condemn her, and He didn't want her to live in fear.

Show me how to overcome this fear, Lord. I don't want to live in fear of Dorothy or anyone else. I'm not proud of what I used to be but I'm forgiven. I'm a new creature in Christ. Show me how to act like one.

Savannah startled at the light tap on her door. She pulled a handkerchief out of her sleeve and wiped her eyes and nose. "Come in."

Mr. Young opened her door, started to say something, and then peered at her. "Are you all right?"

Nodding, Savannah stood up. "What can I do for you, Mr. Young?"

"I need you to take dictation for a letter to Mr. Ewing. Would you come to my office, please?"

"Of course. Let me grab my pad and a pen. I'll be right there." Savannah picked up her things and followed Mr. Young down the hall toward his office.

"Close the door, Savannah."

Mr. Young didn't often close the door, but Savannah trusted him in a way she trusted few men.

She closed the door, sat down and opened her stenographer's pad. Mr. Young watched her but didn't begin his letter.

"Did Dorothy say something to upset you this morning?" Mr. Young's eyes were kind. "I heard her talking when you came in."

Savannah hesitated and bowed her head. *Whom shall I fear?* Taking a deep breath, she looked up. "Dorothy said she heard Mr. Burns asked me to come back to work for him. I don't know how she could possibly have known."

"I've talked to Dorothy before about spreading gossip. Is it true?"

Whom shall I fear? She gazed into Mr. Young's eyes. "It's true he asked but I said no. I might as well tell you what happened. You'll read it in the paper or hear it at the post office anyway."

"Only if you want to tell me."

After a deep breath, Savannah told Mr. Young the whole story, sometimes blushing at the insinuations Mr. Burns had made. "I told him I don't do those things since I've become a Christian. I don't think he believed me."

Mr. Young's gaze never left Savannah's face.

"When I found out Dorothy knew he'd asked me to go back to work for him, I felt like the whole world knew my past—or at least all of Sandy Lake." With an effort, Savannah continued to look into Mr. Young's eyes.

"People will always gossip and talk. My wife says it's as though they're saying, 'I would *never* do anything like that.' If they can make someone else look bad, it makes them feel better about themselves."

"Your wife is so wise. If that's true, people who feel good about themselves probably don't need to gossip."

"Could be. I'm proud of you for turning Mr. Burns down. That's another step in proving you've changed."

"Thank you, sir. You and Mrs. Young have been so kind to me. I'm sorry my personal problems have interfered with my work. I'm ready to do that letter now if you are."

"One more thing. What did you say when Dorothy asked if you were going back to work for Mr. Burns?"

"I just walked away."

"You might want to tell her that if she plans on spreading this story, she should also say you told Mr. Burns no."

Savannah chuckled. "Maybe I should. I know the Lord doesn't want me to be afraid of people—even people who gossip."

♠

The clock on the wall said noon and Savannah's stomach growled. How long until Dorothy left for lunch? Maybe if she moved slowly enough, her office mate would be gone. Savannah covered her typewriter and walked back to get Mr. Young's signature on a few letters. Slowly, deliberately, she donned her outer garments, buttoned every jet black button, and smoothed each finger of her gloves

She glanced at the clock again. 12:05 p.m. Had she stalled long enough? All morning, Savannah had managed to avoid Dorothy, but she hadn't been able to dispel Mr. Young's words.

Opening the door, she listened. Quiet out front. When she

reached the outer office, Dorothy sprang to her feet, obviously waiting for her.

"Savannah—"

Savannah held up her hand. "Dorothy, if you plan to tell your story around town about Mr. Burns wanting me to go back to work for him, be sure you tell them I said no."

Dorothy's face reddened as she turned away. "So you say."

Chapter 35

Snow was falling when Garrett left Black's Clothing Store. The roads were snow covered and slippery. He should have plenty of time to get to the Grist Mill by six o'clock for his appointment with Irv. Had he told Ma he'd be late tonight? He didn't remember, but he thought she knew about his appointment. He wouldn't be able to eat a thing until it was over anyway.

What a day it had been. The confrontation with Mr. Black had left his stomach queasy. He hadn't eaten much lunch. Just one of his sandwiches. What could he say to Irv to make things right? No wonder his stomach rebelled against food.

He braked cautiously as he came up on a horse and buggy. A nasty day to be out in a buggy. On the other hand, horses were sometimes more reliable than cars on bad roads. He'd heard Doc Cooley still used his horses sometimes on wintry days.

Tapping the steering wheel impatiently, he gritted his teeth. Couldn't that horse go any faster?

Too much time on his hands always took him back to his inner debate about Savannah. Maybe he'd been wrong to mistrust her. If Mr. Black's picture had been taken before she moved to Sandy Lake, maybe she hadn't been seeing any of her other former customers either. He'd been so rude when he'd broken things off. Should he apologize and tell her why he wouldn't be courting anyone for awhile?

At last he could see far enough ahead to pass the horse and buggy. He pulled down on the lever and whizzed around them, increasing his speed on the straight, clear road ahead. In a heartbeat, his shiny black Model T skidded to the right. He tried to correct to the left but skidded in the other direction and ended up in the ditch headed back the way he'd come. The engine stalled. He groaned.

Now what? He so wanted to be on time to show Irv he had changed. That wasn't going to happen. He pounded the steering wheel and bit back words he hadn't said in a long time.

The Amish man from the buggy tapped on his window. Garrett cranked it down.

"What can I do to help?" The man wore only a thin denim jacket, not warm enough for this weather.

"I'm not sure." Garrett got out and surveyed his dilemma. It wasn't a terribly deep ditch but too deep to drive out. "I'll probably need someone to pull me out."

"I can do that." The man motioned to his horse. "If we can find someone with a rope or a chain."

Garrett looked at a house they'd just passed and the long lane leading to it. His heart sank. "Are you sure, Mr.—"

"Abe Byler. Chust call me Abe."

"All right, Abe. I'm afraid your family will get too cold waiting."

"We'll be fine. You go see about a rope or a chain."

Garrett turned up his coat collar and strode down the snow-covered lane. He was going to be late.

♠

When Mr. Miller, the elderly farmer, finally found a long enough piece of rope, he insisted on coming back with Garrett to see if he could help. Garrett gritted his teeth as he slowed his steps to the farmer's pace. At this rate, he'd never catch Irv before he left the mill.

At last they reached his car and found Abe waiting with his horse. Mr. Miller handed the rope to Abe who fastened it to the horse's harness. Garrett tied the other end to the Model T's frame. After cranking the engine, he got back in to steer while his rescuer led the horse. The tires spun and resisted the efforts of the plow horse until the farmer moved behind the car and pushed. Then ever so slowly the wheels began to turn. Garrett steered, maneuvering the car back on the road.

He shut off the engine and jumped out to thank Abe who was already pulling the rope off his horse's harness. Garrett grabbed the largest bill he could find out of his wallet and tried to hand it to Abe.

"Nay, nay. I don't want your money. We don't take money for helping our fellow man. It's not our way. Glad I could help you."

"Are you sure?" Garrett looked at the man's thin coat. "I'd like to do something for you."

"Just do a good deed for the next one who needs it." Putting out his work-roughened hand, Abe gave Garrett a firm handshake, and then hitched his horse to his buggy.

Garrett untied the rope from his automobile and handed it to Mr. Miller. "Thank you so much, sir. I really appreciate your help." He reached for his wallet again.

"No, no. Put that away. Happy to do it."

Hesitating, Garrett looked at the elderly farmer, and then at the long lane. Swallowing his impatience, he motioned to his car. "Get in and I'll take you home."

"Not necessary. You're liable to get stuck or slide off in another ditch. Hop in and I'll give you a crank. I've always wanted to do that."

In spite of his misgivings, Garrett got into his automobile. A few minutes later, it roared to life, and he rolled down the window to shout his thanks. Forcing himself to drive slowly, he managed to turn around and crept along the road toward Sandy Lake. No use trying to look at his grandfather's pocket watch. He couldn't risk driving any faster no matter what the time.

As he pulled into the parking area in front of the mill, he saw the lights go out and the front door open. Irv's tall figure bounded down the steps. Garrett opened the door and leapt out of his car, hitting the ground running. But before he could open his mouth, Irv held up his hand.

"I've heard it all before, Garrett. Don't even bother making excuses. I can see that nothing has changed."

"You don't understand. I would have been on time but—"

"Forget it. I should have known a leopard can't change its spots."

Garrett gritted his teeth. His cousin was so unfair. Why wouldn't he believe that Garrett had changed?

As quickly as it had flared, his rage died. Was this how Savannah felt when he'd refused to believe she'd changed?

Chapter 36

"Polly, did you go to the post office today?" Father dropped the Sandy Lake Breeze on the small table in the living room.

"I sent Maggie down after school. Why?" Polly pushed back a stray curl that had escaped again.

"Just wondered if you'd heard the news about George Burns?"

Her father didn't like gossip but news in the newspaper was fair game. "What is it?"

"He attacked Savannah in her room at the boarding house on Sunday night. He's in jail. Paper said William Sider rescued her while most everyone was at the hymn sing."

"Is Savannah okay?"

"I believe William got there before Burns did any harm."

"Hmmm. Wonder why William and Savannah weren't at the hymn sing like everyone else?" As soon as the words were out, Polly bit her tongue. What was her problem, insinuating something going on between William and Savannah?

Father raised his eyebrows. "What are you trying to say?"

"Nothing. I'm not trying to say anything. William is a very nice man, not much older than I am. I always thought maybe... Never mind." Polly went to the kitchen to stir the pot of chili.

Was she jealous that William had rescued Savannah? *For goodness sake, he probably doesn't even know my name.*

Polly hadn't told anyone she had any interest in him. It was none of her business if Savannah and William were friends—or even more than friends.

♠

Savannah dried the last knife and put it in the silverware

drawer. "Anything else I can do, Mrs. Patton?"

"I don't think so. It's your Bible study night with Mildred Young, isn't it? Better not keep her waiting."

Mrs. Patton's face looked lined and worn. Savannah hung up her dish towel and stretched out a hand to her. "Would you like to come with me? I'm sure Mrs. Young wouldn't mind."

Her landlady shook her head. "I might ruin your Bible study. God and I don't seem to have much to say to each other these days. I'm not sure if I've given up on God or if He's given up on me."

"If God didn't give up on me, I'm sure He hasn't given up on you."

Wringing out her dishcloth again and again, Mrs. Patton gazed out the window. At last she shook her head. "I tried my best to live right and be a good person, but that didn't keep bad things from happening. It doesn't seem fair."

"Polly Dye says God never promised bad things wouldn't happen to His children. He does promise to go through trials with us and bring good from them if we trust Him."

"Do you believe that?"

"I'm trying to believe it. I'm such a new Christian and have so much to learn. I'm sure Mrs. Young could explain things much better than I can."

Mrs. Patton sighed. "Savannah, I'm sorry I've been so hard on you. William says it isn't fair to judge everyone to be untrustworthy because one person failed me. I'm afraid that's what I've been doing to you. I want to believe you've changed, but I'm having a hard time."

"It's okay. Mr. Young said I needed to stay in Sandy Lake and prove I've changed, but I know you have a lot at stake with your business here. If you want me to leave, I'll talk to Mr. and Mrs. Young about trying to find another place to stay."

"If I make you leave, that'll just give the old biddies something else to gossip about, just when I'm beginning to believe in you. I can't do that. You go on to your Bible study and ask Mrs. Young to pray for me."

♠

Savannah knocked only once before Mrs. Young opened the door, the smell of fresh bread wafting from her kitchen. She engulfed Savannah in a warm, affectionate hug. "How are you, dearie?"

She shook her head. "I don't know. So much has happened."

"Well, give me your coat and I'll hang it by the stove. I have some tea brewing so we can enjoy drinking it while we talk." Mrs. Young set the lovely pink and yellow china teapot on the table where the matching gold-rimmed cups waited.

No sign of Garrett. Savannah'd had mixed feelings about coming tonight after her last encounter with him. Tension oozed out of her muscles as she sank into a chair..

Beaming at her, Mrs. Young sat down and poured her a cup of tea. So much love filled this room. How different her life might have been if she'd had a mother like Mrs. Young. Savannah straightened. No use dwelling on what might have been.

She smiled at Garrett's mother. "I don't know where to start. Did your husband tell you Mr. Burns came back last night?"

"He told me you had a bad scare. He wanted to let you tell me yourself."

Savannah nodded. Not leaving out a single detail, she told Mrs. Young everything that happened the night before.

"So Mr. Burns is in jail, right?" Mrs. Young shook her head. "I don't know what's wrong with him. Has he ever done anything like this before? I never knew him well."

"I don't think so. I suspect it has something to do with his wife leaving. And now all the talk about prohibition has affected his business and has him scared."

"How long will they keep him in jail? I hope a good long time. I can't feel sorry for anyone who treats people the way he's treated you."

"I don't know how long they'll keep him. If I'd never gotten involved with him, this wouldn't have happened. I have to take responsibility for that. I'm afraid of what he'll do next time he's out of jail."

Mrs. Young took Savannah's hand. "Has Mrs. Patton decided if she's going to let you stay?"

"Not for sure. She did say she's starting to believe in me. I don't know what I'll do if she asks me to leave. Did I tell you I wrote to my parents?"

"No, I had no idea. What prompted you to do that?"

Savannah picked up her Bible. "You remember me asking what it meant to acknowledge God in all our ways?"

"I remember." Mrs. Young opened her Bible.

"This is the verse after the one about acknowledging God is all our ways." Turning to verse 7 in Proverbs 3, Savannah read, "Do not be wise in your own eyes; fear the Lord and shun evil."

Savannah explained how the Holy Spirit had convicted her about always thinking she was smarter than her parents and how that had prompted her to send an apology. "I haven't heard from them yet, but it's only been about a week."

"What will you do if they ask you to come home?"

"I—I don't know. It depends on whether or not Mrs. Patton allows me to stay."

"Your new faith is certainly being tested. I'm proud of how hard you're trying to follow Jesus."

"I have something to show you." Savannah dug around in the bag she'd brought. "Look." She pulled out Sarah's diary and laid it on the table.

"What's this?"

Savannah told her about Polly giving her the diary. "Soon after I began reading, I noticed that when Sarah even thought about something bad happening, *her* first thought was that only God could get her through it. *My* first thought would probably be to blame Him."

Mrs. Young nodded and took a swallow of tea. "That's very perceptive of you."

"After Mr. Burns attacked me, I wanted to blame God. The words were on my lips, but I didn't let them come out. Instead, I cried out to God to help me." Savannah leaned toward Mrs. Young. "Do you think I'm making progress?"

Before Mrs. Young could answer, a few loud backfires disturbed the peaceful atmosphere.

Chapter 37

Mrs. Young and Savannah both looked at the door. "Garrett had an appointment with Irv this evening after work. That's why he's so late." Garrett's mother stood up.

Savannah pushed back her chair. "I'd better go. I don't want to cause trouble."

"No, no. Garrett knew you were going to continue coming for Bible Study. Don't go."

Footsteps pounded up the stairs and the door burst open. Garrett came in, stamping snow from his feet. Mrs. Young went to greet him.

"How was your appointment with Irv? Can I get you something to eat?"

Ignoring her first question, Garrett shook his head. "I'm not hungry." He removed his coat. "A lot on my mind. Hello, Savannah."

Savannah nodded and stood up again. "I should go. You probably want to talk to your mother."

"Actually, Savannah, I want to talk to you."

Mrs. Young's eyebrows rose. "All right. Umm... I'd been thinking about going to bed early tonight. Your father has a late appointment. I'll go on upstairs and you two can talk." She turned to Savannah. "I'm sorry we didn't have our usual prayer time."

"Oh, that reminds me. Mrs. Patton wanted me to ask you to pray for her." Savannah cleared her throat. "I invited her to come tonight but she refused. She's pretty upset with God because of all she's gone through."

"I will pray for her. She's had a hard life. Sometimes it's difficult not to blame God." Mrs. Young picked up the teapot. "Would you like a cup of tea, son?"

"Thanks, Ma. I think I would."

Garrett's mother got another teacup and poured some tea while Garrett hung up his coat. He sat down in the chair she'd vacated and squeezed her hand. "Thanks, Ma."

His mother patted his shoulder and walked around the table to give Savannah a hug. "See you next week or sooner if you want."

Savannah nodded, her eyes brimming with tears. *What a great friend.* "Good night, Mrs. Young."

♠

Quiet filled the kitchen as Garrett's mother, the one who so embodied to him the meaning of *love always believes the best*, went into the hall and up the stairs. Garrett and Savannah stared into their tea as though expecting to find answers to life's mysteries.

At last, Savannah cleared her throat. "You wanted to talk to me, Garrett?"

He lifted his gaze to meet her amazing eyes. He had forgotten how beautiful they were. "I don't know where to begin."

"That's what I told your mother this evening. Maybe the beginning would be a good place."

Nodding, Garrett looked into his tea again. "First, I want to apologize for being so rude to you last week."

Savannah's eyebrows rose. She opened her mouth, but then closed it without speaking.

"A great deal has happened since we talked. I've been unfair to you. I took the word of a man who was drunk over yours, even though my mother warned me not to. I chose to believe the worst instead of believing the best."

"What happened to change your mind?"

"For one thing, I got a taste of my own medicine. My cousin, Irv, chose to believe the worst about why I was late for my appointment. He doesn't believe I've changed. At first I was angry. But I realized I've done the same to you. I'm so sorry."

"Does that mean you believe me now?"

"I think so. I don't want to misjudge you anymore."

"Thank you, Garrett. I'm far from perfect, but I'm not the same person I used to be. Mr. Burns came to my room last night—"

Garrett jumped to his feet. "Again?"

"Let me finish."

Slumping into his chair, Garrett gripped the edge of the table.

"He came to offer me a deal to come back to the tavern. I turned him down. When I said no, he tried to force himself on me. He's in jail."

Garrett let go of the table and sat up straight. He groaned. "Savannah, there's something else I have to tell you."

"What is it?"

"Last week Mr. Black told me what your occupation used to be. He didn't think I knew."

Savannah's gaze dropped to the table.

"While he was telling me, I thought I saw a picture of you under some papers on his desk."

Red crept up Savannah's neck and cheeks. She buried her face in her hands. Her voice was muffled. "I should never have let him take that picture. He said he'd develop it in his dark room so I didn't think anyone else would ever see it."

Garrett swallowed hard. "When my boss left the store one day, I searched his office and found it. I was desperate to know if that picture had been taken before or after you came to Sandy Lake."

Savannah's head jerked up. "That picture was taken months before I moved to Sandy Lake. I haven't seen Mr. Black or any of my other customers since I came to Christ."

"Mr. Black agrees the picture was taken before you moved and that he hasn't seen you since you left Jackson Center. He told me about your past, hoping I'd break up with you so you'd go back into business and he could start seeing you again."

Savannah groaned and lowered her head once more.

"My boss says every time he looks at your picture, he's determined to see you again. I don't know what he'll do but I think he'll try. And Savannah, he's married."

Tears rolled down Savannah's cheeks. She sobbed out loud. "What have I done? I always told myself I wasn't hurting anyone. It was just a job. I tried to keep the names of the men a secret so no one would know. I never dreamed there'd be men who still... I hate myself." She shuddered. "I don't think I've ever been truly sorry because I never faced the extent of the damage I've done. All the men I've tempted."

Garrett nodded. "I know what you mean. Recently I understood that my repentance had been too shallow. I hadn't really faced what a selfish, irresponsible, deceitful person I was." He rubbed his face with both hands. "I didn't tell you this to make you feel bad. I'm just worried that Mr. Black might come to your room. He knows where you live. One of his customers, William, I think, said someone named Savannah lived at the same boarding house he did."

"William Sider. That's why he thought my name sounded familiar. Just a matter of time, until he finds out my past. No decent man will ever want anything to do with me, and I can't blame them."

"You know William?"

"I don't know him well. He's the man who rescued me when Mr. Burns attacked me last night."

Garrett was silent. Then he gazed into Savannah's tear-stained eyes. "I don't know if you'd call me a decent man, but I want you."

"How could you after all I've done?"

"Because I have a lot of character flaws of my own. I'm no better than you. But even though I want you, right now I can only be your friend. God's made it clear He wants me to stop distracting myself with women while He changes me."

CHAPTER 38

Polly curled up in Mother's gray chair cradling her dark blue journal against her chest. She and Maggie had put the little ones to bed early and the rest of the family soon followed. Even Father had turned in early. Being alone in the living room was a rare treat.

She picked up Chartreuse and dated her entry: *February 26, 1912*. Then she stopped and put down her pen. How honest did she want to be? She sighed. If one wasn't honest, what was the use of keeping a diary?

I'm afraid Mother would be so disappointed in me. Tonight I found yet another reason to be jealous of Savannah. I thought I was doing better at overcoming those feelings until Father told me William Sider rescued her last night. I don't even know if they know each other, but when Father told me, an ocean of animosity almost choked me.

No one even knows I have feelings for William. I've never even been honest with myself about this. He was a year ahead of me in school, and I admired him so much. Smart, handsome, strong. He was popular and didn't even know I was alive. Then I got involved with Garrett and forgot about William. Until recently.

I know Mother would tell me to pray about it, but I'm even ashamed to tell God how I feel. Not that He doesn't know already...

A tear dripped onto the cream-colored page, leaving a shimmering drop on the green ink. Polly blew on it gently. At last she swung her legs to the floor, leaned over to put her journal on the table, and dropped to her knees. She buried her face in the worn upholstery of Mother's chair.

"Oh, Mother..." She shook her head. She didn't want to turn

out like Sarah's children who had never learned to depend on the Lord. Swallowing a sob, she began again. *Father, I'm sorry. You know how much I miss my mother, how hard it is for me to* be *the mother. I want turning to you to be my first impulse when life is hard.*

Polly pulled a handkerchief from the pocket of her faded blue work dress and blew her nose. *"I'm sorry about being jealous of Savannah. She has plenty of problems, more than I do. But I can't seem to stop being jealous. I think it started the day I saw her snuggled up to Garrett in his car while he and I were courting. Forgive me and help me see her through your eyes.*

"Florence, are you all right?"

Polly looked into her father's worried eyes. "I'm okay."

"Anything I can do?"

"I don't think so. I've been talking to God and I'm feeling a little better. I miss Mama so much and life is hard. I'm sorry to worry you."

"I miss your mother, too. She left big shoes to fill, but you're doing a grand job."

Polly's shoulders drooped. "She wouldn't think so if she could read my mind."

Her father frowned. "Florence, what's going on? Your mother wouldn't expect you to be perfect and neither do I."

Polly gazed at her father, then shook her head. "I can't talk about it. It's too embarrassing. We'd better head for bed. Morning comes early."

♠

Garrett locked the door of Black's Clothing Store behind him. Mr. Black had left earlier saying he had an errand to do. Neither had mentioned their discussion about Savannah the day before but tension had run high. Garrett was happy to see him go.

He hurried across the parking lot, and then slowed down. No reason to rush. Why couldn't his appointment with Irv have been tonight when he would have been on time? Garrett's first attempt to follow Reverend Caldwell's advice had been a total failure.

So now what, Lord? Do I go on to someone else or keep trying to see Irv? Maybe I should try to make an appointment with Pastor Caldwell.

He couldn't believe he'd said that. He'd never made an appointment with a pastor in his life. How did one make appointments with itinerant preachers?

♠

Savannah hurried up the boarding house steps. Garrett had said last night he still wanted her even though they could only be friends. That piece of good news had brightened her day. It had needed brightening after Dorothy read aloud the article from last night's newspaper to the entire office.

She opened the door and almost ran into William.

"Savannah, how are you doing? Are you getting over the scare Mr. Burns gave you on Sunday night?"

Closing the door behind her, Savannah nodded. "I guess so. I'm still worried about what he'll do when he gets out of jail. The newspaper said he'd only be there a week."

"Doesn't seem long enough. Someone downtown said Mr. Burns came to ask you to go back to work for him. What kind of job did you do at the tavern?"

Savannah's cheeks flushed. She fastened a wave of hair more securely, looking anywhere but at William. At last she lifted her head and looked him in the eye. "Do you remember what Mr. Burns called me the night he was arrested?"

It was William's turn to blush. "I do. I should have punched him."

"No, actually that's what I was. That's what I did at his tavern." A huge weight lifted from her shoulders as the words left her lips. "But not anymore. Not since Jesus forgave me for my sins and gave me a new beginning. I'll never earn a living that way again."

William's mouth hung open, his eyes wide. "Wow. I really admire your honesty. I've never known anyone to be so honest about their past. I did some things I wouldn't want anyone to know before Jesus changed me."

"I'm tired of worrying about people finding out about my past. Tired of living in fear. I just need to be honest."

"Good for you, Savannah. Do you think you and I could have dinner at the restaurant some time, or go to a concert at the Opera House?"

Now Savannah's eyes grew wide. "You mean you'd want to

be seen with me after what I told you? It might ruin your reputation."

"As long as we're not doing anything wrong, I'll let the Lord take care of my reputation."

Two decent guys were interested in her. What would Garrett think of her going out with William? He'd said they could only be friends. "I guess we could do that some time just as friends. I'm not ready for a serious beau."

"Okay, we'll take things slow. Sort of get to know each other first."

"That sounds good."

"Oh, by the way, did you notice you have a letter?" William pointed to the small table near the door. "The post master must have given it to Mrs. Patton today."

"Thanks. I didn't notice." Savannah picked up the small square envelope. She frowned.

"Something wrong?"

"I don't recognize the handwriting—and there's no stamp and no return address." Savannah turned the envelope over but found no clues to the sender on the back. "Someone must have hand delivered it. How strange."

"Why don't you open it and see who it's from?"
Savannah hesitated, then tucked the envelope in her bag. "I'll read it later. I'd better see if Mrs. Patton needs me."

CHAPTER 39

Savannah hurried up the stairs to her room to drop off her handbag. Maybe she'd take one quick peek at the letter. She couldn't explain her reluctance to open it in front of William, just a bad feeling. Grabbing a letter opener from the top of her dresser, she slit the envelope and pulled out a heart-shaped card. Who would be sending her a Valentine a few weeks late? She'd suspect Garrett if he hadn't told her they could only be friends.

Pulse racing, she opened the card.

Roses are red, violets are blue.

Sugar is sweet, and I miss you.

She turned the card over.

Please meet me tonight at midnight at the rear entrance of the Cottage Hotel. I have discreetly reserved a room. I'll make it worth your while. Devon Black.

Savannah dropped down beside her bed, covering her mouth to muffle her sobs. *Oh, God, is this never going to end? Is this what Mrs. Young meant when she told me we reap what we sow? First Mr. Burns and now this—I just want to disappear.*

Garrett mentioned his boss knew where she lived. If she didn't meet him, would he come looking for her? That would be the end of her arrangement with Mrs. Patton. Who could she trust? If Garrett or his parents got involved, Garrett might lose his job.

She dragged herself up, pulled a handkerchief from her bag and blew her nose. Hiding the card under Sarah's diary, she hurried down the steps to help Mrs. Patton. Life had to go on.

Her landlady looked up as Savannah entered the kitchen. "You're late. Are you okay?"

"Not really. Life is so complicated."

"It is. Come peel some potatoes." Mrs. Patton touched her shoulder as if to show she wasn't as heartless as her words conveyed.

Savannah sniffed back fresh tears. "How was your day?"

"Not much better or worse than usual. Got two new boarders coming in tonight. That's good news."

"I'm happy for you." Savannah tried to sound happy. "Better than two leaving I guess."

Desperate to come up with a solution to her problem, she peered at the potato she was peeling as though it required all her attention. Mrs. Patton fell silent. Who else could she ask to help her? She certainly couldn't ask Polly or Kitt to meet Mr. Black at midnight.

William stuck his head through the kitchen doorway. "Want some help setting the table?" Savannah took a second look at him. None of the other boarders had ever offered to set the table.

"Certainly. We'd be happy for some help." Mrs. Patton handed a stack of heavy white plates to William. "Thanks for offering."

When he went back to the dining room, Mrs. Patton nodded at Savannah. "I'm sorry I was suspicious of William and you. I've known his parents for years, and I think they raised a good one. Not many like that around."

William. Maybe he could help her. He was big and strong and probably not afraid of anyone. She smiled at Mrs. Patton. "I haven't known him long, but he seems like a fine person."

She could try to sit near William at dinner and ask him to meet her later.

♠

The dining room was filled with the usual hubbub as Savannah carried in two bowls of mashed potatoes. She touched William's shoulder. He tilted his head as she spoke softly. "Save me a seat, okay?" He nodded as she scurried back to the kitchen.

After several more trips, Savannah slipped into the empty chair beside him. "Thanks."

"Sure. Everything okay?"

"I'll tell you after we say grace."

Even though Mrs. Patton was angry at God, she still insisted her boarders go through the motions of bowing their heads and returning thanks.

When the normal chatter resumed, Savannah told William about her dilemma. "I really hate to ask, but could you meet Mr. Black so he doesn't come looking for me?"

"We could ask the Sheriff to meet him. What he's doing is against the law."

Savannah bit her lip. "This is the first time he's done this, so I'd just like to turn him down without getting him into trouble. If I go and Mrs. Patton sees me, she's liable to think the worst."

William nodded. "All right. I'll do it."

"Just tell him I'm not interested in meeting him tonight or any time in the future. Make sure he understands I'm a Christian now."

"I can do that. But what do I tell Mrs. Patton if she sees me leaving?"

"Could you tell her you have some business... No, it's not fair to ask you to be less than honest. I'll tell her myself." Savannah's heart pounded painfully. Would this cause more trouble with her employer?

Even though William tried to make small talk, dinner seemed to go on and on. One minute she wanted it to end so she could talk to Mrs. Patton, and the next she wanted it to go on forever so she wouldn't have to talk to her. At last people began to carry their plates to the kitchen. Savannah stacked a pile of serving bowls and followed.

Soon the kitchen was quiet except for the clinking of cups, plates, and bowls as Mrs. Patton washed the dishes and Savannah dried. Mentally she rehearsed how to explain the situation, but nothing seemed quite right. She waited until Mrs. Patton had almost finished.

"Did you notice the letter I received today?"

"Can't say I did."

In as few words as possible, Savannah told her what the letter contained, withholding the name of the writer. "William is going to meet him, so he doesn't come looking for me. I don't want anything else to happen to give your boarding house a bad name.

Sighing, Mrs. Patton rubbed her eyes. "Why are you telling me this?"

"I don't want you to think poorly of William if you see him going out late."

Tapping her toe on the hardwood floor, Mrs. Patton met Savannah's gaze. "Thank you, Savannah. That's very honest of you. I'm going to choose to believe you're telling me the truth. I can't think of any reason for you to lie."

♠

After Savannah dried the last dish and returned to her room, the evening dragged interminably. Maybe she should write another letter to her parents. She dismissed that thought as soon as it came. She'd wait for their response to her letter. It seemed unlikely they'd forgive her, especially her mother, but time would tell. Nothing to do but wait.

In the silence, she couldn't escape the lingering sadness from her talk with Garrett the night before. Even if her parents forgave her, could she ever forgive herself for all the damage she'd done?

Wiping more tears, she opened her bedside table drawer and withdrew the little diary Polly so treasured. She was grateful her friend had trusted her enough to loan her something so precious. Turning to the silky marker, Savannah read about the series of losses and celebrations Sarah recorded one after another. Shaking her head, she kept going back to the words Sarah had written after the loss of their first child, "The Lord gave and the Lord hath taken away; blessed be the name of the Lord."

How could Sarah face losses with that attitude? How could she praise God and call His name blessed even when her heart was breaking?

CHAPTER 40

Garrett stared into the darkness. It was almost midnight and he still hadn't slept. Normally he slept well, but not tonight. He groaned and turned his pillow again. Savannah's face seemed indelibly etched on his brain whether his eyes were open or closed.

"Father, I know you said you wanted me alone for awhile to deal with character flaws. I'm willing to do that, but I can't stop thinking about Savannah. Are you trying to tell me something or is Satan attacking me?"

Pray.

The word wasn't audible but it was clear. He got out of bed and knelt on the cold floor. "Is Savannah in some kind of danger? What's happening?"

Pray.

"Father, I pray you would surround Savannah with your angels. Cover her by your blood. That's what Ma often prays. Keep her safe from harm and danger. Lead her and guide her in paths of righteousness. Make her into your image. Fill her with your Spirit."

The words poured from Garrett's lips, surprising him. He reached for his Bible and turned to Romans 8 where he'd been reading that morning. *...we know not what we should pray for as we ought but the Spirit itself maketh intercession for us...*

"I don't know how to pray for Savannah, Father, but your Holy Spirit knows what she needs. Thank you for praying through me. Even if that's all I can do, help me be faithful."

♠

Savannah huddled on her bed fully dressed with a quilt wrapped around her. Somehow she couldn't go to bed knowing William would be leaving to face Mr. Black. She looked at the ticking alarm clock. 11:45.

Down the hall, she heard a noise. She scrambled off the bed and bounded to the door in a few short steps. Turning the knob gently, she pulled the door open and peeked out. William's eyes widened when he saw her.

"Still up?"

"I couldn't sleep. Thanks again for doing this."

"Sure. Your job is to pray, you know."

"What shall I pray for besides your safety?"

William squinted. "Pray for Mr. Black's salvation. He needs Jesus."

Nodding, Savannah watched him tiptoe down the stairs. She shivered and closed her door. Immediately she imagined the worst. What if something happened to him? What if Mr. Black became violent and William needed assistance? She opened the door and glided down the steps.

He looked back and mouthed one word. "What?"

"I'm going with you." Even her whisper sounded loud to her ears. "I'll watch from a distance in case I need to go for help. I don't think Mr. Black would hurt you, but we can't be sure."

Frowning, William stared at her. "I don't like this. What if he sees you?"

"I'll hide in the side entrance to the blacksmith shop beside the Hotel. Let's go. We don't want to be late."

They hurried down the deserted main street and turned right at the Cottage Hotel, staying close to the building. William peered around the back of the Hotel, and then motioned for Savannah to cross over to Osborne's black smith shop. He disappeared around the back of the Hotel. She ran to the small entryway of the shop and flattened herself against the inside wall.

Not a moment too soon. From her prime vantage point, Savannah saw the back door of the hotel open and Mr. Black step out. He must have been waiting inside. At first she couldn't make out any words. Then Mr. Black clearly said, "I don't believe it." His tone even at this distance was aggrieved.

A few minutes later, William raised his voice. She heard the word "sheriff" and "jail." In spite of the louder voices, neither man made any move to attack the other. Savannah began to breathe easier. Then William grabbed Mr. Black's shoulders with both hands and shook him. He outweighed the older man by at least fifty pounds and stood a head taller. When William let go, Mr. Black teetered and backed into the entryway. The door closed.

She had been so caught up in the drama unfolding that she'd forgotten to pray, but God had answered anyway. William came around the side of the Hotel and Savannah rushed to meet him. "Are you all right?"

"I'm fine. I'm glad that piece of slime didn't say anything else or I'd likely have punched him."

"I heard him say, 'I don't believe it.' What was he talking about?"

"He doesn't believe you're a Christian. I told him I had no doubt that you are and that he isn't. He didn't care much for that."

Together they retraced their steps the short distance to the boarding house and let themselves back into the darkened building. "William, I don't know how to thank you."

"I was glad to help. Let me know if anyone else from your past raises his ugly head."

"God has been so good to me. I don't deserve His mercy or your kindness."

"None of us deserve it, Savannah. That's why it's called mercy." William took her arm to guide her to the staircase.

♠

As soon as Savannah and William disappeared onto Main Street, Polly emerged from where she'd been concealed at the far end of the black smith's shop. What in the world had they been doing? She hurried to the street in time to see them open the door to the boarding house.

Polly hadn't been able to sleep and had snuck out for a walk. She'd been strolling down Walnut Street when she glimpsed William and Savannah slinking along beside the Cottage Hotel. She had cut across the block to hide beside Osborne's shop where she had a good view. Even so, she hadn't recognized the man William was talking to, and she'd been too far away to hear what they'd said.

Shaking her head, she turned around and started for home, battling jealousy at William and Savannah's apparent closeness. Father would have a fit if he discovered she'd been out walking in the middle of the night. What good reason could William and

Savannah possibly have for meeting someone at the Cottage Hotel at midnight? Maybe she'd been right thinking there was something between them.

Love always believes the best. She resisted her mother's words. She didn't know what William and Savannah had been up to, but only a fool would believe they had a good reason to be together at this hour.

CHAPTER 41

Garrett breathed a sigh of relief as he left work on Friday. Mr. Black had seemed subdued since Wednesday morning. The tension had eased for reasons Garrett didn't understand. On the surface nothing had changed. He was still holding his breath waiting for his boss to contact Savannah. Maybe he'd changed his mind. Regardless, Garrett was glad the week was over. *I guess I'm still waiting for the other shoe to drop—whatever that means.*

He pulled out his grandfather's pocket watch. Still about half an hour until his appointment with Reverend Caldwell. Although the pastor was originally from Ohio, his mother had discovered he was boarding with a family in Jackson Center. So convenient to stop by on his way home from work. The itinerant preacher had received permission from the pastor of the Jackson Center Presbyterian Church for them to meet in one of the classrooms.

What would he say to the pastor? His hands went clammy. This was a huge step from his *don't anyone tell me what to do* approach. Did he really *want* anyone telling him what to do?

He twisted the crank of his automobile, and then climbed into the driver's seat. *It's not about what you want*, he reminded himself. *It's about what God wants.*

♠

Reverend Caldwell was waiting for Garrett when he stepped into the vestibule. He stuck out his hand. "Garrett, so good to see you."

"Thanks for meeting me, Reverend."

"Please call me Jim."

"Really? I thought pastors wanted to be called reverend."

The pastor led the way to the basement stairs. "In some situations, that's probably best. But I think we might be more comfortable on a first name basis."

When they were both seated in one of the classrooms downstairs, Reverend Caldwell smiled. "So what can I do for you?"

Garrett squirmed. He didn't like asking for advice. "I'm having a hard time putting into practice the things you told me last Sunday." He explained his situation with Irv, frustration building. "I tried to make things right, but everything went wrong. Now I'm stuck." He slammed his fist on the table. "How can I make things right if Irv won't talk to me? Is it enough that I tried? Can I give up?"

The young pastor traced his thumb along the grain in the heavy wooden table in front of him. "What do you think?"

Garrett was startled. He'd expected answers, not questions. His anger at his cousin rose. "Irv's not being fair. Maybe he doesn't deserve to have me keep trying."

"How many chances did Irv give you before he fired you?"

Garrett cringed. He was silent a long time, his anger receding. "More than I deserved. We're related."

Reverend Caldwell nodded but stayed quiet.

"I see what you're getting at, but what if he won't give me another appointment? What if he won't give me another chance to make things right?"

"How about writing a letter?"

Garrett nodded. "That might work. He might read a letter from me." He grinned. "I could make sure I don't put my name on the outside so he won't throw it away without opening it."

Reverend Caldwell laughed, his dark brown eyes lighting up. "Good thought. You could also pray for him. Ask God to help him forgive you and restore your relationship."

"I bet my mother is already praying, but I'll pray too."

"How are things going in your life otherwise?"

The young pastor acted like he had all the time in the world. Maybe he did. "You asked me to pray about what it would mean for God to get me alone while he deals with my character flaws."

The pastor watched him. "I remember. Did you pray?"

"I didn't have to pray. I already knew." He squirmed again.

"I've always used women to, well, to distract me from loneliness and from God's dealings with me. He wants me to be alone right now, even though there's someone I love."

Thoughtfully, Reverend Caldwell rubbed his chin. "I see. Does she know you love her?"

"I think so but I explained why we can only be friends."

"I'm proud of you for the progress you've made." The pastor paused, his gaze roving over Garrett's face, eyes thoughtful. "What do you do for a living?"

The change of subject took Garrett by surprise. "I work at Black's Clothing Store in Mercer."

"Are you happy selling clothes?"

"I was until Mr. Black and I had a disagreement."

"What kind of disagreement?"

"About a woman." Garrett sighed. "I might as well tell you the whole story." Trying not to leave out any important details, he explained how he and Savannah had met and how Mr. Black was involved.

Reverend Caldwell remained silent for so long that Garrett prodded him. "What are you thinking, Reverend... Uh, how about I call you Pastor Jim?"

"That's fine, Garrett. I'm thinking that in time, God may have other work for you to do. But I want Him to tell you when the time is right. In the meantime, how would you like to travel with me to the churches where I preach?"

Garrett's eyebrows raised. "Why?"

"I'd like to get to know you better, and it would be good for me to have a Timothy."

"A what?"

"A Timothy. The Apostle Paul had a young man named Timothy who he guided in the faith. It was good for both of them." The pastor steepled his fingers on the table. "You don't have to give me an answer today. Think about it. Pray about it. Talk to your parents."

Garrett nodded. "All right. I can do that. You took me by surprise."

"Maybe I'm getting ahead of myself but I don't think so. I'm excited to find out what God has in store for you."

"Some days I get discouraged and think I haven't changed

at all. Other times, I look in the mirror and hardly recognize myself. Not because my outward appearance has changed. It's the inward person that's changing and somehow it shines through. Savannah says it's because we're new creatures in Christ."

"That you are. It's a process God will continue for the rest of our lives. Have you ever watched a potter at work?"

"I don't think so."

"He begins with a lump of clay. It takes a long time before that clay looks anything like a bowl, a pitcher, or a vase. Only the potter can tell what he's making." The pastor worked an imaginary piece of clay on the table.

"He puts that clay on his potter's wheel, and keeps working until he reaches his goal, even if he has to crush it and start over." Pastor Jim smiled. "God is like that. He's a patient Potter who acts like He has all the time in the world, and He never gives up on us."

Garrett bowed his head. "Just pray I don't jump off the wheel."

CHAPTER 42

Garrett hesitated at the top of the stairs outside his bedroom, and then descended, one slow step at a time. Should he go to the church in Jackson Center where Rever—Pastor Jim was preaching this morning? He'd been wrestling with this decision all weekend. *Is this something you want me to do, Lord?*

His mother would be surprised if he didn't go with her, but he didn't think she'd mind. He stopped at the bottom of the stairs. Ma was singing.

"Trust and obey for there's no other way to be happy in Jesus, but to trust and obey."

He lifted his head and nodded. *Father, I believe you brought Pastor Jim into my life, and I'm going to trust that you prompted the invitation to be his "Timothy." I'm going to obey and accompany him to the churches where he preaches.*

As he made his decision, peace came. Entering the kitchen, he whistled along with Ma's song.

She smiled and kissed his cheek. "You sound happy."

"I'm usually happy when I make a good decision." He hugged Ma's plump shoulders.

Pa came into the kitchen dressed for church. He raised his eyebrows at Garrett. "What decision did you make?"

Garrett stared at his father. "Are you going to church?"

"Don't look so surprised. I go to church sometimes."

Garrett swallowed the sarcastic words on his tongue. "Reverend Caldwell invited me to go with him to the churches where he preaches. I've decided to go. Today he'll be in Jackson Center."

"Why did he invite you? Are they having a special service?"

Ma set a bowl of steaming scrambled eggs on the table.

"He said it would be good for him to have a Timothy." Garrett sat down and took a drink of juice.

"A what?" Pa sat across from him and helped himself to the platter of bacon.

"A Timothy—like the Apostle Paul had a younger Christian named Timothy he was training." Garrett reached for the scrambled eggs.

Ma beamed. "That's wonderful, son. The pastor must see your potential."

"Potential for what? You aren't thinking of becoming an itinerant preacher, are you?" Pa's brows drew together in a dark scowl.

"Calm down, Pa. This will be a great way for me to grow in my faith, getting to know a man of God."

His father's face flushed.

"That wasn't a put down, Pa, but you've never claimed to be a believer. Ma has done most of the spiritual training, and I think it would be good for me to have some Bible training from a man."

Ma patted Pa's hand. "It's never too late to become a man of God."

♠

The drive to Jackson Center passed quickly compared to his drive to Mercer for work. He parked his car among the crowded horses and buggies and stepped out. A balmy day for early March. Much of the snow had already melted.

People stared in his direction. Was it his car? Some called greetings to him. What questions would they ask about why he was here? Garrett took a deep breath and headed for the entry. Pastor Jim stood inside the door, and his face broke into a huge smile.

"You came."

"I would have called but I didn't make up my mind until this morning. When I heard Ma singing, 'Trust and obey,' I knew I was to come and be your Timothy."

Pastor Jim smiled again and shook his hand. "Let me introduce you to some of these folks."

Garrett got so much attention he was almost embarrassed

as the pastor introduced him to the friendly congregation. Pastor Jim even invited Garrett to sit with him on a front pew. When Garrett objected, he clapped him on the back. "You can do what you want, but I'd consider it a blessing if you'd sit with me. I'm usually alone."

How could he refuse? After they were seated, Pastor Jim bowed his head. Garrett did the same, praying for his friend as the chatter flowed around them.

♠

"I'm happy to have my new friend, Garrett Young, with me today." The pastor beamed at the people in the pews. "I'm thankful to say he's accepted my invitation to be my 'Timothy' and accompany me when I preach. I'm praying it will be a blessing to us both, as well as to the churches we visit."

Relieved that he wouldn't have to explain to people why he was here, Garrett picked up his Bible and settled back to hear Pastor Jim's message.

"As we read the Bible, we discover that God spoke to people in very real ways. Although He may not always have spoken in an audible voice, we find the words, "Then the Lord said to Moses," "The Lord said to Joshua," "The angel of the Lord spoke to Philip," or "The Lord said to Ananias." He also spoke to other Bible figures in both the Old and New Testament.

"Few Bible scholars would debate the truth of this, and yet many live their lives as though Almighty God no longer speaks."

Someone behind him coughed. Someone else cleared their throat. Feet shuffled. Had Pastor Jim touched a sore spot?

"I'm here to tell you our God still speaks, but often we don't recognize His voice. Or we prefer to be the master of our own fate, to choose our own course."

Garrett crinkled his brow. This was a new thought. Although he believed the Holy Spirit had led him at various time, he'd assumed God only spoke to pastors or very godly men and women as clearly as He had in Bible times. All his life he'd preferred to be the master of his own fate. Did he really want God to speak to him?

"If God spoke to you, how would you respond? Let's turn to Chapter three of first Samuel and read verses one through ten."

Pastor Jim paused, allowing people to find the place. When

pages stopped rustling, he read the verses in a clear, carrying voice. Then he bowed his head and prayed the words from Psalm 19 as he always did before his message. "*Let the words of my mouth and the meditations of my heart be acceptable in thy sight, O Lord, my strength, and my redeemer.*"

Opening his eyes, Pastor Jim gazed at the congregation. "The first three times the Lord spoke to Samuel, he thought it was Eli. As is true for many of us, he hadn't learned to discern God's voice from the voice of someone he held in high esteem."

Was that why the pastor had said he wanted God to tell Garrett Himself when the time was right if He had other work for him to do?

"Verse seven tells us: *Now Samuel did not yet know the Lord, neither was the word of the Lord yet revealed unto him.* Perhaps you've been going to church all your life, even gotten stars and awards for perfect attendance, but could it be said of you as it was of Samuel that you do not yet know the Lord?"

More coughing and feet shuffling. Even a few whispers. Were people who'd been coming to church for a long time offended by the pastor's words? Garrett had gone to church with his mother for years before he'd come to know the Lord.

Pastor Jim cleared his throat and ignored the distractions. "When the Lord called Samuel for the third time, Eli realized God was speaking to the child. He gave Samuel the best advice possible. *If God calls again, say Speak, Lord, for your servant is listening.*"

The congregation was quiet now, and Pastor Jim gazed at them. "It was late, and Samuel was probably tired from serving Eli. Wouldn't it have been tempting to pretend he didn't hear? Yet three times, he got up and ran to ask what Eli wanted.

"Then when God called for the fourth time, Samuel responded exactly as Eli had directed. *Speak, Lord, for your servant is listening.*"

Those had been the exact words Garrett had spoken before hearing Reverend Caldwell preach for the first time. A baby cried toward the back of the church and Garrett gazed at the Bible in his hand. Had he really meant what he said?

"When God speaks to us, we have a choice. Will we listen and obey or will we go in the opposite direction as Jonah did? If we listen and obey, there's no guarantee our lives will be easy, but at least we won't end up in the belly of a whale."

CHAPTER 43

Garrett beat a rhythm on the steering wheel with his thumb. The silence in the automobile was getting on his nerves. He couldn't escape Pastor Jim's words: *When God speaks to us, we have a choice whether to listen and obey or to go in the opposite direction as Jonah did.*

Did he really want God to speak to him? What if God asked him to be an itinerant preacher, maybe even stay single all his life? Was he really willing to listen and obey regardless of what God asked of him?

Garrett shifted in his seat. Would the trip to Sandy Lake never end? His inner peace had fled. He pulled off the road, bowed his head and groaned. *Savannah.* Another groan escaped. It was hard enough staying away from her for a couple months, but to give her up forever? That was too much to ask, too much for God to expect.

He needed to calm down. Jumping to conclusions before he even knew what God's plan was for his life solved nothing. Taking slow deep breaths, he pulled back on the road. But what if... He shook his head. He needed to think about something else. Maybe his letter to Irv. What should he say? *Dear Irv?* Maybe just *Irv.*

"Help me find the right words, Lord."

Irv, I'm really sorry about being late for our appointment on Monday.

Quiet words interrupted his thoughts. *Why were you late, Garrett?*

Garrett paused. Then he sighed and nodded. "You're right, Lord. *I* was to blame." The tightness in his chest eased and his apology to Irv flowed.

I don't blame you for being upset or for thinking nothing has changed. In a way, you're right. I have a lot of growing to do as a Christian. If I hadn't been so impatient, I wouldn't have been driving too fast on the slippery road. I wouldn't have slid off into a ditch and needed to be pulled out. I wouldn't have been late.

I know I don't deserve another chance, but I'd still like to apologize in person for all the trouble I caused. But if you'd rather not get together, please allow this letter to be my apology. I appreciate all the chances you gave me to change, and I'm sorry I disappointed you so many times. Please forgive me.

"Thank you, Father, for helping me see that I was to blame for being late. I put the blame on the slow horse and on the bad weather, but if I'm honest it was my fault. Refusing to take the blame when I'm wrong is one of my character flaws, isn't it? Probably because of my pride. I guess Polly was right. I'll write this letter to Irv when I get home and send it in morning."

♠

George Burns tossed and turned on the narrow cot, furious at the poor accommodations. Surely most people who spent a night in jail wouldn't fit comfortably on this small bed. And the mattress... a straw tick of all things. Every time he got reasonably comfortable, a piece of straw poked through the cotton cover making him itch.

He'd tried daily to talk the sheriff into letting him leave, claiming his business couldn't survive without him. He had no idea what was happening at the tavern in his absence. His employees were probably robbing him blind. The sheriff had allowed him to call a couple of times but no one answered. It wasn't unexpected. When George had gotten behind in his bills, he'd told his workers to stop answering the telephone.

Then there was Savannah. Why had she reacted as though his advances were unwelcome? Maybe he'd been a little rough but he didn't think women like her minded a little roughness. It wasn't like she was a decent woman who needed tender coaxing. She was a whore.

He sat up and swung his feet to the floor. No lights at all in this stinkin' place. How was he supposed to find the chamber pot? Sheriff Donley locked him in and went home so he couldn't use the outhouse. You'd think the sheriff oughta be required to stay at the jail when they had a prisoner. What were they paying the man?

A prisoner. He'd never spent even an hour in jail in his life. Now he'd been in here a week. He shuffled over to the locked gate and rattled it as hard as he could. Donley had even made him empty his pockets so he couldn't pick the lock.

He needed a drink. This was the longest he'd gone without alcohol since before his wife left. He'd had nothing to drink but water in here. Alcohol wasn't all he needed. Inching his way back to his cot, he flopped down on his back and immediately a piece of straw poked through his shirt. He had to come up with a plan to get his needs met as soon as they let him out. Monday evening couldn't come soon enough. There had to be a way to get Savannah back. If not back to the tavern, then somewhere more private.

♠

Savannah picked up her Bible and stowed it in her quilted bag. Slipping on her coat, she left her room and ran down the stairs. She could hardly wait to get to the Young's for Bible study. She wanted to talk to Mrs. Young about everything that had happened. How thankful she was for a friend who never treated her like inferior goods.

She breathed in the fresh air. Hopefully March meant spring was on its way. It was nice to walk on nearly bare sidewalks. Though the solitude of the deserted street was peaceful, Savannah yearned for the days to get longer so she wouldn't have to walk in the dark on Monday evenings.

Maybe Garrett would be home. Hurrying along Main Street, Savannah couldn't help but hope. They could only be friends, but friends were allowed to see each other and talk, weren't they?

Savannah crossed Main Street just as a horse and buggy stopped at the end of Mill. She glanced up. *Oh no! Mr. Burns! Why hadn't the sheriff told her he was out of jail?*

He leaped out of his buggy and grabbed her before she could turn around. His left hand covered her mouth, his right arm scooped her off her feet. He clambered into his buggy and flung her inside, knocking the wind out of her. Before she could catch her breath to scream, he tied a huge, red handkerchief tightly over her mouth.

Mr. Burns bent over her. His hot breath made her cringe as she struggled to get away. He was too quick. Pain stabbed at her shoulders as he wrenched her arms behind her. His body pressed hers into the unyielding floor of the buggy. The rough burn of the rope pulled at her wrists. She kicked at him. He chuckled as he grabbed her feet tying them next.

"This time's gonna be different. You won't get away as easy as you did last time." Mr. Burns stared at her. "You really owe me now. More'n a week in the slammer all because of you."

Twisting her head back and forth, Savannah tried to speak. The handkerchief allowed nothing but guttural sounds.

Mr. Burns nodded and leered at her, foul-smelling breath wafting into her nostrils. "It's okay. We'll have plenty of time for talking later. Plenty of time to get to know each other better."

♠

Mildred Young looked at the red and white wall clock as she hung up her dish towel. Savannah was late. She always arrived early or at least on time. Garrett's footsteps resounded as he ran down the stairs and came into the kitchen.

"Where's Savannah? I thought you had Bible study on Monday evenings."

"We do. She's late. Something must have come up. She's never been late before."

Garrett sat down and drummed his fingers on the table.

She gazed at him. "Did you want to talk to Savannah about something?"

"Not really. I was just looking forward to seeing her. I miss her."

Mildred nodded. "I'm sure she misses you too."

"I apologized last week for the way I'd treated her. I want to be her beau again, but... I guess I didn't tell you..."

Garrett told his mother of God's dealings with him when Reverend Caldwell had preached at their church. "No matter how much I want Savannah, I know it's not the right time." He shook himself and stood up. "Well, I guess she isn't coming. You'd think she could have at least called."

His mother frowned. "I can't believe she wouldn't have called. Maybe the party line was busy. Maybe I'll call Mrs. Patton."

"Don't bother her, Ma. We're probably just not as important to Savannah as you thought we were."

Mildred gazed after her son as he left the room. Why was it

so hard for him to believe the best?

CHAPTER 44

The wall telephone rang in the hall outside Mildred Young's kitchen. Who would be calling at ten o'clock at night? She bustled down the stairs, with Garrett on her heels.

"Hello."

"Hello, Mildred. This is Innis Patton."

"Oh, Innis. How are you?"

"I'm fine. Is Savannah still there?"

"Savannah? She didn't come to Bible study tonight."

"Really? She left here for your house at 6:45.

"What, Ma? What?" Garrett mouthed his question.

Mildred held up one finger and shook her head.

"She never came back to the boarding house." Innis sounded worried. "I was waiting for her because I wanted to talk to her about something."

"Oh dear me. Where could she be? I hope something hasn't happened."

"Ma, come on. What's going on?" Garrett grasped his mother's arm, as she continued to shake her head and point to the phone.

"I've been working really hard at trusting her. I hope she hasn't done something to make me regret it."

"Let's not jump to conclusions, Innis. Savannah isn't the same person she used to be."

"I hope you're right. I'm not sure what to do."

"I'll ask Garrett to look for her. Make sure she didn't fall and break her ankle or something. I'll call you back."

Garrett already had his coat when Mildred hung up the telephone and told him what Innis had said.

"Please hurry, son. I'm very concerned."

♠

As they left the houses of Sandy Lake behind, George untied the handkerchief from Savannah's mouth. "No one around to hear ya screaming."

"Mr. Burns, why are you doing this? This will only get you in more trouble. Just take me back to the boarding house, and I won't turn you in."

"Nah, I got plans for you and me. I been awful lonely in jail, so I come up with an idea for you and me to spend some time together."

"Mrs. Young will be concerned because I didn't show up for Bible study. "

"Bible study. Is that where you was going? I got things planned that'll be a lot more fun than Bible study."

"If I don't come back to the boarding house, Mrs. Patton will call the sheriff. You'll be the first one he'll suspect."

"Ah, but they'll never find ya where I'm taking ya."

"You're not taking me to the tavern?"

"Oh no, I have a better plan."

"Wh—where are we going?" Savannah's voice quivered.

"You'll find out soon enough. No one'll ever think to look there."

♠

Garrett stumbled along weaving back and forth, checking along both sides of Mill Street to make sure Savannah hadn't fallen beside the road. Where could she be?

What if Mr. Black had come and convinced Savannah to go somewhere? What if she'd gotten discouraged with her life at the boarding house and decided to accept his offer?

He shook his head. He wouldn't go there. "Love always believes the best. Love always believes the best." This time he'd choose to believe the best for once until he'd been proven wrong. He hated being proven wrong. His pride talking.

Turning onto Main Street, Garrett continued his search until he reached the boarding house. If Savannah was coming to their house for Bible study, she wouldn't have gone in the opposite direction. He ran up the steps to the boarding house and tried the door knob. It was unlocked so he went in. Mrs. Patton was sitting on a chair inside the door with a gas lamp on the table beside her. She jumped up, her eyes hopeful.

Garrett shook his head. "I didn't find her. I think we need to call the sheriff. Do you know when George Burns was getting out of jail?"

"I think someone said he was to be released today. Do you think he might have—have kidnapped her?" Mrs. Patton's eyes widened in her pale face.

"I wouldn't put it past him. For some reason, he thinks Savannah owes him. He says he'll get it out of her one way or another."

Mrs. Patton bit her lip. "You don't think there's any chance she just went out with someone for the night, do you?"

Garrett bowed his head. "I'm tempted to believe that, but I'm choosing not to. My mother's always telling me to believe the best, and this time I'm determined to do it."

Nodding, Mrs. Patton stood up. "I'm fighting the same battle. I'll call the sheriff."

Rocking back and forth, Garrett tried to pray. *Father, you know where Savannah is. Please help us find her before it's too late.*

Mrs. Patton's quick footsteps interrupted his prayer. "George Burns was released from jail earlier this evening. The sheriff will ring the fire alarm and organize a search team."

"That's good. May I use your telephone to call my parents?"

"Of course. I'm going to get William. He's the one who rescued Savannah from Mr. Burns before."

Bile rose in Garrett's throat. He wanted to be the one to rescue Savannah. He groaned. Pride again. What did it matter who rescued her?

♠

Polly jumped out of bed and dashed into the hall, almost running into her father. "What is it? Was that the fire alarm?"

"Nothing for you to worry about. I'll get dressed and go see what I can do."

"But, Papa, I want to go with you. For some reason, I feel like I should." Polly grabbed her father's arm. "Maggie and Ben can take care of the children if they need anything."

"All right. Hurry up. There's no time to waste."

Five minutes later, they dashed down the stairs, grabbed

coats, and ran out the front door. "It'll be faster to run into town than to hitch up the buggy. Come on."

In front of the Potter place, Kitt was running down the steps to Broad Street. "Do you know what's wrong?"

"Probably a fire. I don't know why you girls think you need to go." Father frowned.

Polly and Kitt gazed at each other. "I don't know either." Kitt shrugged. "Let's go." They broke into a run.

CHAPTER 45

People milled around in front of the boarding house while the sheriff shouted orders without much success. Polly's gaze fastened on William as he stood on the top step. He gave a piercing whistle that effectively stopped the escalating noise. "Let's listen to what Sheriff Donley has to say."

The sheriff climbed to the top of the stairs beside William and cleared his throat. "Tonight around six forty-five, Savannah Stevens left the boarding house to go Mildred Young's for Bible study. She never arrived and hasn't returned to the boarding house. Mr. Burns, who has made threats against Savannah, was released from jail shortly before Savannah left for Mrs. Young's. We're concerned that he may be involved in her disappearance."

Polly gasped and grabbed Kitt's arm. "Oh no." Kitt began to shake.

A shrill voice from the back of the crowd rose above the chatter. "You oughta check the bedrooms of the Cottage Hotel and the boarding house. That's likely where you'll find them."

"Stop it." Mrs. Patton's diminutive frame appeared beside William and the sheriff. "I'll not have you badmouthing one of my boarders. She's working hard to change her reputation. Seems to me we ought to try to help her, not smear her name with rumors."

When the chatter of the crowd became deafening in response to Mrs. Patton's comment, William whistled again. The sheriff nodded his thanks. "We need to organize a search party. It's likely Mr. Burns may have headed for Jackson Center since that's where he's from, but it's also possible he's still in Sandy Lake." He gestured toward William. "William's family are bringing a hunting dog who can track by scent. Mrs. Patton is gathering a few articles of Savannah's clothing to help the dog pick up the trail."

Sheriff Donley gazed at the crowd. "I'd like six of you to spread out and search the north end of Sandy Lake, six the south end. The rest of you head for Jackson Center and keep your eyes open for clues. When you come to side roads, a few of you search those while the rest of you keep going. If any of you women want to help, always make sure you have a man with you. Don't stray away alone. Always go by twos.

"Garrett and Doc Cooley, maybe you could each take someone with you and head for Jackson Center since you can get there faster in your automobiles."

Polly turned her head. Garrett stood at the edge of the crowd with his parents. Of course they'd be here. She looked at Kitt, who was still trembling. "Are you okay?"

"This brings back memories of all the bad stuff that happened in Atlantic City, except I think Mr. Burns is worse than Dr. Girard."

"Polly, do you want to go with me to look for Savannah?" Garrett, hair standing on end and face pale, met her surprised gaze. "If we find her it might be nice for her to have a woman her own age."

"I was going to ask Polly if she'd go with me." William towered over them as he smiled at Polly. "My parents will meet us here with the dog. If Liesel can pick up the scent, we'll follow with my parents in their horse and buggy."

Tongue-tied, Polly looked from one to the other. Her father stepped between them. "Florence—"

Polly interrupted. "I've never watched a tracking dog. Maybe I'll go with William. I'll be fine, Papa." She glanced at Kitt. "What are you going to do? Do you think you should go home?"

Kitt stood up straight. "If that bully has kidnapped Savannah, then I'm going to help find him and make him pay. I'll go with one of the groups in town."

Doc Cooley strode up to Polly's father. "Do you want to ride with me, Bob? You can be looking around while I keep my eyes on the road. If we find George, I may need your help to bring him in while I'm driving."

"Sounds like a good plan, Doc. Garrett, you should probably take another man with you in case you need to subdue George."

"I'll go with you, Garrett." Sheriff Donley joined their little group. "I think I'm more likely to be needed in Jackson Center than here." He returned to the top of the stairs and shouted to the crowd. "If Savannah and George are found in Sandy Lake, ring the fire alarm bell and call the sheriff in Jackson Center. If we find them in Jackson Center, we'll return here."

Polly looked at her father. "What if we don't find them at all?"

♠

People broke into groups, some getting in buggies, some on foot, spreading out in different directions two by two. Polly glanced at William. Why had he chosen her to go with him?

He turned to look at her and answered her unasked question. "Someone told me you'd been a good friend to Savannah. I thought that would be a comfort if we find her."

So that was why he'd asked her, for Savannah's sake, not because he... She gave herself an internal shake and nodded. "Savannah and I have become friends although..."

"Although what?" William raised an eyebrow.

Polly sighed. "She's so beautiful. It's hard..." She bit her lip. What was she doing, baring her soul to William who hardly knew her?

"She is beautiful." William smiled. "Beautiful girls need friends too. Just because she's attractive doesn't mean her life is easy."

Before Polly could respond, a large buggy pulled by two black stallions turned onto Main Street without stopping at the intersection.

"That's my parents. Look at Liesel. She has a great nose. I'm counting on her to find Savannah."

"What kind of dog is she?"

"A German Shorthaired Pointer. They're used mostly for hunting birds. But I'm hoping she'll be able to pick up Savannah's scent. I worked with her some on tracking before I moved to town."

When the horses pulled up beside the boarding house, William snapped his fingers and Liesel leaped to the ground. "Pa and Ma, I'd like you to meet Polly Dye. She's a friend of Savannah Stevens." He helped Polly into the back seat as Mrs. Patton approached them with a bag.

"Here's a scarf and a pair of gloves that belong to Savannah."

"Thank you. We'll see how Liesel reacts to these." William pulled out a red scarf and held it in front of the dog's nose. "Find, Liesel. Find Savannah."

Liesel sniffed eagerly at the scarf and dashed to the boarding house steps. After a few minutes of sniffing, she took off up Main Street. William jumped into the buggy beside Polly. "Follow her, Pa."

The dog made a right turn at Mill Street, then stopped. After a few more minutes of sniffing, she turned and ran back to Main Street and turned left.

♠

"What did you say?" Harold Young looked at his wife, plodding along beside him as they covered some of the side streets of Sandy Lake.

"I wasn't talking to you, I was talking to God. He knows where Savannah is and I'm asking Him to protect her." Mildred stopped to catch her breath.

"With all the bad things happening in the world, do you think God can be bothered about one lost person?"

"Jesus told a story about one sheep who was lost on a stormy night." Mildred tightened her scarf. "He said the shepherd left his other ninety-nine sheep and went after the one that was lost. If a shepherd cares about one lost sheep, surely Jesus cares about one lost person."

♠

Savannah had tried to keep track of all the turns they made but she was completely lost. They jounced along by the light of the moon which appeared to be full, but the road had deep ruts that rattled her teeth. "Where are we?"

"Don't matter to you. You ain't goin' nowhere without me, and I'm making sure anyone trying to follow us will have a merry chase. I know every side road in Jackson Center and a few that ain't nothin' but foot paths."

Chapter 46

Mrs. Patton made another pot of coffee. Searchers dribbled into the dining room, long faces revealing their lack of results. No one wanted to go home until Savannah was found or until they received word from the searchers in Jackson Center. People spoke in low voices or folded their arms on the tables and rested their weary heads.

Occasionally Savannah's landlady allowed herself to focus on how angry she'd be if her missing boarder pranced into the boarding house in the morning from some liaison, but mostly she was angry at George Burns who might have kidnapped Savannah. Just because he was bigger and stronger. Just as her ex-husband had mistreated her because he was bigger and stronger.

♠

With no predetermined plan, Garrett and the sheriff pulled into the tavern parking lot in Jackson Center. They were followed by Dr. Cooley and Bob Dye. Eventually, other horses and buggies from the search party pulled into the lot, all filled with grim-faced people. They hadn't found Savannah.

The sheriff tried the door to the tavern but it was locked. No amount of pounding produced a response. Finally, he opened the door with a skeleton key he carried. Garrett wanted to help search the tavern, but the sheriff only asked Doc Cooley and Bob Dye to go with him. Garrett stood in the doorway, listening to the snarls and complaints of the people they'd wakened who rented rooms at the tavern. George and Savannah weren't there.

At last the buggy carrying Polly and William's family pulled into the parking lot with their dog close behind. William joined the disgruntled group of people outside the tavern. "We chased back and forth all over the back roads of Jackson Center but some of them were only foot paths, very soggy because of the melting snow. Liesel got confused. Maybe I expected too much. She's a bird dog."

In spite of desperately wanting to be the one to find Savannah, most of all Garrett wanted her to be found. Even William and his dog hadn't been able to do it. He closed his eyes. "Oh God..."

"Let's go home and get some sleep. Tomorrow we'll try again." Sheriff Donley turned toward Garrett's car. "Come on, Garrett."

"But sir—"

"We need to go back to Sandy Lake to tell folks we haven't found Savannah."

Should he insist on continuing the search on his own? But he had brought the sheriff and was responsible to get him home. He got back into his car.

Garrett silently talked to God on the way home, while the Sheriff snored with his head tilted back on the seat.

Lord, I'm sorry I wasn't faithful to pray for Savannah tonight. This isn't a competition, but I wanted so much to find her. Finding her seems much more important than praying for her. Pride again.

The rest of the way back to Sandy Lake, Garrett focused on praying for Savannah, that she'd be found, that she'd be safe, that Mr. Burns would be brought to justice if he was responsible. Still he had no peace.

♠

Mr. Burns's chestnut mare stopped and Savannah jerked awake. She couldn't believe she'd fallen asleep. The little cabin deep in the woods looked like it hadn't been used in years—no glass in the windows and the door partially detached from its hinges. A strong smell told her a skunk had been in the neighborhood.

Mr. Burns cursed as he scrambled out of the buggy. "Nobody has no respect for people's property. Who broke out them windows and the door? Even smells like a skunk's been using my place."

Holding her breath against the odor, Savannah talked silently to the Lord while Mr. Burns went into the cabin. *I trust you, Lord. I trust you. I'm not blaming you for this happening. I'm running to you because I trust you.*

Mr. Burns came back to the buggy. "You're gonna have to stay here while I go get something to cover the windows and fix the door. I heard it's to snow again this afternoon. I can't risk taking you into town." He lifted her out of the buggy and carried her into the filthy, stinking cabin. "We'll have to put up with the smell. We'll get used to it."

Sobs built in Savannah's throat, but she wouldn't let Mr. Burns see her tears. She pressed her lips together as he set her on a wobbly, broken chair. He pawed through her bag. What was he looking for? Making sure it contained nothing to help her escape? At last, he set it on her lap.

"I'm not sure when I'll be back. I might have to go to Mercer in case the sheriff is lookin' for me in Jackson Center." At the last minute, he turned and tied the handkerchief around her mouth. "Not taking any chances."

Closing her eyes, Savannah took a deep breath, then regretted it. She gagged and her eyes watered. She twisted her ankles and wrists, trying to loosen the knots. How much time did she have until Mr. Burns returned?

With a little jerk, she discovered that even with her wrists bound, she could reach into her bag and pull out her Bible and Sarah's diary. She clasped them tightly—a lifeline from others who'd survived hard times.

♠

Polly climbed out of the buggy. She thanked William for inviting her to go along, said goodbye to his parents, and walked toward Doc Cooley's car. Tears stung her eyelids. Where was Savannah? She regretted every jealous, envious thought she'd ever had about her. *I'm so sorry, Lord. Please rescue her and help me love her the way you do.*

Her father got out of Doc Cooley's car, and they walked arm in arm toward home. "What will happen to Savannah, Papa? We can't just go home. What if she's alone somewhere with Mr. Burns?"

Patting his daughter's hand, he smiled. "So like your mother, Florence."

"Am I? How?"

"She was like that good shepherd in the Bible who went out

looking for one lost sheep. She cared so much for others. Especially people society didn't care about. I see some of that in you."

Polly shook her head. "I have a long way to go, Papa. Too often I let bad feelings toward people rule my heart. But I want to be like Jesus, and I know that's what Mama wanted for me."

Her father stopped in mid-stride. "Wait..."

"What? What's wrong?"

Breaking into a run, her father panted, his words coming out in short gasps. "Hurry. I just... had... an... idea. George Burns had an old hunting cabin in the woods around Jackson Center. We used to pass it when we hunted there years before we moved to Sandy Lake. Maybe that's where he took Savannah."

"Oh Papa, maybe that's where she is."

"I don't want to get people's hopes up in case I'm wrong. Let's take Jasper and our buggy and see if we can find the cabin. I'll take my rifle."

♠

Polly scanned the countryside. It was almost morning. All the side roads were beginning to look alike. "Are you sure this is right road, Papa?"

"Almost. There. I think that's the lane that leads to the cabin. Take the reins, and I'll hold the rifle in case we find George. Don't let Jasper go too fast. We'll try to be quiet. You should be ready to duck below the seat if you need to."

"Look, tracks. Horse and buggy tracks, fresh ones." Polly could hardly contain her excitement.

"I see them. I think this is it. Let's pray we can rescue Savannah without anyone getting hurt."

"I don't see a horse and buggy." Polly looked around the clearing. "There's no one here." A tear rolled down her cheek.

"Don't be too sure. Let's be quiet in case George hid the horse and buggy somewhere." Leaping out of the buggy, Polly's father ran to peek in the window.

"She's here. Come on." They ran to open the door.

"Savannah!" Polly raced to her friend and untied the gag. "Oh, Savannah, we were so worried about you."

Tears rolled down Savannah's cheeks as she leaned into Polly's hug. "You came, Polly. How did you know where I was?"

"Let's get her out of here." Polly's father gently lifted

Savannah into his arms, her Bible and Sarah's diary clutched in her hands. "We can untie you and talk on the way home."

CHAPTER 47

Polly arranged Savannah on the back seat of their buggy. She put the two books back in her bag and began working on the knots as her father flicked Jasper's reins. "Did Mr. Burns bring you here?"

"Yes. He left to get something to fix the door and windows. How did you find me?"

"We used to live in Jackson Center, and my father remembered George Burns had an old hunting cabin out here. I'm amazed Father could find it, but I'm sure God helped us. Lots of people have been looking for you and praying."

"Really? Lots of people? I didn't think many people cared what happened to me."

Polly explained how Mrs. Patton had called Mildred Young and eventually the sheriff, who had arranged a search party. "William Sider's parents even brought a dog to try to track you, but it didn't work."

Savannah shook her head in disbelief. "I can't believe all these people cared enough to come out in the middle of the night to look for me."

"Mother would be so proud of our town. There, you're free." Polly tugged off the last of Savannah's ropes.

"Girls, get down on the floor. I think someone's coming."

As Polly and Savannah hurried to obey, the clip clop of a horse's hooves became louder.

"It's him." Father whispered the words although Mr. Burns couldn't have heard. He pulled his rifle onto his lap.

"What are you doing here?" Mr. Burns's voice had a nasty edge.

Polly peered out the side of their buggy. The road was narrow and Mr. Burns's rig was in the middle of it.

"I had some errands to do this morning." Father acted like he drove out to Mr. Burns's hunting camp every day.

"Is that right? What kind of errands could you possibly have out here?"

"It's private. If you'll move your rig, we'll be on our way."

Mr. Burns stood. "I'll have a look in your buggy first."

Father lifted his rifle and stepped out of the buggy, his gun aimed at Mr. Burns. "You'll do no such thing. Florence, come hold the gun on George while I tie him up. We'll take him back to town."

Mr. Burns took a step. "I don't think you have the nerve—"

Polly and Savannah jumped at a loud explosion from Father's gun. George Burns cursed.

"That was a warning shot, Burns. I only miss on purpose, and I'm not likely to miss on purpose twice."

Mr. Burns sat down, still shouting oaths at Father. "I'll teach you to meddle in things that are none of your business, Robert Dye."

"Savannah, does Mr. Burns have a weapon on him?"

"I don't think so. He came straight from the jail to kidnap me."

"All right, girls. Bring me the rope Mr. Burns used to tie up Savannah. Florence, you remember how to use this gun?"

"I remember, Father."

♠

Nearly everyone had gone home but Mrs. Patton continued to nurse a mug of coffee. She sat in a chair at the dining room table where she could see the outer door. William sat beside her, and Kitt on the other side of him. Garrett paced in the hallway, praying that God would show him what to do. It was impossible to sit still. Should he go looking for Savannah? If so, where?

The truth was, he wanted William to go to bed. If Savannah was found, he didn't want her to come back and find William waiting for her. If Garrett left, she might think he'd gone home to bed. Maybe he should invite William to go with him to look for Savannah.

At last he dropped into the chair by the door, and bowed his head. He quieted his heart. In spite of all his prayers, he'd been acting as though he had no faith in God at all, as though finding Savannah was all up to him. He pictured Jesus speaking, "Peace be still" to his troubled thoughts.

Out of the stillness, he heard again Reverend Caldwell's words:

When God speaks to us, we have a choice whether to listen and obey or to go in the opposite direction as Jonah did.

So he was back to that. He could sense the Holy Spirit waiting for his answer. As he surrendered control, his resistance melted.

Father, I know you've been waiting for me to give up my will. I'm sorry I've been so double-minded—willing to do anything you ask, anything except give up Savannah. Oh, I'm willing to give her up for a few weeks or months, but I haven't been willing to give her up forever.

Garrett knelt beside the chair. *If you'll bring Savannah safely home, I promise I'll do anything you ask, even if it means being a single, itinerant pastor for the rest of my life. Just please watch over Savannah, and I'll do anything you say.*

The battle was over. Peace at last. Garrett would obey God no matter what the cost.

The door burst open and Savannah, Polly and Mr. Dye swept by Garrett without noticing him kneeling beside the chair. Curses and swearing wafted in behind them. The door slammed. Before Garrett could get up, William reached the hall in three huge strides. He gathered Savannah into his arms with Mrs. Patton and Kitt right behind them. Polly and her father completed the circle. Garrett stood alone by the door. Was this the way it would be for the rest of his life?

Chapter 48

After the excitement of Savannah's homecoming, the dining room was quiet. The Dyes had gone home, leaving just Mrs. Patton and William at the table with Savannah. She rested her head against the back of her chair. All the stories had been told, and she was exhausted. She should go to bed. She straightened. Where was Garrett? He would have known she didn't show up at his mother's house for Bible study. Hadn't he helped search for her?

"What's wrong?" Mrs. Patton's eyes were kind. "It's all over now. Sheriff Donley took George Burns back to jail. Later, they'll move him to the Mercer County jail until his trial."

"It's not that. It's just...well, I—where's Garrett? Didn't he help look for me?"

William nodded. "He was here. The sheriff rode with him to Jackson Center. Garrett didn't want to give up the search, but the sheriff insisted on coming back to Sandy Lake. I don't know where Garrett went after that."

"He was here for awhile, pacing up and down the hall. I suppose he got tired and went home." Mrs. Patton touched Savannah's hand. "I'm sure you're exhausted. Why don't you go to your room and get some sleep? I don't think Mr. Young will expect you at work."

Savannah pushed out of her chair. She should be joyful and excited that God had delivered her from Mr. Burns. Instead, sadness weighed her down like a heavy rock. Surely even a friend would stay to make sure she was okay. Why would Garrett leave without talking to her?

"Savannah?"

She turned around. William was behind her on the stairs.

"I know it's only been a week since we talked about this, but when you were missing, it made me realize how much I like you. Do you think you might be ready to go out with me on Friday evening?"

She looked into William's eager eyes. Apparently Garrett wasn't even interested in being friends. "Yes, I believe I'm ready."

♠

Savannah dried the last cup and saucer as Mrs. Patton wiped the counter. The week had passed quickly. Many people who'd never spoken to Savannah before had asked if she was okay. She could hardly believe all the love and compassion poured on her. Polly and Kitt had stopped a couple times to check on her, too. For the first time, Sandy Lake was beginning to feel like home.

"Could I talk to you for a minute, Savannah?" Mrs. Patton motioned for her to come into her sitting room behind the kitchen. She'd never been invited to the sitting room.

"I have a date with William a little later, but I can come for a few minutes."

Mrs. Patton sat in the small rocking chair, nodding for Savannah to sit on the loveseat. "I believe I owe you an apology."

Savannah's eyes widened. "Me? Why?"

"William told me it wasn't fair to take it out on other people because one person failed me. He was right. I was afraid to trust because my husband betrayed me. I'm so sorry I didn't treat you well. I was suspicious and unkind when all the while, you were trying to turn over a new leaf, as my mother used to say."

Tears rolled down Savannah's cheeks. "I don't blame you, Mrs. Patton. You gave me a chance when I'm not sure anyone else would have. I had nowhere to go. I can never thank you enough."

She knelt beside Mrs. Patton's rocker and took her hands. "I will always be grateful that you took me in and gave me a job. With my reputation, I don't blame you for being suspicious."

Her landlady stood and pulled Savannah to her feet. "I never thought of it that way. I'm glad I was able to help give you a new beginning. I want you to know I do trust you. I even stood up for you when someone said unkind things about you when you were missing." Mrs. Patton gave Savannah a few awkward pats. Her landlady wasn't given to demonstrations of affection, but Savannah wiped her tears and hugged her anyway. Amazing what

God had accomplished through something as bad as being kidnapped.

♠

Garrett drove into Sandy Lake after a long day at work. They'd needed to restock the shelves which they didn't usually do on Friday evenings. Mr. Black hadn't mentioned Savannah again since they'd talked, and he hadn't closed his door at unusual times either. For Savannah's sake, Garrett was glad.

He turned onto Main Street, stifling a yawn, and then sat up straight. Was that William and Savannah walking down the street toward the Opera House? A sign out in front advertised a special musical presentation. Savannah loved that sort of thing. Why hadn't he taken her more often when they'd been seeing each other?

Of course the answer was that he didn't personally care for musical presentations. How selfish of him. Yet another flaw floating to the surface. As an only child, it hadn't been necessary for him to share or play games that others wanted to play. Ma had always been happy to play whatever game suited him.

"You've got quite a job on your hands, Lord. Good thing you're a skilled Potter."

Seeing William and Savannah together haunted him. Is this how Polly had felt when she saw him with Savannah? No, she'd probably felt worse because she and Garrett had still been courting at the time. He had repented of what he'd done and he knew he was forgiven, but he still cringed at the memory.

♠

When Garrett came into the sunny kitchen, Ma glanced at him with a puzzled frown. Probably wondering which side of the bed he'd gotten up on today. His moods had been as changeable as the March weather. "Just orange juice for me. I need to get on the road to pick up Pastor Jim to be on time at the Methodist Church in Mercer."

"Reverend Caldwell is preaching there today?"

"Yes, and then a potluck dinner afterward. Don't plan for me for lunch. I'm hoping to talk to Pastor Jim about something afterward. Don't worry if I'm late."

"Is everything all right, Garrett? You haven't been yourself lately."

Garrett glanced at his father already seated at the table. He must have been acting odd if his father had noticed. "Just have some important decisions to make. Sorry if I've been acting strange."

This was the third Sunday in a row his father had come downstairs dressed for church. Garrett was especially glad Pa was going with Ma since Garrett would be attending wherever Pastor Jim preached. Pa seemed to want everyone to act as though going to church was his usual thing, so Garrett didn't say a word. How would his father respond if it turned out God wanted Garrett to be a single, itinerant pastor for the rest of his life?

CHAPTER 49

Oh God, I can't stop thinking about William and Savannah going into the Opera House. If only I had been more sensitive to her likes and dislikes. Garrett groaned. *Not that it matters if you want me to be single my whole life.* He groaned again.

Would this trip to Jackson Center never end? If only there was a switch to turn off his mind.

At last he drove into town, but the hat shop on Main Street set off another series of images. The first time he'd seen Savannah she'd been coming out of that very shop. He'd been smitten from his first glimpse. He was still smitten.

He took a deep breath and turned onto the side street where Pastor Jim lived. As he pulled up in front of the house, the door opened and his friend appeared. Apparently he'd been watching from the window.

Garrett sensed the positive aura that always surrounded Pastor Jim even before he got into the car. He didn't have any of the things Garrett had always thought necessary for happiness—a girl friend or wife, a nice house, a good job, plenty of money—and yet he nearly radiated some indefinable quality. How did he do it?

"Good morning, Garrett. How are things in Sandy Lake?"

Putting the car in motion, Garrett shook his head. "I don't know where to start."

Reverend Caldwell was a good listener, and Garrett told him all that had happened over the past week beginning with Savannah's kidnapping.

"I'd heard the owner of the tavern had kidnapped a woman, but I had no idea she was a friend of yours."

Garrett nodded, then sighed. "I'd been wrestling with God

all week. Last Sunday morning you said when God speaks to us, we have a choice whether to listen and obey or to go in the opposite direction."

Pastor Jim turned his head, gazing at Garrett. "Did you think God was asking you to do something you didn't want to do?"

"I was afraid he might ask me to be an unmarried, itinerant preacher. I was willing to give up Savannah for a couple weeks or months, but not forever." Garrett gripped the steering wheel tighter.

"Ah...so did you win the wrestling match or did God?"

"When none of the searchers found Savannah, I made a promise to God that if He'd bring her safely home, I'd do anything He asked—even be a single, itinerant preacher the rest of my life."

"I see."

"The words were hardly out of my mouth when she and some of the searchers came in the door. They didn't see me kneeling by the chair, and before I could get up, one of the boarders who's interested in her, came and gave her a big hug."

As they pulled into the parking lot, Garrett shuddered. "I've never felt so alone in my life. If God holds me to my promise, is that the way my life will be from now on?"

Pastor Jim's eyes were kind. "We'll talk about it after church. God is faithful. If He calls you to that kind of life, His grace will be sufficient."

♠

Garrett sank into the pew beside Jim. "What are you preaching about today?"

"The pearl of great price. Do you know that parable?"

"I think I've heard of it, but I don't remember what it's about."

"It's about a man who found a costly pearl that was so wonderful, he sold everything he had to buy it. The Bible says the Kingdom of heaven is like that."

Those words exposed Garrett's heart like a sharp scalpel. What had he read in Hebrews the other day? *The word of God is quick, and powerful, and sharper than any two-edged sword...* When faced with the prospect of losing Savannah, *she* had become that costly pearl that he'd give anything to have. Now God was asking him to make Jesus and His kingdom the most important thing.

He heard little of Reverend Caldwell's message. Finger by finger he released his hold on the pew he'd been gripping, just as God was loosening self from the throne of his life. At the end of the service, the congregation sang an old Swedish hymn that was new to Garrett. Pastor Jim gave an altar call as they sang.

O that Pearl of great price! Have you found it?
Is the Savior supreme in your love?
O consider it well, ere you answer,
As you hope for a welcome above.
Have you given up all for this Treasure?
Have you counted past gains as but loss?
Has your trust in yourself and your merits
Come to naught before Christ and His cross?

Garrett remained in his seat until the Pastor asked the congregation one last question. "Can you say with the Apostle Paul, *I have suffered the loss of all things, and do count them but dung, that I may win Christ...*"

Those words, the sharpest scalpel of all, catapulted Garrett from his seat to the altar, not caring what anyone said or thought. He vowed to keep fighting this battle until Christ was first in his life. "Forgive me, Jesus, for placing a higher value on my relationship with Savannah than on my relationship with you. I choose to make you my pearl of great price, whatever the cost."

♠

After a sumptuous potluck dinner, Garrett and Pastor Jim went into a classroom to talk.

"How are you feeling about your promise to God, Garrett?"

"Much better. All through your message the Holy Spirit was taking me off the throne and putting Jesus on it. I don't want anything or anyone to be more important to me."

"So you're willing to allow God to win this wrestling match?"

"I am."

Pastor Jim sat quietly for a long time, his eyes closed. He appeared to be listening to something Garrett couldn't hear. At last he opened his eyes. "I don't know what future God has planned for you. But sometimes when we're obedient and surrender something very dear to God, He gives it back to us."

Garrett stared at him. "You mean to say that after I went through all this to give Savannah up, God might give her back to me?"

Nodding, Pastor Jim picked up his Bible and turned to the book of Genesis. "God gave Abraham a son, Isaac, for whom he had waited many years and who Abraham loved very much. Yet one day God told him to take Isaac and sacrifice him on Mount Moriah. Can you even imagine how difficult that was for Abraham? And yet Abraham set out to do what God asked."

Now Garrett was nodding. "I remember the story. After he'd put Isaac on the altar, God provided a ram for the sacrifice."

"Yes. God allowed Abraham to keep the son whom he loved after Abraham proved that God was first in his life. In the same way, now that you've proven to God that He is first, He may give Savannah back to you."

Looking down at the table, Garrett shook his head. "I'm afraid it's too late. Savannah is already seeing someone else."

CHAPTER 50

Polly kissed Twila's chubby cheek and tucked her into bed. Elsie was already nestled in her bed. *Maybe the girls will take a long nap, so I can take one too.* How long did it take to catch up on missing a night's sleep?

She crossed the hall to the bedroom she shared with the other girls. Throwing herself on the bed, she sprawled crosswise—a rare treat, and closed her eyes. She slowed her breathing and waited for sleep to come. Nothing happened.

At last Polly got up and grabbed her journal from its hiding place under her bloomers in her dresser drawer. She propped herself against the headboard with a couple of pillows. Maybe if she wrote things down, her mind would stop swirling.

She traced the gold letters on the dark blue cover, then reached for Chartreuse.

March 11, 1912

I want to empty my brain. Maybe then I'll be able to sleep. I keep reliving all the awful things that happened to Savannah on Monday night. I asked God to help me love her like He does. Maybe that's why I can't get her out of my mind.

She seems to be doing okay, but I'm still worried about her. I'm praying she'll remember God didn't promise bad things wouldn't happen to us, only that He'd be with us. She was holding her Bible and Sarah's diary when we rescued her. That has to mean something.

I've also asked God to forgive me for the jealousy and envy I had toward her and told Him I'd do all I can to help her. It was foolish of me to be jealous about William. I don't have time for a beau anyway. The only way I could marry would be if Father remarried.

Polly shuddered. *I'd much rather stay single all my life than have Father bring another woman into Mother's house. He loved our mother so much, surely he'd never want to remarry.*

♠

Garrett stepped into the warm, cheery kitchen just as Ma came in from the sitting room.

"How was the service, son?"

"It was good, Ma. How was yours?"

"Good, although probably not as exciting as yours. How's Reverend Caldwell?"

"He's amazing, Ma. He's poor in every way that matters to the world, but he's one of the happiest people I know."

"Maybe that's because he's like the man who found the pearl of great price and sold everything he had to get it. He found what gives a person true happiness."

Garrett's mouth dropped. "How in the world... Ma, that's what Reverend Caldwell preached about today."

Ma smiled. "The Holy Spirit is working overtime, isn't He?" Her eyes sparkled.

"I guess so." He took off his coat. "I keep forgetting to tell you, I wrote a letter to Irv last Sunday. I didn't remember to tell Pastor Jim either."

"That's wonderful, Son. I've been praying he'd be willing to let you make amends."

"Do you have a few minutes to talk?"

"Sure. How about a cup of tea? Did you have lunch at the church?"

"We had lunch but tea sounds good." Garrett plopped into a chair.

His mother threw a few pieces of wood into the stove and filled the teakettle. Garrett tilted his chair back on two legs as she bustled around getting out tea cups and spoons. When the tea was ready, she filled their cups with steaming liquid. Then she sat down and smiled at Garrett.

"What is it, son?"

He brought his chair down on all four legs, trying to decide whether to ask his father to join them. No, he wasn't ready to face his father's possible opposition to anything he had to say spiritually.

"I've been wrestling with God again, Ma."

"About what?"

"Reverend Caldwell preached last week about being willing to do anything God asked of us."

Garrett went on to tell his mother about his promise to God when Savannah was missing, and then Pastor Jim's message and their talk afterward. "So I still don't really know what God wants from me, except that He wants to be first in my life."

Ma reached a hand to cover his on the table. "If you get that right, son, all the rest will follow. God is using Reverend Caldwell in your life for sure. For now, if I were you, I'd just concentrate on being his Timothy. I'm praying for you."

♠

Garrett glanced out the window at the softly falling spring rain. Almost three weeks since he'd made his promise to God. How long did it take for a butterfly to come out of its chrysalis? Ever since he'd stepped down from the throne of his life, each day was a new adventure. Each day he affirmed that he would do whatever God asked of him. Each Sunday he devoured the truths from God's Word as Pastor Jim preached. Yesterday had been no exception. He was so blessed to have this man as his friend.

Ma bustled into the kitchen. "Oh, you're home, son. I have a letter for you."

She hurried to the small desk where she kept the mail. "Let's see. That's a bill, those are ads, and... here it is." She handed him an envelope. "There's no return address, but it looks like Irv's handwriting."

"I'd given up on ever hearing from him."

"He's always pleasant to your father and me at church but never stops to talk."

Garrett turned the envelope over and over in his hands. "I almost hate to open it. If he refuses to forgive me, I'll have to deal with all the negative feelings again."

"I've been praying he'd choose to believe the best and accept your efforts to make peace." Ma handed him a pearl-handled letter opener.

Garrett slit the top of the envelope with one quick slice and pulled out the letter. Glancing at his mother, he took a deep breath.

Garrett, I'm sorry it's taken me so long to respond to your letter. I guess you might say I've been wrestling with my pride. Out of my own stubbornness, I didn't want to believe you'd changed because I always said I'd never believe it. But the Bible says if I want God to forgive me for my sins, I have to forgive you. I'm impressed that you admitted it was your fault you were late and that you still want to talk in person. I know you work in Mercer now, but if you want to stop by the mill at 6:00 some evening, we can talk. Irv

He looked at Ma with the sting of tears in his eyes. "God's been so good to me. Much better than I deserve."

♠

George sat in his cell in the Mercer jail. He'd been here for almost a month and still no word about when his trial would start. He'd closed the tavern because he had no close family members to run it, and he wasn't about to turn it over to his unfaithful wife.

"Mr. Burns, you have a visitor." The guard stood by the door of his cell. "You can come this way to talk to him."

"Who would want to visit me? And who says I want any visitors?"

"You can refuse, if you like, but if I were in your shoes, I'd be thankful for a visitor." The guard kept his tone level and his expression neutral.

It was George's choice. "Oh, all right, I'll come. But if someone's here to harass me, I won't stay."

"Fair enough."

In the small, drab room where visits took place sat a man George had never seen. "Who in the world are you? And why are you here?" George's tone was gruff.

"I'm Reverend Caldwell, an itinerant preacher. We've never met but I came to see if there's anything I can do for you."

"Do for me? I doubt it unless you have a file I can use to break out of this joint."

"No files, Mr. Burns. But I did bring a kit with soap, shaving cream, and a few other permitted items. I also brought you a Bible."

"I'm much obliged for the practical stuff but what would I do with a Bible?"

"You could read it, or I could read it to you. Getting to know the author has helped a lot of people make a fresh start."

George's shoulders drooped and his chin sagged. "I never

thought I'd be saying this, but I'll take it. The hours in here sure get long with nothing to do."

"I recommend you start in the book of Psalms or in the Gospels—the first four books of the New Testament. There's an index in the front. Every week on Wednesday evening, I come here to hold a service in the chapel. I haven't seen you there, but I'd sure be happy if you'd come."

Silence filled the room. Then George nodded. "We'll see. I might come. I got nothin' better to do."

CHAPTER 51

Savannah glanced at the calendar on her desk as she prepared to go to the post office during her lunch break. Tomorrow would be the first day of June. More than three months since she'd written to her parents. She didn't expect to hear from them. But out of habit, she checked her mail every day.

At the post office, her mouth dropped when Mr. Boyd held out an envelope with her mother's handwriting. Gulping, Savannah reached for the letter, then drew back her hand. Since Mr. Boyd had already let go, the letter fell to the floor. "I'm sorry. I thought you had it." Mr. Boyd peered over the counter at the envelope.

"Not your fault." She smiled at Mr. Boyd. "I've been waiting a long time for this letter. But now that it's here, I'm not sure I want to read it." Since her kidnapping, people had been so kind that Savannah had stopped assuming everyone in Sandy Lake was nosy.

The post master leaned over and patted her hand. "I understand. I'm sorry I can't guarantee good news in the letters I give out."

Savannah smiled and picked up the envelope. "I know. That's not your fault either. Thank you."

Turning to walk away, she held the letter with the tips of her fingers, as though she could protect herself from what it contained. Giving herself a shake, she stuffed it in her beaded handbag and walked out of the post office. "The Lord is my light and my salvation, whom shall I fear?"

♠

Dinner was over and the dishes put away. Savannah had told no one about her mother's letter, and she still hadn't opened it. She sat on the edge of her bed. Why had she even written to her parents, giving them another chance to reject her? There was always a possibility her father would forgive her if not for her mother's influence, but he did nothing her mother didn't approve. Otherwise, Ma made his life miserable.

Slowly she picked up the letter opener and slit the envelope. Still she couldn't bring herself to pull out the single sheet of paper. Instead, she opened a drawer and drew out a clean handkerchief. Might as well be prepared. She should probably try to believe the best of her parents since she wanted people to believe the best of her, but the rock in the pit of her stomach made it difficult.

At last, she pulled out the letter and began to read.

Savannah, I told you before that you shamed us and you shamed God by what you did. I don't know why you're trying to make us believe you've changed. I always knew you were poor white trash just like your father's side of the family. Now that you've proved it, don't waste your time trying to make us believe otherwise. We have no use for the likes of you.

Her mother had signed the letter, *Gertrude and Edgar Stevens.* Clearly her mother no longer considered her their daughter. Savannah stifled a sob. What had she expected? Tears poured down her cheeks. She dropped to her knees. *Oh, God, thank you that you're with me. Thank you that you'll never turn me away.*

Sobs continued to shake her body. Who could she talk to? William was only a few doors away. Savannah shook her head. They had dated for more than two months, but her heart wasn't in it. Last Friday she'd broken things off, knowing he'd never be more than a friend.

Although she was always welcome at the Young's, things had been awkward since Garrett had seen her with William. He was definitely avoiding her. She didn't want to surprise him by showing up without warning. Her heart still hurt because he hadn't stayed to talk to her the night she was kidnapped.

She couldn't talk to Mrs. Patton who'd gone to visit her sister in Sharon. Maybe she could talk to Polly. But what if Savannah told her about her mother's letter and Polly believed what her mother said?

♠

Polly hung up the dish towel just as a knock came on their front door. She hadn't heard horse's hooves or a car engine. Who could it be? She walked into the living room as her father opened the door.

"Savannah, come in. It's always good to see you." Her father gave Savannah her usual hearty welcome. Raising his voice, he called to Polly. "Florence... Oh, there you are. Savannah's here."

Giving Savannah a hug, Polly took a second look at her. Had she been crying? "I'm so glad to see you. Let's go to the front room so we can talk."

She followed Savannah into the sitting room and closed the door behind them. "Sit down, my friend." Plopping down on the loveseat beside Savannah, Polly reached for her hand. "Is something wrong?"

Repressed sobs shook Savannah's body, and fresh tears rolled down her cheeks. She pulled a handkerchief out of the pocket of her modest dark blue dress. Polly suspected she'd been replacing her fancier dresses one by one as she could afford to have new ones made.

At last Savannah blew her nose and told Polly about the letter she'd written to her parents. "They don't want anything to do with me. I really thought God wanted me to write to them. Do you think I misunderstood Him?"

"Why did you think God wanted you to write to them?"

"Because I owed them an apology for always thinking I knew better than they did. I didn't honor them as the Bible says we should."

Polly nodded, silently praying for wisdom. "You obeyed God by sending your parents an apology, but you can't control how they responded. You were only responsible for doing what He asked you to do. I'm so proud of you for doing what was right."

Savannah sighed. "How can you be proud of me when even my mother wants nothing to do with me? She says... " She swallowed hard and ducked her head.

"What does she say?"

Standing up, Savannah started toward the door. "It's no use. If my own family doesn't believe in me, I can't expect anyone else to. Maybe not even God."

♠

Garrett sat cross-legged on his bed and reached for his Bible. He'd formed a habit of reading before he went to bed and first thing when he got up. It was a good way to end his day and a good way to begin. He'd been reading through the book of Genesis and the book of Proverbs. He opened to the satin black marker where he'd left off the night before.

And it came to pass after these things, that God did tempt Abraham... Pastor Jim had told him that word meant "test" in this context. *And he said, Take now thy son, thine only son Isaac, whom thou lovest...*

Ah, this was the scripture Pastor Jim had talked about when they'd discussed Garrett's promise to God. What had the Pastor said? "Sometimes when we're obedient and surrender something very dear to God, He gives it back to us." Garrett read to the end of the Chapter 22 as Abraham demonstrated his obedience, only to have God allow him to keep his son.

I've been obedient to you, Father, putting Savannah on the altar of sacrifice. I won't take her back, even should she ask, unless you make it clear that's your plan.

He sat, head bowed, heart open to the Lord for some time. At last he turned to Proverbs eighteen. The Proverbs fascinated him, especially the many references to characteristics of a fool. Those verses described well the man he used to be. He read each verse, praying for wisdom to apply it to his life. At verse twenty-two, he stopped and reread the verse. *Whoso findeth a wife findeth a good thing, and obtaineth favor of the Lord.*

The verse might as well have been written in bold print and branded on his heart. He could hardly breathe. *Father... Father... Are you giving Savannah back to me?*

CHAPTER 52

Savannah opened one eye and groaned when her alarm clock chimed. Breakfast was served later on Saturdays. Why was she so tired? The sun was shining but she didn't care. It changed nothing in her world.

I always knew you were poor white trash just like your father's side of the family. Now that you've proved it, don't waste your time trying to make us believe any different. She shut off the alarm and pulled her pillow over her head, desperate to shut out the hateful words.

Minutes ticked by. At last, she groaned and threw back the covers. No matter what her mother thought of her, she still had to help Mrs. Patton with breakfast and go to work. She didn't usually work on Saturdays, but Mr. Young had some important documents he wanted her to type.

She dressed, washed her face, combed her hair, and avoided looking at herself in the mirror, not wanting to see the face her mother had always loathed. As though it were Savannah's fault she had inherited the good looks of the woman her mother despised. Grandmother Stevens.

As she picked up her bag and opened the door, she hesitated. She was late but maybe she'd have a few minutes to read before beginning work at the office. Opening the drawer of her bedside table, she pulled out her Bible and Sarah's diary and stuffed them in her handbag.

♠

Savannah pulled the cover off her typewriter and checked the time. Ten o'clock. Plenty of time to finish the documents Mr. Young wanted by Monday morning. Really no excuse for not spending some devotional time, as Mrs. Young called it. She opened her bag and reached for her Bible.

You shamed us and you shamed God by what you did. I don't know why you're trying to make us believe you've changed.

Was that how God felt about her? That she'd shamed Him and she couldn't make Him believe she'd changed? A sob caught in her throat. She closed her bag, stuffed it in a drawer and opened the file with the information for the documents she needed to type.

The office was quiet without Mr. Young or Dorothy, and no agents or customers coming in and out. Quiet was good. Hard work would take her mind off her mother's letter.

An hour later, the Sandy Lake fire bell clanged. She sniffed. Someone's leaf fire must have gotten out of control. Wait, it was June. Didn't people burn leaves in the fall?

She shrugged and stretched. None of her business anyway. Nothing she could do. These documents were taking longer than she'd thought.

A half hour later, a siren drew her to the window. Stoneboro's chemical fire engine with many feet of hose thundered past. The fire must be serious. She sniffed again. The smell of something burning was stronger. Should she go find out what was happening? She glanced at the work on her desk. Probably better finish what she was doing. It wasn't lunch time yet anyway.

Determined to shut out all interruptions, Savannah concentrated on her work. She pulled the last sheet from the typewriter as a train whistle blasted in long continuous bursts. She peered at the clock. Twelve-twenty-one. No trains ran through Sandy Lake this time of day. Alarmed, she ran to the front door of the office, then sprinted to the door that opened onto the sidewalk. Huge puffs of dark smoke billowed on the other side of the intersection of Lake and Main Streets. She choked and coughed.

Two teams of horses with a group of men sprang into action as a locomotive and a flat car stopped at the train station. The flat car carried a huge steamer fire engine and hundreds of feet of hose.

"What are they doing?" Savannah shouted at a tall, dark-haired bystander.

"They're taking the equipment to Sandy Creek where they can pump water on the fire through the hose."

Savannah turned around and squinted at the raging inferno. "Is that the Feather building burning? I thought they said it was fireproof." Her blood ran cold. The Feather building wasn't far from the boarding house.

The man looked in the direction she pointed. "It's the Feather building, all right. That's Mr. Feather they're dragging away. I just came from there. He wouldn't leave. Just kept saying the building was fireproof. I'm glad they got him out."

Savannah started to run, calling over her shoulder. "What about Mrs. Patton's boarding house?"

"You mean the old Sandy Lake House? It's too late to save that. They're just trying to keep the fire from jumping across the street to Doc Giebner's old office."

Savannah sprinted up the sidewalk. Sobs choked her as smoke engulfed her, and her side ached. Men, women, and children carried water in buckets, trying to quench the flames. The fire devoured everything in its path as it raged on. Others climbed up to throw wet carpets on the roofs of buildings across from the fire, hoping to keep it from spreading. A continuous stream of people followed them, bringing more water to throw on the carpets.

Everyone seemed to have a job to do. Everyone except her. She tried several times to ask how she could help, but no one paid any attention to her. Why would anyone want the help of someone like her?

Every building in the Feather Block was blazing. The Cottage Hotel in the Muse Block looked like it had been blown up. In the next block, the boarding house was engulfed in flames. What would Mrs. Patton do? What would Savannah do? As she gazed at the remains of the boarding house, hopelessness settled over her.

Although the fire chief from Franklin appeared to be getting things under control with water gushing from two hoses, it was too late for her. She was homeless, left with nothing but the clothes she was wearing and the money she had put in the bank.

She turned, head drooping, and walked back the way she'd come. Going back to Georgia wasn't an option now that her mother had disowned her. Mr. Burns's tavern was closed. The clothes she might have used to start a new business had been destroyed in the fire. Had God washed His hands of her, too?

♠

Garrett finished his lunch and looked up as a man entered Mr. Black's clothing store. He was a friend of Garrett's father.

"Good to see you, John. What can I do for you?" Garrett sniffed. The smell of smoke became overwhelming as the man approached.

"I just stopped by to let you know there's a bad fire in Sandy Lake. Your father asked me to tell you."

"Are Ma and Pa all right?" Garrett's voice rose in alarm.

"Oh yes, they're fine. I didn't mean to scare you.

"Where did it start?"

"I heard it started in the Bach Brothers' livery stable. I helped fight it until I had to get ready for work." John pulled out a handkerchief.

"How far had it spread when you left?"

"It spread fast because there was a brisk wind blowing. Everything was in flames up through the Feather block and everything else on the left side of the street clear up to the old Sandy Lake Hotel."

"Mrs. Patton's boarding house?"

"That's right. I think the old Cornplanter steamer from Franklin got there just in time to keep it from spreading, but not in time to save the boarding house—"

"I'm sorry, sir. I have a friend living there. I have to go."

Garrett raced to his car, cranked the engine, and jumped in. Mr. Black would be back in a few minutes. The store would be fine. *Oh, God, please take care of Savannah. Please watch over her and keep her safe. Don't snatch her away from me now that I thought you might be giving her back.*

Pulling down on the accelerator, Garrett drove as fast as he dared. He prayed nothing got in his way. If only he could get a message to Pastor Jim to ask him to pray. He knew God heard his own prayers, but he had more confidence in the Pastor's.

He rolled down his window and smelled smoke the minute he reached the outskirts of Sandy Lake. Riding through town, he shook his head at the devastation. He turned right onto Mill Street and parked beside the road.

Trotting down Main Street, he questioned everyone he met. "Have you seen Savannah Stevens?"

Each time the answer was negative. The fire appeared to be

under control, but people on the left side of the street continued to carry buckets of water to throw on carpets on the roofs. He caught Polly Dye's arm as she handed a sandwich to one of the firemen. "Have you seen Savannah?"

"No, I'm a little worried about her. I've been looking for her, too."

"You don't think she's still in the boarding house do you?" Panic threatened to choke him.

"No, they said there was no one in the building. I thought she'd be here helping Mrs. Patton. She doesn't work at the office on Saturdays. Have you talked to her lately?"

"Not for weeks."

Polly bit her lip. "You don't know then."

"Know what? Has something bad happened?" He had hurt Savannah enough already. She didn't need more pain. His emotions were a tangled mess.

"She wrote to her parents to apologize for how she'd treated them." Polly told him about the letter Savannah had gotten and her state of mind the night before. "That's why I'm worried. Losing everything after getting that letter, I'm afraid she might run away."

CHAPTER 53

Savannah walked past the office where she worked, then turned around, walked back and went in. She hadn't even locked the door or taken her purse when she left. Putting the neatly typed documents on Mr. Young's desk, she scanned his office and then hers. Would she ever see this place again? How could she keep her job without a place to live. People had been nice enough after she'd been kidnapped, but that didn't mean they'd be willing to rent to her. Would she be able to afford it if they did?

She picked up her purse and the keys Mr. Young had entrusted to her, and then locked each of the doors. What should she do with the keys? If she left town without returning the keys, he might think the worst. There were no answers. Dropping the keys in her handbag, she headed south, walking away from town. Almost immediately she came to a fork in the road. Should she go to Jackson Center or Grove City?

Pausing, she glanced at the fork bearing left. The Methodist Church where she'd attended with Garrett and his parents was only a few steps away. Although it had been several months since she'd been there, she felt drawn to it.

Someone had said the doors were never locked. She took a tentative step in that direction, then another. Soon she was climbing the steps and trying the door. It opened.

After a moment's hesitation, she went in. She drew deep breaths of peace and walked down the center aisle to the front row of benches. Sitting down and bowing her head, she tried to pray. No words came. She reached into her bag, pulled out her Bible and Sarah's diary. She opened the diary at random. *The Lord gave and the Lord hath taken away; blessed be the name of the Lord.*

The words stole her breath. Could she say that? Could she look at her losses and still say "Blessed be the name of the Lord?"

Her gaze moved up the page. *If I turn against God, to whom will I go for comfort and strength to get through the days ahead?*

A sob caught in her throat. She stood and walked to the altar, then dropped to her knees. Tears slid down her cheeks. What had happened to her decision to run to God rather than blame Him for her trials?

In her diary, Sarah had said, *Only God could get me through the loss of a child.* And He had. "Forgive me, Father, for allowing my mother's words to erase everything I'd learned from Polly and Sarah. Only you can get me through the losses I'm facing. Only you can enable me to still trust you with all my heart.

"By faith, I'm going to say, *The Lord gave and the Lord has taken away; Blessed be the name of the Lord.*

The outer door opened and clanged shut. She stood and looked toward the back of the sanctuary.

Garrett raced down the aisle. "Savannah! I've looked everywhere for you. Praise God, I've found you." He reached to take her in his arms, then stopped. "I'm sorry. I was so excited about finding you, I almost forgot you're seeing William."

Savannah touched his cheek. "I can't believe you're real. How did you find me?"

"I came in here to pray for guidance. Polly told me you were upset last night. She thought you might have run away."

"When I found out I was homeless, I didn't know where to go until I saw the church. I felt drawn to come here. Then God began speaking to me about things I'd learned from Sarah's diary."

"Whose diary?"

"It's a story for another day. Garrett, I'm not seeing William anymore. I knew we could never be more than friends."

"Do you think you could still have feelings for me?"

"I never stopped having feelings for you, but I was so hurt when you didn't stay to talk to me after I was kidnapped. I didn't think you cared about me at all."

"Oh, Savannah." Garrett drew her close. "I'm so sorry I left."

They sank down on the front bench. Garrett told her about his promise to God the night of her kidnapping, and how he'd stood and watched William rush to greet her. "I'd never felt so alone in my life. I thought God was asking me to give you up forever, to be a single, itinerant preacher."

Savannah gulped. "Do you still think that's what He wants?"

"I don't know about the itinerant preacher part. But last night I believe God said He was giving you back to me."

"But Garrett, I have nowhere to live. I can't afford to rent an apartment even if someone was willing to rent to me. I don't know what to do."

Garrett dropped to his knees and took both Savannah's hands. "Savannah, I fell in love with you the day we met, and I've never stopped loving you. Will you marry me?"

Savannah gazed into his blue eyes. "I love you too, and I want to marry you. But it's too soon. You can't propose to me just because I don't have a place to live or because you feel sorry for me."

"No, no, that's not how it is. I want to marry you because I love you."

The door at the rear of the sanctuary banged open. Polly, red hair in disarray and dark brown work dress smudged and stained from battling the fire, appeared in the doorway. "Savannah..."

"Polly..."

The girls raced toward each other, meeting halfway. "I was so worried about you, Savannah. I looked everywhere for you. Where have you been?"

"I was working at the office. When I found out about the fire, I tried to help fight it, but no one wanted my help. I had no place to go since the boarding house burned. So I started walking out of town, and then came here to pray. How did you find me?"

"I don't know. The Holy Spirit must have led me."

Savannah pointed at Garrett. "He led Garrett here, too, when he couldn't find me."

Garrett stood and joined them. "God is amazing, isn't He?"

Polly smiled. "He is amazing. I have some good news, Savannah. When we discovered the boarding house had burned, our family had an emergency meeting. We want you to come live with us."

"Oh, Polly, I can't do that. You don't have room for me."

"Ben said he'd move in with Robert and George. You can

have his room. We really want you to come."

Savannah glanced at Garrett, a question in her eyes. When he nodded, she looked back at Polly. "Garret asked me to marry him, but I didn't want to rush things. Maybe I could live with your family for a few months until we get married."

"I think that sounds like a perfect plan." Polly hugged Savannah again.

Tears rolled down Savannah's cheeks. "You and your family have already done so much for me. I don't know how I'd have survived all that's happened if you hadn't befriended me and shared Sarah's legacy with me."

"That's the very essence of a legacy, isn't it?" Polly swiped at Savannah's tears. "A legacy is meant to be shared."

EPILOGUE

August 3, 1912
2:00 p.m.

Polly straightened Savannah's simple white veil and smoothed the satiny fabric of the gown she and Mrs. Young had helped Savannah make. Never had Savannah looked lovelier and Polly couldn't wait to see Garrett's face when he got his first glimpse of her. After two months of sharing their home with Savannah, not even a trace of jealousy or envy marred Polly's love for her.

Opening the sitting room door a crack, Polly peeked into the living room. The rest of the Dye family, Kitt, Mrs. Patton and Mr. and Mrs. Young were already assembled, chatting quietly. There would be a larger reception later at the Methodist Church, but Garrett and Savannah wanted only a small private wedding in the Dye home.

Closing the door, Polly leaned her forehead against it.

"What's wrong, Polly? Aren't you feeling well?"

"I'm fine. I just can't believe that not quite a year ago we held Mother's funeral in this very place."

"I'm so sorry. It was thoughtless of me not to recognize how difficult this would be for your family." Savannah's violet-blue eyes darkened. "We should have gotten married in the church."

"It's okay. Mother would have wanted you to have it here. She'd be so pleased that you chose to be married in our home. Maybe she and Sarah are smiling down on us today. Memories just overwhelmed me for a minute."

Polly opened the door a crack again. Reverend Caldwell,

Garrett, and his best man, Irv, walked out of the kitchen door into the far end of the dining room which had been rearranged for the occasion. The beginning notes of the wedding march came from the table top Victrola Mr. Young had rented. Music filled the rooms. Maggie, standing on the landing to the stairs, gave Elsie and Twila each a little push. Faces wreathed in smiles, they began dropping flower petals on the path Savannah and Polly would follow.

"Do I look okay?" Polly smoothed the shimmering pale green of her gown. She'd been so busy helping Savannah, she hadn't given much attention to her appearance.

"You look beautiful. A dream in green." Savannah hugged Polly.

Polly left the sitting room and hesitated beside her father who waited outside the door to give Savannah away. Tears pooled in her eyes as her gaze met his. She was so proud of how he'd stepped up to be a father to Savannah over the past two months. She walked on. Would he ever walk Polly down the aisle? Would he ever give her away?

She smiled at Reverend Caldwell and took her place on his far right. Then she turned to watch Garrett's face. His eyes filled with love and complete devotion as Savannah stepped out of the sitting room. His face glowed.

♠

Savannah smiled at Bob Dye and mouthed the words, "Thank you" as she took his arm. The words didn't begin to convey how much she appreciated all the family had done for her these past months. *I never thought I'd find out what it felt like to be loved just for myself, but the Dye's showed me it was real. I hope Garrett and I have a home as filled with love as this one.*

As they stopped in front of Garrett and Reverend Caldwell, her gaze met her groom's. Tears of joy gathered in her eyes as his gaze conveyed a promise of many bright tomorrows. Reverend Caldwell cleared his throat. "Dearly beloved..."

The End

AUTHOR'S NOTE

The setting of this second book in the Sarah's Legacy series is once again Sandy Lake, Pennsylvania. The fire in Sandy Lake on June 1, 1912, was very real and the information is factual as derived from newspaper reports at that time.

The two main characters, Garrett Young and Savannah Stevens, are fictitious, as are Garrett's parents, Mildred and Harold Young. Also fictitious are George Burns, Mr. Black, Reverend Caldwell, William Sider, and Irv. As far as I know, Sandy Lake never had a sheriff or a jail.

The Dye family and the Davis family were real people, as noted in Sarah's Legacy, as was Innis Patton, who ran the boarding house where Savannah supposedly made her home. Post Master Boyd, Dr. Judd Cooley and his wife, Lulu (Potter) and Dr. Thomas Cooley and his wife, Sarah, were also real people, as were Kitt Potter and her mother.

However, in spite of the fact that the Davis's and the Dye's and others I've mentioned were real people and that some of the events are real, the characters I've created, conclusions I've drawn and the story I've written are a work of fiction. I've loved researching and writing about Sandy Lake, a place that became more home to me than where I was raised. I hope you're also enjoying the journey.